THE COCOA-VAN SUMMER

John Coquet

*For Margaret
With my best wishes.

John Coquet.*

Published by New Generation Publishing in 2015

Copyright © John Coquet 2015

First Edition

The author asserts the moral right under the Copyright, Designs and Patents Act 1988 to be identified as the author of this work.

All Rights reserved. No part of this publication may be reproduced, stored in a retrieval system or transmitted, in any form or by any means without the prior consent of the author, nor be otherwise circulated in any form of binding or cover other than that which it is published and without a similar condition being imposed on the subsequent purchaser.

www.newgeneration-publishing.com

CHAPTER ONE

'Is it...was it a close friend, the dead person, Mr Baxter?'

'No, not a friend at all, Brenda,' Alan said, trying to sound less resentful than he felt. 'I never even met him. He was a member of my golf club over at Wendmore. I'm going to the funeral service only because the club asked me to represent them at it. Two of us, that is. The other one's due here soon.'

His voice still carried a good deal of its suburban London origins. Enough, he knew, to be thought rather lah-de-dah by those locals whose feet had deeper roots in the Somerset soil than his own. Brenda, his cleaner, had an accent like theirs.

'That's not so bad, then,' she said. 'You need a bit of company at a funeral, I always think. And didn't you say it was at Upper Mendham? Of course we're Chapel ourselves but that's a nice church, that one. Nicer than the one here, anyway.' She nodded in agreement with herself before saying: 'Well, I'll be getting off now. You won't forget I'll be here a day later than usual next week, will you?'

'I won't.' He supposed he ought to ask about her husband. 'And how is Geoff?'

At nearly seventy, Geoff claimed never to be really well. But whatever his health problems were, real or imagined, he rarely let them interfere with his paid work in gardens like Alan's.

Brenda and Alan were in the front room of Myrtle Cottage which formed one end of a short terrace down a lane off Stratfield's main street. The fourteenth-century village church she disapproved of had been updated by Victorian architects who left its interior looking merely old-fashioned instead of ancient. Not far from it was her dour Noncomformist chapel – never a by-word locally for fun and frolic. There was a pub, once The George. Alan hadn't been inside it since new owners modernised it beyond the call of duty and re-named it The Firkin. The one-time village shop was now a house.

'It's only his annual check-up,' Brenda said, 'what he likes to call his M.O.T. The trouble is they usually do find something not quite as it ought to be, so I like to go with him – give him a bit of support, if you like.' She pulled a disapproving face and gestured at the lower reaches of her apron. 'And he's been so tender down there we're wondering if it might be a rupture or even one of those hernias.' She sighed before saying more brightly: 'I hope you don't mind me saying so, Mr Baxter, but you look very smart today. I don't see many of my gentlemen wearing suits of a morning. Or ever, come to think of it.'

He recognised this as a way of reminding him that her cleaning skills were also valued elsewhere in the village and that he was far from being her sole client. It made her worth hanging onto.

'Thanks, Brenda, I do try sometimes.'

Now that she'd mentioned it he realised he couldn't remember the last time he'd worn his suit which was old but still serviceable. It must have been years ago, probably for another funeral.

After he paid her she nodded to him and left the room, closing the door softly behind her. He thought this might be a token of her respect for the day's special event, but a few moments later he heard the vacuum cleaner being noisily shoved into the cupboard under the stairs, followed by the cottage's front door banging shut. So he was wrong about that.

It was almost time for Maxwell Tyler, his co-mourner, to turn up. Alan didn't know him, either, other than by sight, and not to speak to except for the first time on the phone a few days earlier.

In the meantime, it couldn't do any harm to wish Reggie Hallows, today's deceased, all the best for his future if he had one. And if he had, that it might be somewhere pleasant. Alan knew what he was now doing came close to praying and the trouble with that was knowing when to stop. Not much later, the clatter of the door knocker saved him from having to decide for himself.

'Just coming,' he called, levering himself from his chair. He didn't bother to glance in the wall mirror for reassurance about his appearance. There was no need, not today, and especially not after Brenda's comment. And he knew he looked in reasonable shape for his age, maybe even better than that. There were lots of chaps in their sixties or even younger who looked worse.

'I'm on my way,' he called, hearing the knocker again. He opened the front door, saying: 'Sorry to have kept you, Max. Do come on in.'

Tyler took up most of the narrow doorway and exuded the smell of bread pudding. He was middle-aged and fat with hardly any hair on his head but compensated for its loss by having a big moustache.

He came in and shook Alan's hand, saying loudly in a plum-laden voice: 'Bloody cheek, I call it.'

'What's that, then?'

'The way we've been dragooned into turning up at this do, willy-nilly. I've never heard of a funeral rota, don't know about you. And I've been a member at Wendmore for the better part of thirty years and done my stint on the committee as well. It must be one of the secretary's closely-guarded secrets if it exists at all other than in his mind. I wouldn't be surprised if he didn't just pluck our names out of a hat. You weren't ever on the committee, I take it?'

'No, I wasn't.'

He was glad never to have been invited. The thought of being closeted with those old duffers endlessly debating nothing much at all held no appeal.

Tyler went on: 'It's not as though Reggie and I were really close. Friends, yes, but not what you'd call bosom friends. And I don't believe you were, were you?'

'No.'

Tyler shook his head. 'Didn't think so, somehow. Oh, I admit I enjoyed his company in the bar, listening to his yarns and so forth, but that was as far as it went. All his real pals, the ones who went back years with him, are taking advantage of this weather and swanning about on the course as we speak. You can depend on it, and that's in spite of the club flag being flown at half-mast today. I noticed it when I drove past.'

Rather than let Tyler take root in the hall, Alan intervened to stem the flow of booming indignation by leading him into the front room, no great distance. The bread-pudding smell must be coming from after-shave lotion.

'Do sit down, Max. Do you fancy a drink before we set off?'

'That's very civil of you. Yes, I think I might manage to force one down. And we do have a moment or two in hand. What, half-an-hour's drive from here at most? Service at noon? Mind you, we don't want to fetch up there at the last minute, do we, not in our unsought role of official mourners?' Without waiting to hear Alan's view on that, he said, 'No, we don't,' and sat down heavily, stretching out his legs.

'If you can manage it I'll have a pink gin, if I may. No ice, thanks, and perhaps you'd better go easy on the gin as I've drawn the short straw for the driving.'

Alan was expecting some additional moaning on that score, having been made to listen to a preliminary summary of it on the phone.

'Yes, I thought you sounded rather put out when I rang.'

'It's not that I object to doing the driving, not as such. No, it's just that you're miles out of my way. Had to come over here, then have to go all the way back again and on to the church at Upper Mendham, and then the whole thing again in reverse. That's all.'

'No, I quite understand,' Alan said, relying on the tone he'd used for years to calm displeased headmasters and angry parents. 'But as I explained, I booked my Ford in at the garage a fortnight ago and it'd take ages to get another date if I cancelled. You know what they're like round here.'

Tyler nodded, his jowls quivering. 'Indeed I do. Though the Mercedes dealership's an honourable exception.'

Alan knew from experience that berks like Tyler were always eager to get their patronising in early. It was their way of ensuring listeners knew at once where they fitted into the local scheme of things. Nor had Tyler called him by his first name, despite Alan having called him Max right away. It was a classic berk ploy.

He handed Tyler the drink he'd been preparing from a range of bottles on a small Pembroke table. Luckily one of them contained bitters and was still almost full after a lengthy period of lying fallow.

His visitor was looking unexpectedly funeral-smart, he reflected as he sat down. And looking smart was a hard trick to pull off by someone of Tyler's size. It was easy to imagine he was already deep in heart-attack territory, the area so recently vacated by Reggie Hallows according to the Wendmore secretary.

Before Tyler's arrival, Alan was half-expecting, half-hoping, to have another chance to see the suit he once glimpsed him wearing while doing what presumably was his job, auctioning cows and sheep at a local livestock sale. Rob Roy himself would have approved of its bold plaid-like check. Apart from that occasion, Alan had seen him only rarely, either in the Wendmore car park or out on the course in golfing attire so striking it must have been worn for a wager or as a forfeit.

But Tyler was wearing an unimprovable dark blue suit. It was teamed with the Wendmore club's red tie which looked like an open wound against his white shirt. Alan thought how inappropriate the tie was for a funeral while he made inroads into the ample glass of whisky he'd poured for himself and already started on while doing some fake busying at the table.

'Do you want to borrow a black tie?' he asked

pointedly, hoping to gain or regain some sway over Tyler. 'I think I may have a spare one upstairs.'

'No, I don't think that's necessary. After all, we're representing the club so at least one of us ought to advertise the fact, don't you agree? Cheers, by the way.' After telling Alan to mark his words, Tyler said, 'Half the male mourners won't even have bloody jackets on, let alone black ties. If they bother with ties at all, that is.' He drained his glass. 'Thanks for that, my first today.'

The pink gin, no more than a mean man's double, had deepened the flush he already had when he arrived. He got to his feet with an effort and ran his hand, its weighty signet ring much in evidence, over what little remained of his faded ginger hair. Then he told Alan it was time they started to think about making a move.

In what Alan saw as a deliberate afterthought, Tyler said, 'Nice little place you've got here, quite rustic with all these beams and crannies and so forth. That's a good inglenook, too. And a bread oven, I see. Labourer's cottage, was it?'

'I think it must have been, yes.' Unlike Tyler's house, Alan didn't doubt.

'Unusual, though, to favour the labouring classes with cottages of this size. With a hall, I mean. The front door usually opens straight into a room. Must have been a generous squire here in the old days. A Quaker in all probability. They liked to go in for do-gooding.' Abruptly, he said, 'Just you here, is it? No wife or anything?'

'Not now, not for a while now.'

'So sorry. Not a loss, I hope?'

'No. Though I suppose it's a loss of a sort.' Not that much of a one, Alan thought, more like a blessing in easily-penetrated disguise. 'Been on my own for six years, four of them divorced.'

'Shame. But having said that, it happens to most of us. Well, not to me, though it did once but so long ago now I doubt if it still counts.'

There were several pieces of antique furniture in the

room; a bureau and a small bow-fronted chest-of-drawers as well as the Pembroke table, all of them in mahogany and all bought at the behest of Alan's ex-wife, Susan, during the years when such things were expensive and desirable. They were still in place now, their value having halved and then halved again.

'I've got one rather like that,' Tyler announced, looking at the bureau. He moved closer to it, bending down with a grunt and peering at parts of it through his half-moon spectacles.

'Yes, I thought so. They're not the original handles, are they? Replaced, when? In Victorian times, would you think? Such a pity.'

Having found he'd already conceived and then given birth to a sharp dislike of Tyler, one based on his size, voice, moustache, and abundant sense of well-being, Alan said nothing about that. For all he knew, Tyler could have been having him on and luring him into saying something stupid.

They walked together down the front path in the warm mid-May sunshine and out through the gate. Tyler's gleaming Mercedes was parked nearby, well away from the kerb. It was the same car Alan had seen him hauling himself into and out of in the Wendmore car park.

'What's that bloody delivery van doing outside your place?' Tyler asked accusingly. 'I noticed it when I drove up. Couldn't whoever it belongs to park it in front of his own place, spoil his own view?'

The van complained of was primrose-coloured with the words Coq au Vin sign-written on its flanks in a flowing script, each word in a different colour of the French tricolour. Alan knew Tyler would have something to say about it and had been using the walk down the path to rehearse the explanation he'd prepared earlier.

'Yes, it's a bit embarrassing that, Max, I'm afraid,' he said glibly. 'It belongs to a friend of mine and I mentioned to him that my car was off the road. I don't suppose you know him, Jimmy Hargreaves, but he owns that bistro place over in Netterton. Anyway, he was quick off the mark to suggest I borrow his van for a couple of days. Very kind of him, too. Saved me a lot of trouble.' Knowing Tyler would disapprove, and not caring much one way or the other, he added: 'I eat over there fairly frequently, you see. It's a good place to go when you're on your own and don't want to do much cooking for yourself.'

Tyler was frowning while Alan spoke. Now he opened his mouth for a comment Alan could have scripted for him; he was going to say the van could have been pressed into use for the trip instead of his doing all the driving.

Sticking to his plan, Alan said, 'Yes, I know what you were going to say but I couldn't have used a van like that to ferry us to the church. That's why I had to suggest you drove. It wouldn't have looked very dignified or respectful for us to be seen driving there in that. It'd look as if we were delivering a shipment of communion wine.'

That should do the trick, he thought. Getting Tyler to drive saved him the cost of the petrol as well as letting him take full advantage of the free drinks that were sure to be on offer at the wake.

'I suppose so, I daresay you're right,' Tyler said, sounding reluctant to admit it. 'But I'm surprised your garage didn't fix you up with a courtesy car. No, actually I'm not, but my Merc fellows always let me have one. For a client in good standing, you see. But, yes, I've seen that bistro place. Never eaten there, of course. Establishments like that aren't often known for their authentic Gallic cuisine, are they? And I've often seen that van being driven about the area. What's more, I know what the locals call it, both the bistro and the van. The cocoa van. Did you know that?'

'I did, yes,' Alan admitted. 'It's just the local way of pronouncing the name.'

Tyler let out a braying laugh. His moustache started life inside his nostrils and he now threw his head so far back that all of it was on show.

'And you realise if you're seen driving it they'll start calling you the cocoa-van man, don't you?'

Still snuffling, he let himself into his car and Alan got in beside him. Then he started it and drove off smartly.

'But whatever you do, don't drive up to the club in it. They won't let trade vehicles use the car park there. Do you remember the fuss when that taxi-driver fellow was finally allowed to join? An endless debate as to whether his taxi was a trade vehicle despite it being a saloon car. Caused a hell of a to-do, and the committee eventually decided it was trade after all and wouldn't let him use it.'

He drove on in a silence broken only by his comments on fellow road users. After passing through a couple of villages and past a succession of fields with sheep in them, he said, 'Reginald's a queer name to saddle a chap with, wouldn't you say? The sort of name you'd expect to be dished out much earlier than when he was born. It's a name a subaltern might have had in the first war. Did you ever play with him at all?'

When Alan told him that to the best of his knowledge he'd never spoken to Hallows, wouldn't even know him by sight, Tyler said, 'You do surprise me. Anyway, he was the sort of fellow who'd have been called a bounder in days gone by, a bit of a cad.'

'How do you mean?'

'He had something of a reputation, you see. Nothing ever proved, of course, but when he hacked his ball into the rough – no rare event, let me tell you – he always declined offers of help and insisted on doing the ball-hunting on his own. And as you can guess, he often found it in a surprisingly advantageous position quite clear of obstructions and so on. Once you get an inkling of that sort of caper you tend to keep an eye out for it.'

'Didn't anyone ever say anything?' He knew he'd have done and what he'd have said.

'No, far too easy for him to deny it so no one ever mentioned it. He was a pretty popular chap at the club for all that. Gregarious, you know, never backward in coming forward in the bar. I think it was looked on as nothing more than a mild eccentricity. To do him credit, I don't think he ever tried it on in competitions, only in friendly matches.' He gave Alan a sharp sideways look. 'Are you sure you never came across him? Or heard about it on the grapevine?' When Alan shook his head, Tyler said, 'And then there were his lady friends. Surely you've heard about them.'

'No, I'm afraid not.'

That was because he never did much mingling with the crowd that used the bar as a refuge from whatever horrors awaited them at home. By his own admission, Tyler was one of them. Hallows was bound to have been one as well, holding forth and being entirely at ease among the solicitors, the accountants and the retired military men. Alan didn't know what Hallows had done for a living but it was bound to have been something professional involving payment by fees rather than salary, and nothing to do with trade. Teaching children would never have come into it.

'That's really strange. I thought it was very widely known. Not that any of it ever reached his wife's ears, I believe, but even so…Yes, he was a bit of a Lothario by all accounts, including his own, and always had been. Not bad going at his age, wouldn't you say? I suppose he was in his mid-seventies or even a touch older. No, not bad going at all.'

'Are you sure he wasn't just spinning you a yarn?'

'No fear of that. Some of the lady members could certainly tell you a tale about him. But the odd thing is that he had moral scruples. The one he made most of was his claim never to have had sex with his wife in the same twenty-four-hour period in which he'd done the deed with another woman. Remarkable, isn't it?'

'Especially to have been able to get away with it for so long.'

Hallows ought to have shared his reminiscences with Susan, Alan thought. She'd got away with it for years before leaving to set up home with her lover from the public library where she worked part-time. And avoiding having sex the same day with her husband wouldn't have put too much of a strain on her.

'An example to us all,' Tyler said. 'He was impeccably turned out, must have had more clothes than Beau Brummel. Always managed to keep the weight off and was never short of the readies. In fact I had the impression he was very well-heeled indeed. And quite a fine-looking chap when all's said and done. For his age, I mean. Could make the ladies laugh, always had them in fits. He said that was half the battle when it came to making a play for them.'

Almost at once, he drew up in someone's private parking space outside that someone's cottage, about a hundred yards from their destination. Several cars slowly passed them, the drivers looking around in search of somewhere to park.

'That's a bit of luck,' he said. 'No point in trying to get any closer than this. Those fellows are going to have to retrace their steps.' He switched off the engine.

To Alan's surprise after what had gone before, Tyler now said, 'Best not to labour the point, though, about old Reggie's foibles. Not really the day for that, wouldn't you agree? *De mortuis,* something or other, if you take my meaning.'

The word "twat" sprang to Alan's lips but he snared it there with an effort. He'd forgotten most of the Latin drummed into him as a schoolboy. The only complete sentence he could still remember was the Latin for "I go to the city to buy bread" which was a news item he'd never needed to share with anyone. Besides, a different Latin tag such as *Caveat Emptor*, the auctioneer's cop-out, ought to be more familiar to Tyler.

'As we used to say in ancient Rome, yes,' he replied quickly enough to feel pleased with himself. 'It's about speaking only well of the dead. I knew that.'

'Not far off. Look, I suppose we'd better get over to the

church now, bag ourselves a good place.'

'But not too near the front. The first few pews are bound to be reserved for family only. We don't want to make a show of ourselves by marching up there and then being made to slink back with everyone watching.'

Tyler shrugged his bulky shoulders. 'Wouldn't make any odds to me. When I said a good place, I meant a good place at the back.'

CHAPTER TWO

Penny Hallows was sixty. She'd been a married woman for just short of forty years, and a widow for ten days.

She delayed getting dressed in case she changed her mind at the last minute about what to wear. She'd got only as far as choosing a black woollen skirt as suitable for what was to come. She put it on and looked at her reflection in a cheval mirror, twisting round so she could see how it looked from behind. That was the view most people would have of her later that morning and into the early afternoon, so it was important to get it right. She was slim, a comfortable size twelve, several sizes smaller than most of the women who'd see her today. Her bobbed hair was coloured only days before the hospital gave her the news about Reggie. It had been one less thing to think about.

On the way back to her wardrobe she passed the other one, Reggie's one, remembering with a pang that it was hers now, too. Later, when she was ready, she'd have to clear it out and get rid of its contents. To where, though? To one or more of those charity shops in Taunton, she supposed. But there might come a time when she'd see some needy or frugal man rigged out in something smart and expensive that used to belong to her husband. That would be hard to cope with. Far better, then, to dispose of his finery much further away in a town she hardly ever visited. People always claimed it was vital to keep busy at times like this but it was hard for it to be otherwise with so much organising to be done. The disposal of bin liners full of clothes and shoes could count as one of those time-consuming tasks said to be beneficial to women in her situation. There was no rush. It was something she might get around to doing much later.

She sat on the edge of the bed to put her shoes on. When she stood up again and smoothed the duvet she realised for the first time that she was still keeping to her side of the bed. It hadn't yet occurred to her to let herself stray into what was always Reggie's side. He'd often strayed into hers but that happened more by accident than desire in recent years.

There was a perfunctory tap at the door.

'Mummy, I just wondered…Oh, sorry, I didn't realise.'

She was relieved to have her bra on. No matter how hard she tried not to be embarrassed, four years weren't proving long enough to stop her wanting to keep the results of her partial mastectomy as private as possible, even from her daughter.

'That's all right, Emma, you mustn't mind me. Did you want anything special?'

Emma was as slim as her mother but with a darker complexion, brown eyes instead of blue, and was attractive in an unthreatening way. She looked smart and businesslike in a dark suit.

'I only wondered if you'd decided what to wear yet. Though I do like that skirt, it's just right. What you need now is, I don't know, obviously something not too bright.' She stood thinking for a moment with her head tilted to one side and her brown hair brushing her shoulder. 'I know, what about dark grey? I'm sure I've seen you in a top like that, one with a round neck.'

'I think I know the one you mean,' Penny said, and sifted through the wardrobe hangers before she found what she was looking for. She slipped into it. 'This is the one, isn't it?'

'Yes, that's perfect, I knew I'd seen it before. You don't want to look too…well, funereal, I suppose.'

'No, I definitely want to avoid that. It does vary a bit, I know, but even people down here tend not to go in for that sort of thing these days. They used to, of course. You remember granny's funeral? All those black clothes, like a gathering of crows. But they're much less formal now. You should see some of them, you really should. Anyway,' she said, doing a complete twirl, 'what do you make of the whole ensemble? Will I do, do you think?'

Evidently she did, because Emma came over and gave her a hug, taking care not to let their faces come into contact and smudge their make-up.

Downstairs, a long-case clock started to strike. When she was newly married, Penny called it a grandfather clock but Reggie soon put her right about that. As its bell rang out for the tenth and final time, she said, 'I think I'm just about ready.' She picked up her handbag from the dressing-table, loosely draped a flimsy black scarf around her neck, took a last look round the room, and walked downstairs with Emma in her wake. They went from the panelled hall into what Reggie always insisted she call the drawing-room, and not the sitting-room or worse.

'I don't know about you,' she said, 'but I could do with a drink.'

Emma looked surprised. 'It's a bit early, isn't it?'

'I don't think it is. Not today.'

After they had a drink – gin and tonic for her and, unusually, a soft drink for Emma – the funeral car arrived. The chauffeur opened the rear doors for the two women and ushered then inside.

It was to be the only funeral car. Penny had wanted as little fuss as possible and decided with no hesitation, regardless of what people might think or expect, she and Emma were to be the only mourners, family or otherwise, at the cremation. She told her neighbours it was being kept very private but, of course, they'd all be welcome afterwards at the service in the village church and then at the Antelope pub.

There were only the two of them in the family now. She was an only child. Emma, though not for a moment intended to be, also turned out to be one. Reggie had a bachelor brother, Gerard, but he was well gone in age and certainly too far gone in any number of other ways to make the necessary trip from Yorkshire, even supposing he could take in the news of his younger brother's death. According to their mother, Penny's mother-in-law, he was named as a gesture of thanks to St Gerard Majella, apparently the patron saint of difficult births. Penny knew all she ever wanted to about them.

But there was a late intervention from the president of the Upper Mendham branch of the Women's Institute that she occasionally attended. She made a point of supporting the bring-and-buy events but not the evening talks by invited speakers who often went on alarmingly about subjects like snowdrop varieties and thimble-collecting.

After a discreet period, Joan Atkinson came to the house to offer her personal condolences as well as those of her members.

Having listened to Penny's plans without interruption, she said at last: 'Look, dear, private's one thing but surely you won't want to be at the crematorium with only Emma for company. It's such a dreary place and it'd be too awful, just too depressing for both of you. Even more so for her, poor girl. She's too young to have got used to being at cremations.' She went on to explain she'd spoken to her members, and many of them would like to attend. 'Just to keep you company, just to be a sort of guard of honour.'

Penny had felt too tired to argue about it. She wanted to say no but the offer was kindly meant, so accepted it reluctantly with as much grace as she had to spare at the time. And Joan was right about Emma. Even at forty, cremations wouldn't have become a regular feature of her life.

The car started off at a suitably stately rate. Halfway up the lane, an elderly man who was unknown to Penny snatched off his cap as the car passed and then stood watching while it turned into the main street.

'Are you all right, mummy?'

'I think so.' As right as I'll ever be till all this is over, she thought. 'You mustn't worry about me.'

She was glad the glass screen was in place between the front and rear seats. Then, rather than say anything about how much Emma would miss her father, she said, 'Daddy was so proud of you, you know. Getting that job in the City and settling down with Giles, especially after those…'

Emma had two long-term ex-partners, both of them useless, not that Giles was much better. Penny was as proud of her as Reggie had been, despite the very few visits she made to her parents who'd done so much for her – or Reggie's money had. Emma might not have done well enough at school to go to university – not just a tarted-up poly, but a proper one, as he'd put it – without his paying for her private education.

Emma was blinking rapidly. 'Don't say anything more or you'll make me cry and I haven't done that yet, not properly, not since you first rang me.' Still blinking but still not crying, she said, 'It was so sad, coming only a few weeks before your Ruby Wedding. I know daddy was quite a bit older than you but you must have hoped you'd be able to go on to celebrate your Golden Wedding as well.'

'I know. It just wasn't meant to be.'

'But look, if it wasn't for…I wasn't planning to say anything until I had some real news to tell you, but I want there to be something nice for you today, something nice we can share.' She let out a long sigh, a sound Penny was used to hearing when Emma failed to get her own way. 'I wish Giles could be here so we could tell you together. And he would have been but for that business trip to Hong Kong coming up at such short notice.'

The mention of sharing made Penny think it must be more than a promotion. She let her hopes rise.

'Something nice to share? Don't tell me you're pregnant at last.'

'No, I'm sorry but it's not that. Not yet, anyway. But you're on the right track. I'm coming off the pill at the end of this cycle and we're going to try to start a family. As you'll have noticed, I've already stopped drinking in anticipation of it.'

'That's wonderful news, I'm so pleased for you.'

It was a relief to be able, even to feel entitled, to have a break from needing to look heartbroken, and for such a good reason. She gladly jettisoned all funeral thoughts from her mind and replaced them with practicalities.

'I do hope it works for you. After all, you're forty now, aren't you? I'd already had you for twenty years by the time I was your age.' Wanting to be sure, she asked if Giles was happy about it. He was such a selfish man that she had her doubts.

'To be perfectly honest, he's not a hundred-per-cent happy, no. He says it's bound to interfere with my career, and having a baby about the house would be inconvenient for him. But I talked him round and I think he agreed with me that at my age we shouldn't put it off much longer. And do you know what he said? Typical man, he said that at forty I wouldn't have too many eggs left to be fertilised.'

That didn't sound at all promising but it was no more than Penny would have expected from him.

'Not very gracious of him, was it? But I'm not only pleased for you and Giles. I'm pleased for myself, too. You know how much I've wanted you to have a family and I only wish your father could have lived long enough to hear about it.'

Another practicality showed itself. 'Dare I ask you if you'll now be upgrading that partnership of yours to a marriage?'

Emma sighed again. 'Do let's take one thing at a time. We'll have to wait and see.'

'I know.' She didn't want to start an argument, not today of all days. 'And I must say I wish you well. It's not as though the genes on both sides of your family are exactly seething with fertility, is it?' More for her own benefit than Emma's, she added: 'But I expect there are all sorts of procedures available now to improve the odds.'

'We'll cross that bridge if and when we come to it. It's far too soon to be thinking of anything like that. I'm not worrying about it, either, as one of Giles's sisters has a child. I'll let you know as soon as we've anything to announce, so try not to be too anxious. And it might take some time, so don't ask me about it every month. Promise?'

'I'll try.'

At Emma's age, her child-bearing potential was limited. As for the languid Giles who now sounded more selfish than ever, he might have a good job but whenever she saw him Penny doubted he had more than two sperms to rub together.

'That's enough about me, really it is,' Emma said. She reached across and took Penny's hand. 'I'm so impressed by how strong you're being.'

It sounded as if she'd only just noticed that, and it became worse when she said, with Penny wishing she hadn't: 'I'd convinced myself you'd be in pieces. But you didn't need to put on a brave face just for me.'

When they reached the crematorium, the driver carefully piloted the car along a flower-bordered path marked Principals Only. Several other cars were parked some distance away. An abandoned and empty invalid chair stood to one side.

As Penny got out of the car she saw a small group of people, women with just a few men, most of them in their Sunday-best clothes. They stood in a ragged semi-circle in front of the crematorium chapel door, ready for the proceedings to come. She recognised the W.I. members but would have sworn she'd never met any of the men. She must have seen some of them before but that was different from meeting them. How they must have resented being dragged from their gardens and sheds to be present on such a fine day to do the driving and make up the numbers.

The women smiled at her and Emma and murmured things she failed to catch but knew would be words of sympathy. The men did nothing apart from nodding to her, staying silent and looking ill-at-ease.

She was grateful now for Joan Atkinson's suggestion. The presence of the W.I. women was intended to be supportive, and Penny now found it welcome as well.

Several of them must have been in her position themselves and been thankful for a similar turn-out. She smiled at them, and more faintly at the men.

It was cool in the crematorium's multi-faith chapel. The light was subdued despite the blue sky and its associated brightness being on show through high lancet windows. Penny and Emma walked up the aisle and into the front pew that was for them alone. The W.I. contingent settled themselves, singly and in couples, in the pews behind. An outbreak of coughing and throat clearing soon died away.

Penny knew the coffin would have been put there before her arrival but was still shaken to see it lying on the open-curtained platform with the rollers just visible beneath it. She heard Emma gasp, and reached out to grip her hand.

The coffin was less ornate than many of those pictured in the brochure at the funeral directors' office where they were referred to as caskets. The handles were made of plastic but looked exactly like brass. Her own wreath and Emma's smaller one which she'd brought down undamaged on the train from London were simple enough for anyone not keen on the Baroque. It was disquieting to think they were now resting only a few inches above Reggie's lifeless body which was dressed in the newest of his bespoke suits.

An organ recording began to play not-too-morose music at low volume. It stopped when a robed clergyman of indeterminate religious persuasion entered from a side room. His presence was only one of the details she'd left to the men at the funeral parlour – though they weren't called funeral parlours any more – to arrange and negotiate.

He bowed towards the coffin before shaking Penny and Emma's hands and telling them he was sorry for their loss. That done, he went and stood behind a lectern with a row of switches on it. One of them, Penny knew, had to be triggered to start a CD track at the close of the ceremony. A reverently-spoken funeral director had suggested to her that *My Way*, the Frank Sinatra version, was a popular choice for the bereaved. Reggie wouldn't have liked that, so it was easy to settle for no CD at all.

After rustling the pages of a thin book, the clergyman found his place and read a long prayer about love, loss and resurrection. He went on to say how sad it was to have to bid farewell to a loved one and how he hoped the sorrowing family would take comfort from the presence of so many mourners to share that sadness. A shorter prayer followed, recited from memory this time, and its ending was marked with a muttered "Amen" from the pews.

Almost at once a switch clicked and the rollers whirred softly as they began to turn. The coffin slowly moved away into what looked like an open cupboard. It shuddered as it went, making the flowers on the two wreaths bobble about till it was lost to sight with the curtains swishing almost completely together behind it. Then all Penny sensed was an emptiness, already existing but somehow impending as well, the one Reggie and his little ways used to fill.

Back in the car, she tried to console Emma whose shoulders were moving about a lot as she cried silently into a handkerchief. 'Be brave,' she said, hugging her. 'We've both got something to look forward to now.'

Apart from reminding Emma of that and wanting to cry because of it and managing not to, she could think of nothing to do or say of any use to anyone.

The Upper Mendham village church was St Michael's, though the notice board outside dispensed with the apostrophe. It was a small building with a tower that no longer housed any bells, and was set in a circular and well-filled churchyard. Both its Norman font and chancel arch were noted without much in the way of commentary in Pevsner's *Buildings of England* volume for that part of Somerset.

Penny wasn't a regular member of the congregation but took her turn on the brass-cleaning rota. When she was alone in the church she liked to trail her fingers around the font's stone moulding while trying to imagine the feelings and faith of the long-dead mason who shaped it nine hundred years or so earlier. In the stillness, she imagined generations of villagers dressed in their odd-looking historic clothes and cemented into their inflexible places in society, dutifully going to and from services.

There were fifteen pews on each side of the single aisle. Today they were filled with people who turned to look as she and Emma made their way to the front. They kept their eyes on the ground as they walked, not out of piety but to avoid catching their heels in the heating grilles set into the stone-flagged floor. It was only when they sat down that Penny noticed the organist was playing something both calming and unrecognisable. It reminded her of the soothing background music that suffused her dentist's surgery and waiting-room.

As soon as they were settled, the vicar appeared from the vestry, bowed low to the altar, and crossed the chancel to the pulpit. He climbed the six steps and spent a few seconds looking out over the congregation as if counting them. Then he made a small hand signal and the music stopped almost at once.

After a short pause he started his address, not stinting himself in telling everyone how welcome they were. Not, it went without saying, to mourn a death, but to celebrate a life. That was fair enough, Penny thought, but it was like the way politicians talked about challenges instead of problems and avoided the mention of anything upsetting.

She felt Emma stir when he began to talk about "Reginald". How Reggie would have hated being called that. He always forbade its use even in jest. She clearly recalled stressing the importance of calling him Reggie during her meeting with the vicar and his wife in the vicarage. During it, as well as being offered commiserations, she was given exceedingly weak tea and such a thin slice of Battenburg cake that its marzipan perimeter had detached itself.

No one was called up to the eagle-bearing brass lectern

to reminisce about Reggie. That was also at her insistence. The vicar made up for the break with tradition by telling the congregation that no words of theirs, no matter how heartfelt or eloquent, could do justice to their late friend.

It was good to have got the cremation over and done with before coming back to the church. She'd have hated to see the coffin brought in on the shoulders of a bearer-party in their dodgy morning-suits and to have it perched on trestles like the ones used to support wallpaper-pasting tables.

There were two hymns to be got through next; *Jerusalem* for the members of the W.I. contingent who'd arrived from the crematorium in plenty of time to occupy their reserved places, followed by *Onward, Christian Soldiers*. Without much surprise, she noticed the hymn book now urged on pilgrims rather than soldiers, and that the singers ignored the change. It just went to show.

The vicar concluded with a prayer. When he'd finished it, he blessed the congregation with an expansive sign of the cross that took in the whole of his upper body from forehead to navel and from shoulder to shoulder. Then, to more and slightly jauntier music from the organist, Penny walked with Emma back down the aisle and out into the sunshine which was warm enough to make her glad she'd not worn a coat. The whole business was over in less than thirty minutes.

The wake was held in the private room of the Antelope, only a short stroll from the church. There was a free bar in the corner. As soon as the guests were supplied with drinks from it, they hurried over to help themselves from a table laden with plates of sandwiches, cold meats and salad.

Having planned to have a late lunch together back at the house, Penny and Emma ate nothing. Instead, Penny dealt gratefully with another large gin and tonic and thought how sensible it was of Emma to stick to an orange juice like the one she asked for earlier. It was reputedly crammed with Vitamin C, a real baby-booster by all accounts.

Every now and then people came up to them singly and in small groups to kiss them and thank them, to say reassuring things and to tell Emma how nice it was to see her again. Several of the men were Freemasons, Reggie's brethren, whom Penny knew slightly from having had to go with him to Ladies' Nights.

Another two men who came up to pay their respects claimed to represent Reggie's golf club. One of them, rather shy, who said his name was Alan something or other, was slim and had nice hair that was grey but not too thinning. The other one was fat and had very little hair at all other than in and under his nose. He said loudly that he was Maxwell Tyler, but please call him Max because that was how Reggie knew him. He claimed he and his companion were close friends of her late husband and would miss him as would all the Wendmore members. The other one backed him up to the hilt. After more assurances and regrets they shook hands with mother and daughter and went back to the bar.

Penny was sure she'd never met either of them before and that Reggie had never mentioned them. Nor did he ever wear the awful red polyester tie the fat one had on.

Much later, alone once more in the double bed, she felt pleased to have got through the day so well and that it was now over.

Emma was asleep in her old bedroom with two soft toys from her childhood lying on top of the covers. Her news was lovely, though how it would resolve itself remained to be seen.

CHAPTER THREE

Alan was in the Wendmore bar the next day. It was a comfortable room with picture windows overlooking the eighteenth green, and was dedicated to sitting and drinking. As always at that time of the morning, the early-bird golfers were still out on the course, so it was never busy before lunchtime.

A few chairs were occupied by inner-circle members who glanced up when he came in but failed to invite him over to join them for a chat about what the world was coming to. As well as leafing through a glossy and current golf magazine he found on the table, he was drinking one of the small whiskies he liked to drop in for on his way to the supermarket.

There was a triptych of varnished honour-boards above him on the wall. They showed in gold lettering the names of past winners and current holders of the Wendmore men's trophies: the Founder's Cup, The Directors' Cup and the Rose Bowl. His own name wasn't featured but, annoyingly enough, Tyler's was there on the Rose Bowl board: M.L.F. Tyler 1982. Alan hadn't noticed it before, and wished he hadn't now. The winners of the Ladies' Challenge Cup competition were listed on a much smaller board on the other side of the room.

'I'm glad to see you here this morning, er...Alan. I hope I'm not interrupting you, but I wonder if I might have a quick word.'

He looked up at the lanky figure who'd stolen silently up to him. It was the club secretary, known to many as Tweedy, in fact Harold Pemberton-Andrews, a lantern-jawed man generally thought to be genial but not particularly so by Alan. He was long past any normal retirement age but still clung efficiently to his job. Apart from being treated to an occasional frown of recognition, Alan had little contact with him until the phone call about the funeral when the secretary was as pleasant and persuasive as could be. Unless Tweedy now wanted a blow-by-blow account of the funeral service, the only likely reason for his approach would be to berate him for some breach of club etiquette, a subject close to officialdom's heart.

There were any number of rules of male etiquette detailed in the Wendmore handbook. Breaches, termed inappropriate behaviour, included entering the bar in the evening without a jacket, or entering the dining-room at any time without a jacket and either a tie or cravat. Shorts, which must be tailored, could be worn on the course only in the summer and had to be accompanied by socks – still termed hose at Wendmore – which must be knee-length.

The only rule Alan thought he might have been seen to break recently was changing into his golf shoes in the club's car park. He was due to pick up his car from the garage later that afternoon and, in the meantime, after Tyler's warning, was relieved he'd remembered to park the cocoa van in a side road some distance away.

'Yes, of course, Harry. Will here be all right, or do you want…?'

The secretary lowered his voice and looked cautiously around the room before saying: 'It's actually a bit delicate, so perhaps it'd be better if we went upstairs to my office.'

The secretarial office was a small room with walls displaying prints of golfers from a bygone age. They were swiping at balls with clubs shaped like hockey sticks, and looking to be having a thoroughly joyless time of it. The only window provided an uninterrupted view of the car park.

Tweedy sat down at his desk and motioned Alan to sit opposite him. 'I'm glad to have caught you. It's not only a delicate matter, you see, but a rather distasteful one as well.'

That might or might not rule out any unpleasantness to do with golf shoes, so all Alan said was: 'I'm sorry to hear that.'

The older man, probably the only one of any age for

miles around to be wearing a tweed suit on such a balmy morning, said, 'But first I must thank you for representing us all at the funeral yesterday, you and our friend Max Tyler. It's much appreciated. Yes, a shocking thing but not wholly unexpected, I believe. But to get to the point, I'd appreciate your guidance on something. I seized on you in the bar because I remembered hearing you used to be a schoolmaster and you might have had to deal with this sort of thing yourself. I don't know if you realise this, Alan, but when a member passes on it falls to me in my official capacity to do some finalising of things, personal things to do with the deceased. For instance I have to arrange for the widow, as it usually is, given that they tend to outlive us men, to have the unexpired portion of her husband's annual fees returned to her.' He sighed. 'And you can't imagine what a can of worms that is if it turns out that they're only partners. Not actually married, I mean. Dear God, there's solicitors and all sorts to contend with.'

'I don't envy you that.'

'Another thing I have to do is opening the member's locker downstairs. I've a master key, you see, like a hotel manager would have. Now normally it's just a question of taking out the deceased's waterproofs, towels, golf shoes and so forth, and getting them taken round to the wife. Or the husband, even.'

This was news to Alan. But now he knew about it he could see something unwelcome coming his way.

'Before I say anything more I must ask you, and I assume you did, whether you met Reggie's wife, Mrs Hallows.'

'Yes, we both did, Tyler and me,' Alan said at once, keen to keep Tyler's name in view. 'But only very briefly after the service, just to exchange a few suitable words.'

Leaning across the desk and planting his elbows on its leather surface, Tweedy said, 'Good. That sorts out one thing at least. Of course I ought to mention at this juncture that, well, with Max being the closer friend of Reggie – I hope I haven't got that wrong, because...'

'No, I didn't even—'

'But Max has had to go away for a couple of weeks at very short notice. To Wiltshire, I believe he said when I rang him. Surveying fatstock for auction, I shouldn't wonder, otherwise I'd have asked him to do it.'

'And what would that be?' Alan asked, playing for time. There had to be a way of avoiding what was coming next, if only he could think of it.

'I'm sorry to burden you with this especially as you were so good about representing us, but could I ask you to drop off Reggie's things with Mrs Hallows? I've looked it up and you don't live far from her, not really. And you having met her makes such a difference, don't you think? More personal, somehow.'

Burden was right. The last errand Alan wanted to run in the near or distant future was to return a golfer's crusty old kit to his distraught widow. But, try as he might, he couldn't conjure up a watertight excuse at short notice for non-compliance. Outright refusal wouldn't do, so he settled for reminding Tweedy they'd already agreed Max was the closer friend of Hallows. Wouldn't Max feel slighted by being denied doing him a final favour?

Tweedy shook his head. 'I don't think so. Waiting till Max gets back would look like an afterthought. Don't want Wendmore to look slack or uncaring, do we? No, it's something that needs to be done as soon as possible so it's best if you do it. In fact, today would be ideal if you can manage it. Get everything tidied away, if you know what I mean.'

Alan knew what he meant all right.

'But I can't see what my experience has to do with it, or why you said it was delicate and distasteful. It's no more than—'

'I was just coming to that. It occurred to me you might have dealt with – what shall I say? – distasteful items you confiscated from your pupils. Contraband, I suppose. Quite apart from the waterproofs and things which don't present a problem, I came across this in his locker. You'll see what I mean.' He selected a small key from a bunch of bigger ones to unlock the top drawer of his desk and took out a large buff envelope. 'Take a look at what's inside.'

As Alan opened it and shook out its contents, the secretary went on: 'Yes, that's right, a packet of French letters. Now what do you make of that? They're also well within their use-by date, I might add, which means they're not old stock. The packet's not full, either. As for those magazines – nothing but sheer filth. I know Reggie had a certain reputation, but really...'

Alan grinned despite himself. Was old Tweedy having him on? French letters? He'd not heard anyone use that expression for years.

There were two magazines; both of Scandinavian origin and fairly vintage, Alan thought. They featured coloured photos of two men identified as Lars and Agnar variously at grips with three blonde women, Ingrid, Freya and Mai. They were noticeably different from the photos he once sent off for in his youth. The advertisement had described them as artistic studies of the undraped female, and the application form began by saying: "Yes, I am a student of the female form and am 18 or over."

'Not terribly so, I wouldn't have thought,' he said. 'Not nowadays. You can download much more extreme stuff from the Internet, and lots of it's free. Or so I've been told.' He pushed the envelope and its contents back across the desk.

'Can you indeed? I can't say I'm totally surprised. But the point is, what on earth should I do with it all? French letters at his age; I don't know.' Tweedy pushed the offending articles back across the desk again as if fearing contamination. 'In my position I have clearly defined responsibilities. *All* the effects of a deceased member have to be returned to his wife. Or partner. It's a legal requirement. So strictly speaking, those...those things ought to be passed on to Mrs Hallows along with his waterproofs and other bits of kit.'

'I'm not—'

'You see my problem, don't you? Although I'm bound to, how can I possibly return those magazines to her? It'd cause real offence and I can't believe Reggie ever intended her to see them. Why would he, after all? And as for the French letters, surely she's beyond the age when...Do you take my point?'

Laughing inwardly, Alan said, 'Yes, I do. And I'm sure you're right, Harry.'

He'd had dealings with what Tweedy called contraband. Having confiscated condoms and porn from both boys and girls, he never considered returning them at the end of term. To their credit or shame, whichever it was, the youngsters never asked him to. Nor did he mention it to their parents. With no personal use for the condoms, he dumped them in litter bins well away from the school and, after looking at or reading the porn, eventually did the same with that.

So it was easy for him to sound confident when he said, 'Look, the thing to do, I assure you, is to dispose of them. Just get rid of them, it's what I used to do. No one will ever know. Reggie's gone, and you and I can rely on each other not to say anything.'

'You're sure about that, are you? I can't deny it would be a relief.'

'Discretion and valour, Harry. It'd save a lot of trouble all round.'

'All right, then, I'll do it. I'll dispose of them somewhere, though God knows where. Yes, I'm sure you're right, and thanks very much for your help.'

'Glad to be of service,' Alan said, allowing himself a glimmer of hope that Tweedy's gratitude would be enough to let him off kit-disposal duties.

But Tweedy said instead: 'There is one more thing. While you're at it, perhaps you'd ask Mrs Hallows if she'd give you Reggie's locker key in return. Would you do that for me? I'll give you her address. It's kind of you to offer.'

CHAPTER FOUR

After an early lunch the next day, Penny drove Emma to the station. She waited on the platform with her while the train came in and helped her lift her case into a compartment before hugging and kissing her goodbye. She waved till the train was well on its way even though Emma couldn't have seen her after it had travelled more than a few yards. They were unlikely to meet again until the late summer at the earliest. Unlike the way her own life was going to be from now on, Emma's was always busy.

She was already having doubts about her prospects of becoming a grandmother. Emma had said nothing more about her plans and it was difficult but sensible not to press her for more details after being warned off. She'd sounded happy enough to divulge her news but, in all honesty, no happier than when she announced she was getting her first company car. It left Penny wondering if it was no more than an attempt to lighten the sadness Emma assumed her mother was feeling, and the overt avoidance of alcohol was merely a way of backing up her story. The absence of a future pregnancy could be explained away as nothing more than bad luck.

It was sunny enough for her to deploy the sun-visor while she drove the Range Rover back from the station. The car and all its optional extras were examples of Reggie's many self-indulgences. She hardly ever had a chance to drive it herself and was enjoying doing so now, free from his usual insistence that it was too big for her compared with her own small but powerful BMW sports car.

After passing Upper Mendham's roadside sign which vainly urged motorists to drive carefully through the village, she stopped at its last remaining shop to buy a replacement bottle of gin.

The woman behind the counter recognised her and ditched her customary resigned tone in favour of a lugubrious one, asking Penny if she was all right now and telling her what a shame it was. Penny forced a smile, agreeing about it being a shame and confirming she was indeed all right, thank you for asking.

Minutes later she arrived home, left the car in the drive and went indoors.

The house was called Farthing's. According to the deeds, an Elias Farthing was its first owner. His flaking headstone stood askew in St Michael's churchyard where local yobs regularly used mud to obscure its engraved letter H. It said he was born in 1721 and was now mourned, in 1798, by his widow, Agnes, and their five surviving children. After his surname the word "gentleman" was still faintly legible. As Farthing's was a farmhouse, Penny reasoned he must have been a man of substance, a gentleman farmer. At seventy-seven, he'd made old bones by the standards of his day and out-done Reggie by two years.

Farthing's was a sprawling building with three reception rooms and a kitchen big enough to suit the sort of giant who liked to grind English bones to make his bread. There were four bedrooms upstairs with two smaller rooms converted into bathrooms, one of them en-suite. Two more bedrooms were in the attic, both of them rather damp. Reggie often said something would have to be done about that but never got round to doing anything, probably because the rooms were empty and never used.

Outside, there were two dilapidated stone barns that any estate agent worth his salt would describe as a range of useful outbuildings but which never proved useful for anything at all. Penny never went into them as they were almost certainly still infested with rats, even more so since Reggie's dog died. It was always his dog, not hers. The aloof and self-regarding Borzoi occasionally deigned to kill one or two and left their mangled remains to be disposed of by the gardener in ways unknown. It was typical of Reggie to insist on having an uncommon dog, the only one of its breed in the village where most dog owners went in for Dalmatians and Labradors. As it was left to her to take it for walks that usually turned into runs, she refused to let him replace it. It was one of her few self-asserting stands.

The whole place with its half-acre of land was far too big for a family of three, then of two, and even more so now for a family of one. She was going to rattle round in Farthing's like a pea in a drum. Reggie said anything smaller, newer or more practical would undermine his standing as a financial consultant who went on selflessly working for his clients long after he could have retired. He claimed they wouldn't trust him to make money for them if they suspected he couldn't do so for himself. 'Besides,' he said, truthfully for once, 'we can afford it.'

The only sound she could hear indoors was the ticking of the clock in the hall. When Reggie was away on one of his real or spurious business appointments and she was alone in the house there was a sense of noise and conversation being kept on hold till he returned. But now he was never going to do that, the near-silence had a more ominous quality.

She went into the dining-room, emptied the old gin bottle into a glass and added tonic. The bottle was a week old but still yielded up a good double. She took her drink into the drawing-room, opened a window, and sat on one of the two sofas that faced each other across a large square Chinese carpet. Kicking off her shoes, she leaned back and tucked her feet under her. After a moment's drinking she got up again, padded across the room and put on a CD. The first track, on shuffle play, was the Rolling Stones' *Gimme Shelter.* Reggie hated it, and she never played it when he was within earshot. Today, it felt appropriate.

Back on the sofa again, she soon sensed she was going to start crying because she felt so lonely. She knew the gin had something to do with that but still drank it all. When the feeling failed to go away she went back into the dining-room to make a start on the new bottle.

As she poured herself another drink she noticed

through the front window that a van in an unfortunate shade of yellow was drawing up behind the Range Rover. Moving further along the window while keeping herself well back from it, she realised she'd seen it before. She carried on watching as a man got out, and she grinned when she saw him look in the wing-mirror to pat his hair before making his way along the winding path to the front door.

While she wondered who he was and why he was visiting her, she quickly checked her own hair to make sure it hadn't been crushed against the back of the sofa, but it was okay. Her clothes were fine, too. It was hard to go far wrong with well-cut black trousers and the pale blue silk shirt that went so well with her eyes. It was harder still to go wrong with the heels she could still wear at her age without looking daft, she thought as she put her shoes back on. They weren't what her husband used to call strippers' heels, and he'd certainly have known all about them, but were still high enough to make her feel poised and self-confident. She switched off the CD, went into the hall and waited for the doorbell to ring. Before opening the door, she waited a little while longer so her caller wouldn't think she was desperate for company.

When she saw him more closely she recognised him as one of the men she met after the church service, one of the Wendmore pair. He'd been wearing a suit then, a rather old-fashioned-looking one with wide lapels. Today he had on brown corduroy trousers that were baggy at the knee and too thick, she'd have thought, for this time of year. He was also wearing a thin brown jumper, and brown shoes that had seen better days. A symphony in brown, she thought, while saying: 'Good afternoon, I thought I recognised you,' – and in case it had slipped his mind – reminding him he'd been at the wake in the Antelope.

Before making a thorough job of wiping his shoes on the doormat, he introduced himself. She asked him to call her Penny and he said to call him Alan.

She invited him into the drawing-room, noticing

without comment that he was carrying one of the supermarket's biggest plastic bags.

'What can I do for you, Alan?' she asked as soon as they sat down facing each other. When he crossed his legs she saw he was wearing pink socks which she thought were rather sweet. 'I'd not expected to see you again so soon.' If at all, it would have been true to say.

He wasn't looking all round the room like most visitors did on their first visit. It was a big room and there was a fair bit to see. Only the sofas were modern. The other furniture was all antique and looked it. There were two wing-backed brocaded chairs, a pair of wine-tables, a bureau, assorted lamps and a sofa-table with a deck cargo of silver-framed photos, and they still left the room looking uncluttered. Two glazed cupboards in the recesses on either side of the fireplace housed Reggie's collection – hers now, of course – of austere eighteenth-century Worcester blue-and-white porcelain. Her mother would have dismissed them all as dust-harbourers and too fragile to be of any practical use to anyone. But she knew nothing about antiques and their importance, no more than Penny did till Reggie told her. He wanted visitors to notice and approve of his possessions but pretended not to. 'Mentally pricing everything, that's all they're doing,' he used to grumble. 'Probably casing the joint.'

'I do hope I'm not here too soon, Penny. You know, after the funeral.'

'No, not at all. It's nice to see you again.'

'Just as long as you're sure,' he said hesitantly. 'I could easily come back another time when it's more convenient. I would have phoned but your number seems to be ex-directory.'

'Yes, I'm sorry about that, such a nuisance for you.'

Naturally, that was Reggie's idea to save him, so he said, from unsolicited calls. Embarrassing ones, too, she guessed; calls he might have found awkward to answer with her hovering nearby. They wouldn't have been about business because he insisted his office in Taunton was the only place to talk about that, even though it was apparently perfectly all right for him to invite clients to the house for meals and drinks, often at short notice.

'I'm going to get it changed,' she said. 'It's on my list of things to do. But what can I do for you? Have you come about golf club business or something?' She couldn't think what else it might be.

He lifted the bag onto his lap before saying: 'It's just something we have to do. At times like this the secretary opens the member's locker at the club and he asked me to return the contents to you. Mainly because I'd met you in the Antelope, I suppose.'

'Oh dear, I hope you've not had to come far to do that.'

'Only from Stratfield.'

'Not too far, then, but it's still kind of you to take the trouble. Though I can't imagine there was much of it, was there?'

'No, there wasn't. Not very much at all.'

He took out a moss-coloured waterproof jacket and matching trousers, both carefully folded, and put them next to him on the sofa. He felt again in the bag and put a small hand-towel and a pair of golf shoes on the floor by his feet, assuring her they were all perfectly dry.

'Well, thanks for bringing them over.'

There was a long pause before he said, 'There is just one more thing. I wonder if you'd let me have the locker key, your husband's personal one.'

She opened the handbag beside her on the sofa. 'I think this must be the one' she said, fishing about inside it. 'Yes, the tag's got W.G.C. on it. It was among his effects the hospital gave me and I wondered what it might be for.' She tossed it accurately over to Alan who caught it and put it in a trouser pocket.

'By the way,' she said, 'I couldn't help noticing that van you drove up in. It's the Coq au Vin one, isn't it? From that restaurant in Netterton?'

'It's more of a bistro, really. But yes, it is.'

He then launched himself into a multi-layered account

involving the van, a Ford car, and the Coq au Vin owner. Silently unravelling the details as he spoke, she concluded the van was borrowed. He, Alan, owned the Ford which hadn't been working properly, but now was. He planned to pick it up from the garage later that afternoon, so this was the last time he'd be driving the van. All this was clearly close to his heart, to judge by the effort he put into explaining it.

'Reggie and I went there a few times soon after it opened. Quite good, I seem to remember. And I've often seen the van being driven about. Does the owner do deliveries, do you think?'

'No, nothing like that. He'd hate anyone to think he ran a takeaway. But I imagine he has to go to suppliers, cash-and-carry places, that sort of thing.'

'You do know the restaurant and the van are both known as the cocoa van, don't you?' she asked, overcoming a need to grin. 'That's how they say Coq au Vin round here. So, for the time being, at least, you're the cocoa-van man.'

He could do with smartening up. What on earth must his wife look like if she let him out of the house dressed like that? She asked herself how old he might be. Clearly younger than Reggie; no more than mid-sixties, perhaps. Five years or so older than herself and well-maintained with it, just as Reggie was and took such pains over staying that way. Trim build, the nice hair she remembered noticing before, and a faint smell of something aromatic that wasn't just soap. It was much less pungent than the one that came from the other Wendmore man.

Alan groaned. 'Yes, so I've been told.'

'You've not been driving it to the golf club, have you? I can imagine them being a bit stick-in-the-mud about a van.'

He explained why that hadn't happened. Again he went into more detail than anyone could have wanted, even someone yearning to know all the ins and outs of it. Reggie made the club and its odd ways and even odder members seem boring enough but never went into as much detail as this, not in her hearing at any rate. But now it was time to show some manners and offer her visitor a drink while taking the opportunity to get another one for herself. Without knowing why, she didn't want him to leave too soon.

He'd evidently finished with the cocoa-van saga because he now said, 'Wasn't that the Rolling Stones playing? I thought I heard them as I got out of the van.'

'Yes, it was. *Gimme Shelter*, did you recognise it?' she asked, surprised. It was hard to imagine him knowing about the Stones, looking the way he did. But if she was right about his age he'd have been in his teens when they were starting out.

'I certainly did. When I lived in Kingston they were looked on as a local band. They were called groups in those days, of course.'

'Were they?' She knew that but it was important to establish the age-gap. 'Did you ever get to see them? On stage, I mean.'

He nodded. 'At Tooting in the nineteen-sixties and then again, years later, at Wembley.'

'I wish I had,' she said wistfully. 'Even though I was far too young for that sort of thing, I always wanted to be Marianne Faithfull. Not to be like her, but actually to be her and to be going out with Mick Jagger. Yes, I adored the Stones, too, still do. Emma, my daughter, liked them as well when she was younger, but not as much as I did. More as a curiosity, really. You met her at the wake if you remember.'

'Very presentable young woman, I thought – a credit to you.'

'Thank you.' It was good to hear that. 'Yes, I think she is too, even though I'm her mother and you'd be surprised if I didn't. She's a clever girl, did very well at St Clare's and then at university.'

'St Clare's? After moving from Surrey I was a schoolmaster down here for years, so I know what a good reputation St Clare's has. She was lucky to be able to go there.'

'You were a schoolmaster, were you?' He looked as if he was still wearing his schoolmaster's trousers. 'What did you teach?'

'I came here to be Head of Geography. The kids called me Hog.'

'Not in your hearing, I hope. Anyway, she now works in the City.'

'And what does she do there?'

'To be honest, I've very little idea. She works for some sort of bank but it's not actually a bank as such. Something to do with finance. Travels abroad on business.'

That was more than enough about Emma, she thought, knowing she'd brought her name into the conversation only as a way of prolonging Alan's stay. She was still in no rush to let him go and was beginning to know why.

Setting a new course to the same destination, she said, 'Alan, you must let me offer you a drink to thank you for bringing Reggie's things over here. Or a cup of tea if you prefer it, of course.'

'It was no trouble at all, I assure you. And I don't want to be a nuisance, but if you're twisting my arm I could do with a proper drink.'

'What would you like?' Not to make a point, but because it was no more than the truth, she said, 'I've got most things other than those curious liqueurs you only ever come across in duty-free shops.' She knew as soon as she spoke that it was the first time she'd spoken of possessions as hers and not *ours*.

'Small G and T, then, if I may,' he was saying.

'Don't hold back if you'd prefer something more exotic. I don't drink the stuff myself but my husband was dedicated to obscure malt whiskies. Awful things and fiendishly expensive, too. They make me think of the smell and likely taste of seaweed. Do you go in for that sort of thing, by any chance? Because if you do...'

Alan pulled a face. 'No, I don't, not at all. I often have

an ordinary whisky but at the moment I'll just stick with the G and T, thanks all the same.'

'I think I'll join you by topping this up,' she said, picking up her glass. 'I saw Emma off at the station after lunch and I'm not planning to do any more driving today.'

When she came back with the drinks, Alan took his and made a movement with the glass that looked as if he was raising it as a toast to her rather than to his lips. Looking over it at her, he said, 'If you don't mind me saying so, Penny, you're bearing up remarkably well, considering. When I think of what you've been through, I mean. And so recently.'

'Life goes on, I suppose. But thanks for saying it just the same. To tell you the truth, I don't think it's hit me yet. You know what TV reporters say when some disaster strikes – that the survivors are still struggling to come to terms with it? Well, I'm not conscious of doing much struggling. Not yet, that is. I think I may have come to terms with it already, whatever that means. Though I never expected it to be as…as easy as it seems to have been so far.' She sipped some of her drink before saying: 'It'll probably come to me later as a sort of delayed reaction. Perhaps I'm in denial, but I hope not. After denial, isn't it supposed to go; anger, depression, bargaining and acceptance? So I hope what I'm feeling is already acceptance with nothing else to come. And that makes me feel guilty for missing out the other ones.'

She didn't really feel guilty but knew she ought to sound as if she did. Everything else she'd said was true.

'I don't think you should. You must have had your time taken up worrying about the effect it would have on your daughter rather than on you.'

They drank in silence. She was grateful for what he'd said and for sounding so sincere about it. And, she told herself, for being here to say it.

Alan said, 'I couldn't help noticing that you keep your drinks in another room, not in here. Don't you find it a bit inconvenient, having to keep going in and out?'

'Yes it is, I know. But it's deliberate – to put a brake on my drinking, having to go out of my way to get started and then again to carry on with it.' She smiled. 'Of course, it doesn't always work as you can see. So, how do you manage, then?'

'All my drinks, such as they are, live in my front room more or less to hand.'

There was another silence during which she thought how little she knew about him.

'Are you a married man, Alan?' she asked, startling herself by saying it so abruptly.

He showed no sign of embarrassment. 'Not now,' he said. He sounded relieved to be single which probably ruled him out as a widower. 'But I was married, yes.'

'You say *was*. Do you mean...?'

'Divorced, some years ago now. I've lived on my own since then.'

'I'm so sorry.' Wondering how he filled his time, she said, 'I suppose I ought to start thinking about what I'm going to do with myself now I'm alone. Perhaps you could give me some tips.' Before she could stop herself, she asked if he had any children.

Again there was no embarrassment. 'It never happened, I'm afraid. So I envy you your Emma. She must be a real comfort to you at a time like this.'

'She's done her best, poor lamb. Though she'd be more of a comfort if I could see her more often – if she didn't live so far away. In South London, Wimbledon in fact. Not so far from where you used to live. She says it's got a good postcode, somehow more exclusive than other ones in that area.' Penny shrugged. 'Mind you, I've been there, and parts of it looked pretty ordinary to me. Do you remember yuppies? Do they still exist, do you think? Not that we ever had any down here, of course, but I remember hearing back in Mrs Thatcher's day how particular they were about where they lived in London. One road would be eminently desirable yet an adjoining one with exactly the same sort of houses wouldn't be.'

'Yes, I remember that. They used to do things like pronouncing Streatham as St Reatham to make it sound posher. And they didn't think Clapham sounded posh enough, either, so they pronounced it Clarm instead.' He laughed then, and she joined in.

Afterwards, when he'd left, she realised it was the first time she'd done that since before Reggie died.

CHAPTER FIVE

Since returning the locker key to him, Alan saw the Wendmore secretary only once when they passed each other outside the pro's shop. Tweedy nodded to him but didn't mention his disposal of Reggie's embarrassments. Alan said nothing about his meeting with Penny. With the cocoa van back at the Coq au Vin, he was being extra careful to avoid any golf-shoe misunderstandings in the club car park.

During the last week in May and the first two of June, he ate several times at the Coq au Vin, not only to save him from having to cook but also because he liked to go there and chat with Jimmy Hargreaves who was never too busy to pass up a chance for a spot of mutual abuse. He also read three books from the public library. He made sure he went in there only after a searching look through the window showed neither his ex-wife nor her lover was to be seen. It saved all of them from feeling uncomfortable but he still found it easy to imagine them sniggering together when they made the library computer disclose his choice of books – two about golf and one about India under British rule. He'd have done the same in their position.

The weather had stayed warm enough, even hot on some days, for him to spend time in the garden where Geoff, now passed fit for duty, was turning up weekly to weed and mow. Alan was out there most afternoons, dozing and reading on one of his pair of infinitely-adjustable sun-loungers. In the evenings he liked to drink and watch TV.

Since Susan's departure he'd grown used to being on his own with no one to interrupt or ban whatever he was doing or wanted to do. All the same, he thought sometimes, it'd be comforting to have someone on hand to chat to once in a while, though obviously no one like her. His life was based on sloth, which was fine with him, and changing it would mean becoming like other men of his age. To give their autumnal years a sense of purpose they turned their hands to sparkling new activities like woodturning – why? Or learning foreign languages – why again? His only moments of doubt came when he feared he'd look back on these as the good old days compared with what had followed them.

The supermarket he used was a middle-of-the-road one, not known for bargains in pensioners' fare or for the lobsters and haunches of venison likely to be favoured by the Tylers of the county. It had six checkouts but three of them were mainly for show, being in use only at busy times like Christmas and Easter.

He was in there one non-golfing morning to do his shopping. It was weighted in favour of pies, ready-sliced bread for toast-making, and eggs, cheese and tinned sardines to go on or with the toast. He also picked up a chicken curry complete with rice that needed no more cooking than heating up. It was destined for his Sunday lunch after a spell in his freezer followed by a shorter spell in his microwave oven.

With his credit card at the ready, he was making halting progress towards the checkout when the woman three ahead of him in the queue was snapped out of a private reverie by being told how much she had to pay. Like many an oldster he'd been stuck behind in his time, she only then began a painstaking search through her handbag. Having found and extracted her purse, she took a library card from it and then a bus pass before finding a banknote to hand over. When she was given her change she carefully fed it, one coin at a time, into several of the purse's zipped divisions. She then took up what felt like a sizeable chunk of his remaining life-span by putting her few bits of shopping into a plastic bag before wheeling her trolley away.

'Christ almighty,' he muttered softly, but evidently loudly enough to be heard by the woman immediately in front of him. He'd been too busy silently urging on the old woman to have noticed her while her back was towards him, but when she turned round he saw it was Penny Hallows who was looking at him. He had time to take in the snugly-fitting blue jeans she was wearing and to think how unusual that was for a woman of her age.

Instead of the ticking-off he expected from her, she said, 'You rotten sod, Alan, you'll be old yourself one day.'

'I didn't know it was you, I'm afraid.' Without thinking, he said, 'I didn't recognise you from behind,' and then, faintly embarrassed: 'Sorry about that.'

'I just hope you enjoyed the view.'

It was something only a confident woman would say. No woman in need of reassurance would come out with anything like that for fear of not getting it.

Before he could think of an appropriate response, she said, 'Don't worry about being impatient because I know how aggravating it can be. But you needn't think men are any quicker.'

Her trolley was impressively fuller than his. He noticed the difference when she unexpectedly waited for him beyond the checkout and while they walked together down the slope to the car park. He ought to ask her how she was getting on since he last saw her. Not that there was anything in how she looked or spoke to suggest she was less than perfectly all right.

Cautiously, he asked, 'How have you been, Penny, these last few weeks?'

'Quite busy, to tell you the truth. There's been a lot to do – sorting things out, cancelling things and so on. But I'm surprisingly okay in myself, thanks.'

They reached her Range Rover first. He helped unload her shopping into it before wheeling her trolley away. Then she waited for him to finish going through the same routine for himself. When he returned she thanked him for being such a gentleman and told him how nice it was to have bumped into him so unexpectedly. More casually, she said, 'Are you doing anything special for lunch today?'

'Not really, no,' he said, not making it up. 'I thought I'd have cheese on toast but I've still got half of one of those little Melton Mowbray pies that needs to be eaten this week. I've not decided yet.'

'Well, it's just a thought, but I wondered if you'd like to have something along those lines at my house – save you the trouble of doing it yourself. We could have a drink at the Antelope on the way if you like. It'll be nice and quiet there. Would you fancy that at all?' She added lightly: 'No pressure, though.'

Which meant exactly the opposite, of course, while giving her a chance to do some face-saving if he turned her down. But that wasn't going to happen. She was an attractive woman with a good figure who clearly had no objection to spending more time in his company and showed none of the neediness that normally made him wary of the bereaved. Best of all, and he marked her highly because of it, she was nothing like Susan, and at the very least he was now in line for a better lunch than he'd expected to have.

'It's not often I get an invitation like that. But yes, thank you for asking, I'd love to.'

'Good. Why don't you follow me there so you don't get lost on the way?'

The Antelope was as quiet as she said it would be. A chalked notice on a blackboard said there was still half an hour to go before customers were let loose to order food. As soon as he'd settled her at a table by a window, he went to the bar and was eventually served with drinks.

'I see you finally got rid of the cocoa van.'

He laughed. 'Yes, I told you I would. And normal service has now been resumed, so I can hold my head up in society again.'

'Speaking of society, I had a most pleasant letter from that golf club of yours only a few days after you came to see me. It was from someone calling himself H something Pemberton something, if I remember rightly. Claimed to be the club secretary.'

'Yes, he's not wrong about that. He's old-school, if you know what I mean, but his heart's more or less in the right place. His name's Pemberton Andrews, with a hyphen. First name's Harold, though not many people use it.'

'I can imagine. As well as sending me his condolences, very nicely expressed, I must say, he sent me a cheque for the unexpired part of my husband's membership fees. I'd not been expecting that, it never even occurred to me. Good to have, though. Best part of four hundred pounds, a really nice surprise.'

'I'm sure it was.' Tweedy must have been at peak secretarial efficiency to get it to her so quickly.

She asked him if he'd been playing much golf during the long spell of good weather.

He thought for a moment. 'I must have played about a dozen times since I came to your house. I usually play three times a week, always with the same three friends. You might say we're all creatures of habit because we've been doing it for years. Same friends, same place, and usually on the same mornings each week. Never on a Tuesday, of course. That's when the lady members have precedence on the course, so the men don't usually bother.'

He didn't explain it was also because the women took so long over everything; hitting the ball such short distances, endlessly chatting before and after each stroke, and paying leisurely visits to the clubhouse to freshen up before starting on the inward nine holes of their rounds.

'Don't they?' Penny looked puzzled. 'I never knew that. I'm sure Reggie sometimes went there on Tuesdays.'

He realised he'd inadvertently nudged her husband into an exposed position where his memory could be raked by hostile fire. He had to be careful to say nothing to alert her to Reggie's goings-on, particularly in view of Tyler's claim that she knew nothing about them.

'He was probably going to practise on the putting green or just to chew the fat in the bar. Lots of members do that, even when they're not playing themselves.'

She nodded thoughtfully while he prepared to fend off a question about how well he'd known Reggie.

Instead of asking him that one, she asked another: 'And what are they like? Your friends, I mean. Are they retired like you?'

It was a relief to get away from the Reggie topic and to tell her about them; that two used to work in the local offices of building societies, and the other one, though rarely unavailable for golf, still worked as a salesman but was reticent about what he sold. And how, to make things fair, they switched partners each time they played. Also, to make the matches more stimulating, they played for small cash stakes; a couple of pounds each half and a fiver on the match.

'Isn't that a recipe for squabbling, playing for money?'

'Not really, no. Hardly at all, in practice. We've reached a sort of gentleman's agreement not to criticize our partner of the day during the post-mortems we have in the bar afterwards. If someone's made a hash of things, he's normally allowed to put it down to bad luck or an unexpected gust of wind. Saves a lot of trouble in the long run. Not that we have much time to go over the match in any detail as we only ever stay for the one drink. Two of the chaps have to get back to their wives for lunch and the salesman has to get off to do some selling of whatever it is he sells. The two married ones never say anything much about their domestic lives but I get the impression their wives are glad to get them out from under their feet three times a week.'

'I can well believe it,' Penny said, laughing. 'And do the four of you socialise much?'

That was easy to answer. 'Just twice a year. It's another example of us being creatures of habit. We go for a curry, always to the same restaurant, once in August and once in the run-up to Christmas. No one's ever suggested we do more than that.'

'So do you never play with that...what was his name,

the one who was with you here after the service? Heavily-built man. Max, wasn't it?'

It was Alan's turn to laugh now. 'Tyler, Max Tyler. Heavily-built, that's one way of describing him. No, but I did see him there a week or so ago. He was wearing plus-fours.'

They sat chatting for a little while, looking up only when two couples came in talking loudly about where they wanted to sit. After noisily scraping their chair legs across the floor, they finally settled down at a nearby table, still talking loudly.

Alan had no hesitation in classifying the two men as long-retired officers from the upper reaches of the armed forces, the type that Upper Mendham was noted for. It was easy to imagine they came into the Antelope for what they'd call pre-prandial snifters with their lady wives, fresh from settling their Labradors in front of the green AGAs in their *Period Living* kitchens. Like their wives, they gave off an air of rarely-questioned authority.

Not much more than thirty years ago, he thought, both these red-faced old buffers could have been at the forefront of the NATO forces opposing the Warsaw Pact hordes. It was lucky the Russians and their allies never knew what faced them or the West European population would be speaking Russian by now.

'Nasty looking foursome,' he said softly. 'You don't know them, do you?'

Penny leaned towards him. 'I've seen them in the village but I don't know them, not even to nod in their direction. They must be newcomers, though they won't be here long. No one of their age ever is.' She lowered her voice. 'It's into sheltered housing within a year or two for them, even if they don't realise it now. And if they live that long.'

He picked up her glass. 'Do you fancy another, Penny? But I won't bother with one myself just now. Perhaps I could have one at your house instead, if you don't mind.'

'I don't mind at all. I won't have another here, either.

So we might as well get back there now and put some of that food of yours into my fridge before it starts going off.'

As he followed her out, he noticed the two women were openly looking her up and down, taking in every part of her but seeming to concentrate on her jeans. When they were done with that, they started to whisper together across their table. He was surprised how protective he felt of her at that moment – recently widowed, with uppity married women visibly discussing her and how she was dressed. Part of that protective feeling included his being pleased she appeared not to have noticed what they were doing. Either that, or she didn't care.

CHAPTER SIX

The entrance to the Antelope's car park was some yards down the street from the pub. Penny felt it perfectly natural to take Alan's arm as they walked there. She guessed correctly he wouldn't flinch or shy away from her when she did it, and would walk on the outside of the pavement without having to manhandle her into position or draw her attention to what he was doing, or why.

It was good to be with him in the sunshine. He looked slightly more presentable than when he turned up at her house in unrelieved brown. Today he was wearing a thin, not-too-obviously OAP, mushroom-coloured windcheater, the sort of top he might wear on the golf course. His rust-coloured needlecord trousers were a little too long for him and crumpled over the same shoes he'd been wearing before. She wouldn't have chosen those clothes for him. In a wood, in autumn, no one would know he was there.

She'd noticed the way he dropped his eyes to look at her jeans when she turned round to him in the checkout queue, and suspected he was having a good look at her rear view before that. When seen from behind, the tight jeans and her loose black sweatshirt would have made him think he was eyeing up a much younger woman. It was good to be able to dress younger than her age. One of the benefits of getting away with it was knowing it must annoy the women who did it without getting away with it.

When they turned into the car park and separated to get into their cars she realised she'd been hoping people would see him with her. Those two horse-faced women in the Antelope were a start. The feeling was already displacing the quite different and less optimistic one she'd nursed since Reggie's death.

Once inside the house they went straight into the kitchen. The cooking area had a workaday look with its substantial gas cooker, extensive work surfaces and double sink. It occupied one end of the room which extended into another large flagstoned area furnished with an old oak table surrounded by enough unmatched chairs to seat a dozen. A sofa stood against one wall. It was as battered as the ones described in auction catalogues as in Country House condition. Reggie never let her replace it or have it re-covered, claiming it was vulgar to have new-looking things in the country. A small table had a slim TV set on it, something he felt was acceptable, country or not.

Alan took off his windcheater and hung it over the back of a chair. The beige shirt he was wearing underneath could have done with a thorough ironing, Penny noticed. She asked him what he'd like to drink to go with the salad she was about to start making.

'A beer would be nice.'

'I think I can run to a bottle of that for you to be going on with.' She pointed to a low cupboard. 'In there, if you don't mind helping yourself while I get on with this. I've got a couple of slices of gala pie to go with it. Could you manage one of them, do you think?'

'Sounds an excellent idea. Gala pie, that's the one with the slice of hard-boiled egg in the middle, isn't it? When I was a schoolmaster the kids used to call it Dead Man's Eye Pie. I can't remember when I last had it.'

She told him where he'd find the cutlery and crockery. 'Perhaps you'd put them out for me.'

'Can I get you a drink while I'm at it?'

'There's a bottle of white wine in the fridge. I made a start on it last evening but I put one of those stopper things in it so it ought to be all right still. Be an angel and dig it out and pour me a glass.'

Later, when they'd finished eating the pie, its accompanying salad and the cheese that followed, she told him she liked his shirt. She was in two minds about its colour and the general state of it but that was unimportant for the moment. He'd be pleased to be given a compliment about his clothes. He probably didn't get many.

He looked up from picking biscuit crumbs out of the creases across its front and putting them carefully onto his plate.

'Really?' he said, sounding surprised. As well he might, she thought. 'It's kind of you to say so. I never seem to know what goes with what. My ex despaired of me. She used to say I was a typical man, which by her lights meant I was permanently in a state of being love-forty down when it came to clothes.'

And his wife wasn't wrong about that. Men liked to think they were a bit out of the ordinary and all the better for it, so Penny told him he wasn't as typical as he might think. It wasn't strictly true but he'd be bound to enjoy hearing her say it, and it made a good follow-up to her fib about his shirt.

After meeting him three times there was still a lot to find out about him and his life. She knew he was a divorced and childless retired schoolmaster who lived a few villages away. He liked a drink; gin, whisky – other than the seaweedy malts – and now beer. They shopped at the same supermarket and if the contents of his trolley were anything to go by he was either too idle or unhandy to do much cooking for himself. He had enough money to be a member of Reggie's golf club, but apparently no interest in owning an expensive car. Like the clothes he'd worn on his first visit to her, his Ford had seen better days.

While she made the coffee she asked him to fill in a few of the gaps in her knowledge but only if he had no objections, of course.

Unlike the last time when he rambled on about the cocoa-van and its part in his recent life, he now sounded more relaxed. In a matter-of-fact way he sketched out brief details of his career and said a few bitter-sounding things about his ex-wife, Susan, who left him not long before his early retirement.

'That must have come as a blow,' Penny said when he stopped.

'It was a blow to my pride, certainly,' he said wearily. 'What little pride she'd left me with by the time she upped sticks and buggered off, I mean. It was the thought that she could fancy a bloke from the library service of all things to share her declining years with. That was hard to take. And knowing she must have been having it away with a date-stamp jockey for God knows how long.'

There was nothing helpful she could say about that, and the ensuing silence lasted long enough for her to conclude no more information was coming her way. Before the silence went on too long, she said, 'I daresay it's been a while since you had a chance to get all that off your chest.'

'Yes, mainly because there's been no one I could confide in. Or who'd listen.'

'You've had no relationships at all, then? Nothing of that nature since you and your wife broke up?' She added quickly: 'Sorry to be so personal. I hope you don't mind me asking.'

'Of course not. But sadly, no, not a single one. Yes, there are women in the area who are unattached by accident or design. Given a following wind, I suppose there might be some mutual attraction, if only for a bit of company. It's meeting them that's the problem.'

In Penny's experience, lunches and dinner parties were the backbone of social life in these villages. They took place quite often but it was rare for more than eight people to sit down to eat at them because the ever-ageing guests found it tricky to follow individual conversations above a drink-fuelled babble.

Reggie used those meals to hone his flirtation technique, she remembered. And there was many a time when a male dinner guest – one she was expected not to upset because of his importance to Reggie's business – wandered into this very kitchen to help her take something into the dining-room and she found herself being grabbed for a surprise kiss, or even a bit more. She was nearly always able to wriggle away from the bit more without giving offence.

Her breasts were always the first target for boys when she was young, but perhaps that was different now like everything else was. Getting to first base was what they called it in those days. With her husband's clients it was as important not to give it too much of a welcome as it was not to make a fuss about it. Men, particularly the older ones, tried it on from habit or as the sort of gift a hostess would expect to receive, rather like the flowers their wives brought with them. An enthusiastic response would have confused them. She soon came to look on it as one-way kitchen traffic, not for repetition elsewhere and not to be spoken of. Younger women like Emma wouldn't put up with it, though. Not these days.

'If you've had enough, would you mind giving me a hand with the plates and things? Then we can go into the other room and have a brandy or something.'

He followed her instructions efficiently enough, even rinsing off bits of pie from the cutlery and then scraping pieces of uneaten salad, mainly hers, into a small recycling bin.

'What about dinner parties, things like that?' she asked him after they moved into the drawing-room, she with a brandy of time-saving size, and Alan with a small whisky. He'd specified its smallness, reminding her he had to drive home.

This time he sat on the same sofa with her. She was trying to weigh its significance, if any, when he said, 'There's a problem with those. When I was married we used to entertain, always on a reciprocal basis. Each couple kept to whatever timetable established itself. One month before reciprocating, or even three months or more. Did you do that, I wonder?'

'I think everyone does, otherwise it gets confusing and all out of sync.'

'One thing I do remember was being told singleton guests were a nuisance so that's why I don't get invitations any more, or I like to think it is. And if I did, they know I can't cook and wouldn't be able to invite them back. What's more, all the single women I'd be likely to meet are probably too old or too young for me to think about dating them, even if I wanted to.' He drank some whisky before asking: 'But can people date at my age? I'm not sure they can.'

'I don't see why not. What we've been doing today is a date of sorts. We've been to a pub for a drink and now we've had a meal together without anyone around to play gooseberry. That would constitute a date in most people's minds.'

He made a puffing sound through pursed lips. 'I'm not sure anyone would actually call it that. Not a date as such.'

'I think they might, you know. Anyway, I'm a singleton now so I've got the same problems as you. Some of my friends – neighbours, that is – have plucked up courage and dropped in to see how I am. You know how it is; it's kind of them, of course it is, and it's something they feel they have to do. It's a social duty, I suppose. They're not the sort you'd ever want to confide in about anything personal. They used to come to lunch or dinner here and we used to go to their places in return, just like you were saying. It was all very pleasant and boozy and gossipy. But that's all they were – pleasant company. No more so in practice than anyone I might chat with in the village shop or see at the W.I.'

'That's a pity. And you've had no invitations since…?'

'Yes, it is, and no, I haven't. They've already started saying things like "When your husband was alive" and "Before your husband died". I tell you, Alan, I don't know what I expected to feel but I do find it upsetting. After all, I have to look to the future. It does me no good to be constantly dragged back to the past.'

'But you must know that they mean well.'

After some thought, she said, 'Yes, I do know that. The trouble is that just when I think I'm making progress, carrying on with what needs to be done, trying to cobble together a sort of timetable for doing things, someone turns up on my doorstep with a caring and sympathetic look I've not seen them wearing before, and I'm back where I started.'

Now she'd begun to unburden herself, she might as

well carry on. It might even do her some good, and at least he was giving her no sign of having had enough of it. There was no covert glancing at his watch and no restless moving about on the sofa.

'And I have to tell you, I wasn't, you know, shocked, by his death. Right from the start I knew I'd be likely to face that one day, what with the difference in our ages. He was fifteen years older than me, almost sixteen. He used to joke about it, said it was half a generation. No, I wasn't shocked, not really. He'd not been his usual self for some time and when his heart finally packed up for good I wasn't at all surprised, only concerned for my future and about how Emma was going to feel. Was that selfish of me, do you think?' She wondered if she was being selfish now by openly canvassing his approval of her feelings.

'I wouldn't have thought so. You were thinking of your daughter as well. That wasn't selfish. But weren't you able to prepare yourself for it if he'd not been well for a while?'

'Not really, no.'

That was enough of that to be going on with. It was time to change the subject.

'Thanks for putting up with me going on – you're a good listener. I tell you, if you lived in this village you'd be very much in demand, singleton or not.'

He looked noticeably uncomfortable to hear her say it.

How strange it was that men found it so hard to accept compliments. Reggie was different. He was forever hawking after them and getting them, too. But he was a one-off.

She said, 'I invited you here today, so you can't be that bad.'

'And for a nice meal.'

'But simple enough in all conscience, so thank you. But you said you weren't much of a dab hand at cooking. Was that right or were you being modest? No shame in it if you're not, most men aren't.'

'I wish I was, but I never got round to it. When I was teaching, I used to have a proper lunch at the school so never needed a cooked meal in the evening.' He patted his stomach. 'And I didn't want to run the risk of plumping up.'

She looked down at what little there was to be seen of his stomach under the creased shirt. 'I can see you've got that under control. You're very slim. I expect it's the golf that does it. You remember how Reggie used one of those electric buggy things? When he was younger he used to walk round the course, uphill and down dale. Claimed it was several miles in all. I went there once and watched him for a hole or two before going off to somewhere more interesting. As far as I could see it was a walk punctuated by swinging a club about like a dervish and then undoing all the good work in the bar afterwards. How he didn't get stopped by the police on his way home, I'll never know.'

Alan laughed. 'It's par for the course – sorry about that. I don't do much apart from the golf. The idea of holidaying on my own doesn't appeal so I spend most of my time reading and watching TV. It's not that I'm uninterested in things – most of my pupils would have said "disinterested" – and I know I've got time on my hands to fit in other activities. Except I can't think of any I'd ever want to do. But going back to what I was saying; at weekends and during the school holidays my wife did all the cooking and I never put up much resistance. The upshot of it is that I can't entertain. I know I could take guests over to the Coq au Vin but—'

'The cocoa van, you mean. I wouldn't mind giving it another try sometime. We could go there together, for instance.' That was pushing it rather, but nothing ventured…

There was no response, which was disappointing. As a stopgap, she could invite him for a meal here if she could scrape some neighbours together, but not too many of them for fear of overwhelming him. She'd have to explain her reasons for his presence in advance, and they'd be bound to think it was too soon after Reggie. Why not, though? They were both lonely, under-occupied, and could do with being taken out of themselves.

She was thinking ahead, very far ahead, but it was possible that one day, if they went on seeing each other, he might want to take matters further with her. He might even think she expected him to. If he did, how was she to respond? Supposing, just supposing, she went along with it or even welcomed that sort of complication – and she didn't want to rule it out – he'd have to deal with the after-effects of her operation when confronted with them. Reggie could never cope with them. The two men were different in many ways but it didn't mean they'd react differently.

CHAPTER SEVEN

Two weeks later, Alan was roused from his sun-lounger by Penny phoning to invite him to dinner at her house. It was good to hear from her but he took no comfort from her claim that the meal was to be only a small and informal affair. In Upper Mendham circles, small probably meant no more than a dozen guests. Informal might mean no more than the absence of the county's Lord Lieutenant.

She went on to say only four of her neighbours were coming; two couples, both pairs unassuming. That was better but still not much of a comfort. And, no, she told him, it wasn't too soon after Reggie's death for anyone to feel awkward. Of course, she'd understand if he declined. But if he could come, and she hoped he'd be able to, she planned to explain his presence by telling the others no more than the truth. He was an old golfing chum of Reggie's and had been a real support to her.

Only half of that was true, he thought, but it was too late now to put her right about it.

A dinner for just the two of them would have been better. He'd have looked forward to that. But inviting other guests as well made it look as if she wanted to prove him wrong about his claim that singletons were a nuisance.

Socializing with strangers was never fun-filled. As they were from her village they could easily be like the braying ex-officer types and their wives whose presence in the Antelope was so irritating. If they were, he'd have to do or say something about them when he had the chance.

Then there was the question of reciprocity. Two meals at her house put him under pressure to arrange one for her. Just the one, though, because a slab of Dead Man's Eye Pie didn't count as a proper meal. Dinner at the Coq au Vin would do.

He asked about the dress code, hoping there'd be no nonsense about what Upper Mendham people would call dressing for dinner.

The meal was to be in the dining-room, she told him, so not gardening clothes but not suits, either. That was something, at least.

Now he'd accepted, she asked him if he'd do her a favour, a personal one. Again, he was welcome to say no.

Free meals were one thing, he told himself, but how free would this dinner be if it involved him in doing a favour? First it was Tweedy looking for help, and now it was her.

The new favour concerned Reggie's ashes. She'd been hanging on to them till she felt up to getting rid of them, not that she put it like that. Would he mind terribly if she asked him to go with her to scatter them at a place called Winyard's Gap? She'd understand if he did mind but it would be such a help for her to have some moral support. And, no offence to him, she'd tried to think of someone else who might fit the bill but he was the only one she felt comfortable about asking.

Having gone along with the dinner invitation, he felt no shame for wanting to avoid this second one. It was worth re-visiting his attempted ploy to get Tyler involved in the locker business. So, with escape in mind, he suggested Emma would want to be there. Ash-scattering was a family affair and not one to be downgraded by an outsider's presence.

Penny sounded ready for that. Too nimbly for his liking, she side-stepped it by explaining that Emma was her first choice but claimed to be tied up at work for the foreseeable future. The disapproval in her voice told him her daughter was less than keen to help, not when it involved a round trip of nearly three hundred miles.

He moved on by hinting that one of Reggie's friends from the village would be a more suitable candidate.

To his unvoiced dismay, she explained she planned to dispose of the ashes at the top of a steep hill. She could think of no one else with links to her husband who was still sufficiently mobile to make it up there alive. Worse than that, most of his old friends were dead or had moved away.

Could there be anything else to come? A memorial service in Wells Cathedral, perhaps, or the installation of a special seat in the Wendmore bar with a brass plate on it testifying to Reggie's love of the place?

Outfoxed for a second time, and squeezing reluctance from his voice, he said he'd be pleased to help her. It was always like that – the thin end of the wedge, the sprat to catch a mackerel. As soon as you agreed to do one disagreeable thing you could bet your life you'd be expected to do a worse one as well.

When he arrived at her house three days later she showed every sign of being pleased to see him but said very little. She looked tense and abstracted as she thanked him for coming and told him it was kind of him and much appreciated. Then she suggested they took her sports car.

He'd not been a passenger in one of those since his Surrey days when a chemistry master took him for a spin in an old MG down the A3 to Guildford and back. He'd enjoyed that experience but didn't expect to enjoy the next one.

But this was the right sort of day to be in one, he found. Even in the early evening it was still warm enough to have the BMW's top down. She drove aggressively, going faster and changing gear more often than he'd have done or thought necessary, yet still managed to swerve around most of the pot-holes that cratered the minor roads. He tried to get comfortable but her driving technique forced him to keep one hand locked round the handle of the passenger door to stop himself from sliding about on the leather seat. His free hand kept a tight grip on the lid of the plastic urn clenched between his thighs and which contained all that was left of Reggie.

'Did the place have any special meaning for your husband?' he asked when he saw a signpost pointing to Winyard's Gap. Like the Wendmore bar did, perhaps.

She turned to him, an action he wished she'd postponed till the car had completed its bucketing course onto a main road, the first they'd been on since setting out.

'Sorry about that,' she said. With her eyes back on the road and driving more slowly now, she continued: 'It's a National Trust place and there's a war memorial at the top of the hill. It's the Wessex Division's one. There are fabulous views from up there and when the weather's right you can see the four counties they recruited from: Somerset, Dorset, Wiltshire and Devon.' She sounded like a well-versed guide dishing out information to tourists.

'And was your husband involved in it?'

'Reggie? Good Lord, no. When he was called up for his National Service he wangled his way into a good infantry regiment but was never exposed to shot and shell. But you wouldn't expect to be, not stuck out in Essex somewhere. He said he spent most of his two years driving officers about in a jeep.'

She abruptly wrenched the steering-wheel to the right and drove past a pub before parking in a shallow lay-by. 'Here we are,' she said, switching off the engine and looking at her watch. 'According to my diary, the sun sets in about half an hour so we needn't have hurried. I'll just put the top up and we'll get going.'

'Sorry, Penny, but what's the time of the sunset got to do with it?'

'At the going down of the sun...' She paused expectantly.

'We shall remember them, yes.'

As they got out of the car, she said, 'It all stems from the Remembrance Day service at the Cenotaph. He was always very moved by it, made a point of watching it on TV every year. His father was in the Division when he was killed in Normandy not long after D-Day, you see. Reggie was only a child then but he always wanted his own ashes to be scattered by this memorial. He often came here, usually by himself.'

'I imagine he must have felt it brought a sense of completion. Closure, as they say now – that sort of thing.'

'Mm, I suppose. Not that he'd have ever used an

expression like that. We went over there once, to Caen, to see where it happened, but his father was one of those with no known grave. Probably blown to smithereens, Reggie said, with nothing left to bury. But we did find his name on a memorial. That meant a lot to him. I say that because it was the only time I saw him cry, poor man. He wasn't one for public displays of emotion, not like these days when no one's thought to be properly upset unless they're seen to be in floods of tears in front of all and sundry.'

'I had two great-uncles in the First World War. Brothers, both killed on the Somme. Their bodies were never found either, but their names are on the memorial there.'

She put her hand on his arm. 'How awful for their parents. I can't imagine what that must be like. To lose one son must have been bad enough, but two…'

After she put the car roof up and locked the doors they walked together to the gate at the bottom of the hill which a National Trust sign said was White Hill. Among other information it alerted visitors to the type of trees to be seen on the hill and the sort of birds that lived up there, though Alan knew he'd be unable to identify any of them, trees or birds. Beyond the gate a few steps led to a rutted path, fortunately dry after the good weather. Two longer flights punctuated the steep rise to the top.

He followed her up the wooded hill with the urn under his arm. The steps had handrails which he soon needed to use, and he was out of breath by the time they arrived at the top and stepped onto a narrow plateau where the stone memorial stood.

The views to three sides were obscured by trees. But to the west, over and beyond the pub, many square miles of Somerset could be seen stretching away in the fading light.

'I don't want the ashes to go on this flat part by the memorial. I wouldn't like to think of people trampling on them, so I'll scatter them over the edge instead. It's close enough.'

They peered over the steep drop. 'I think this might

do,' she said, 'He'll be able to see Somerset from here.'

'Do you want us to say a prayer or anything?'

She looked out over the fields which were starting to lose their definition as a thin mist rose over them. Eventually she shook her head, saying, 'No, but perhaps we could think about him for a moment.'

That was easier said than done, Alan found. He'd no image of Reggie to fall back on. Hoping Penny would take his silence for respectful meditation, he waited before offering her the urn. 'Do you want to take this now?' he asked.

'I think I ought to. Would you be a dear and let me hold your hand while I do the scattering? If you wouldn't mind.'

It was hard to know whether she was asking him out of a sense of solidarity or to save herself from toppling over the edge. He did as he was asked, watching while she leaned over and shook out the ashes. The air was still and they ended up as greyish clumps on and between the brambles that grew where they fell.

'They won't stay like that for long,' she said, looking down. 'There's bound to be a wind up here soon to spread them about. Anyway, that's done now.' She spoke without emotion, or at least with no more than he imagined her using to say she'd finished doing her washing-up.

Turning back to him, she said in a quite different tone: 'Thank you, Alan. I'm so glad to have had you with me. I don't think I could have faced it on my own.'

She gave him back the urn. If anything, she was now holding his hand more tightly than before but it was darker on their way back down the hill, the steps were more dangerous in the gloom, and she could easily have stumbled. He took the lead, still hand-in-hand with her.

Back in the car, she said, 'You made it much more bearable for me. No, really,' she insisted as he started to protest.

'I'm pleased you felt you could ask me.'

More surprised than pleased and more than a shade

pissed-off, he wanted to add, to let her know there was no confusion in his mind about it. She'd said nothing to indicate the date was special to her or ever was to her husband. It was easy to understand why Emma preferred to stay away rather than trail down from whatever she did in the City and then trail back again the next day, thus missing almost two days of wheeling and dealing. He guessed Penny chose today solely to get the ash-scattering business out of the way once she'd decided she couldn't put it off any longer. It seemed plausible to him.

'He was so good for me, you know,' she said suddenly. 'Not good *to* me particularly, but he did look after me very well on the whole. But I want to tell you what I've never been able to tell anyone else.'

That sounded ominous. He hoped she wasn't going to tell him about Reggie's gallivanting. If she did, he'd have to act surprised throughout.

'You don't have to confide in me, Penny. It's really none of my business.'

'No, it's important.'

Important to her, possibly. Even if she showered him with less dramatic marital disclosures, he hoped she'd be quick about it as he was more than ready for a drink after slogging his way up and down the hill.

'The truth of the matter is that I never actually loved him.'

Christ, he didn't want to hear anything of that sort.

'Penny, you mustn't—'

She carried on anyway. 'Respected him, yes. Grateful to him, yes. As you know, I was much younger than him. When we met I was just twenty to his thirty-five, which was a big gap for someone of my age. Back then, twenty-year-olds were really young, not grown up like they are now. He was a man who was worldly-wise and well into his career as a financial consultant and the first man I'd ever been out with. All the others were boys. What's more, he had his own flat. None of my previous boy-friends had one, so you can imagine how quickly I grew up with him there. I think you know what I mean.'

He knew exactly what she meant. Not for the first time he thought how good it must have been to be Reggie in his younger days, not forgetting how satisfying his later years were, the lucky bugger.

'And I was just ordinary, a typist,' she was saying now. 'I'd been to a grammar school but that was a step down from his public school. You used to be a schoolmaster so you'd know all about that. My family was ordinary, too. My father was a clerk in a local department store. Reggie was so different. He knew all about etiquette and how to carry on in public and I absorbed it from him, soaked it up like a sponge. We met at a tennis club of all places. I joined it an attempt to give myself a social leg-up. To get away from boys who drove tractors or didn't have jobs at all. And it worked.'

'John Betjeman wrote a poem about a tennis club, I remember – very middle-class places.'

'I know the one you mean. Of course, Reggie thought Betjeman was sloppy, and as he was Dutch he'd no business to be writing about the English.'

That didn't sound right. 'I don't think he was actually Dutch. The name might be, but —'

'Anyway, Reggie made me pregnant and immediately insisted we get married. It came as a complete surprise to me, I can tell you. I'm sure he could have arranged a termination if he wanted to but he wouldn't hear of it. He went on about duty and honour and moral crimes. Both his parents came from what he called Old Catholic families, guardians of the Old Faith as he called it, but he and his mother never practised their religion. I think they took the view that being of Old Catholic stock didn't necessarily mean they had to go to church. It was just another social asset for them, the same as having Coats of Arms.'

Nor did it get in the way of Reggie knocking up a young girl, Alan thought. The Pope would have had something to say about that, no doubt. But a quick trip to the confessional for absolution would have put it right.

'From his point of view, I was a girl who'd be grateful for all he had to offer by way of money and security, and bound to show my gratitude by spending the rest of my life making it up to him. I *was* grateful too. I might have been young but I was old enough to know which side my bread was buttered on and to have an eye to the main chance. Not like the other girls of my age who had to start from scratch. There was no need to save up to get married and buy somewhere to live, not for me. And in my defence, I wasn't completely unattractive. Not a trophy-wife – I wasn't smart enough or sufficiently well-bred for that. He never loved me, of course, but that was okay.' She shrugged. 'I didn't love him either. Grew to be fond, very fond of him but never loved him, not really.'

She stopped talking at last and Alan did nothing to break the silence that followed. It went on long enough for him to think she wasn't winding herself up to tell him even more. He hoped her disclosures had done her some good because he felt no benefit from them. It sounded from her account that she'd had a gilded marriage, even if it wasn't all hearts and flowers. His own union was like that, apart from the gilding; no hearts, no flowers, and certainly gilding-free. She'd said nothing to change his second-hand view of her husband; presumptuous, arrogant and selfish. Lucky, though – no doubt about that.

She'd found her voice again. 'I know it sounds silly to think of it but you know that Stones' song, *You Can't Always Get What You Want*?'

'Yes I do,' he said, wondering what that had to do with anything. 'It was about settling for what you need instead of what you want.'

'Fancy you remembering. You see what I mean, though. I wanted to be in love and be loved in return, both at the same time. It never happened but I did get what I needed to improve myself and get on in life.'

Hearing that, he wanted to say 'And I bet you made the most of it.' What he did say was: 'I'm pleased for you.'

Good luck to her if she could find comfort in a chunk

of Rolling-Stones-based philosophy. But she'd do well to remember the part of the song about *trying* to get what you need. Apart from joining a tennis club, she'd not had to try.

It was good to hear her say: 'There's just one more thing, Alan,' as he'd had more than enough already. 'I'd be grateful if you ever meet Emma again you won't mention any of that to her. I know she may have guessed the truth but she's never mentioned it, that's all.'

'Okay, then.'

She started the car, switched on its lights and drove off less erratically than before but as silently as on the outward journey.

He used the silence to think Tyler was right to believe Reggie's reputation for philandering, augmented by Tweedy's discoveries in the locker, had passed her by. If not, it was too upsetting for her to tell him about it, even though she'd been unstoppable while telling him about everything else.

When they reached Upper Mendham she drew up in front of the village shop and told him to put the empty urn in the litter bin on the pavement outside. She then drove on and parked her car in the drive of her house without first dropping him off in the lane where his car was waiting for him, conveniently positioned to drive home in.

'You'll come in for a moment before you go, won't you? Have a drink before you go back?'

Once inside she busied herself getting drinks for them, leaving him on his own in the room he noticed she'd made a point of calling the drawing-room. Would the generations of down-to-earth country folk who'd owned the place have called it that? He thought not. They probably called it something homely like the parlour.

He wandered about, taking in the quality of its furniture and fittings. Nothing he saw was in anything like the state of the kitchen sofa. Among the antiquery, there was a table with silver-framed photos on it. He'd noticed them before but had no time to examine them. One of the black-and-white photos showed the head and shoulders of a lean and good-looking man of about forty, presumably Reggie, with a young woman recognisable as a young Penny. So that was what he looked like. It confirmed Alan's belief that he'd never seen Reggie in the flesh, or if he had seen him he didn't know who he was, not even in a more worn version of how he looked in the photo. There was a fierce, almost predatory, look on Reggie's face which made him look more like a military man than the pen-pusher she'd said he'd been.

Alan's library book about the British Raj had photos in it of youngish officers who resembled early Reggies. They looked keen-eyed and ready for action. It was likely to be action that involved shooting animals in general, and skewering pigs in particular, he guessed. Then, after riding back to the officers' mess to dose themselves with whisky and sodas, they probably changed for a chukka or two of polo. They were the sort of public-school men with broad ancestral acres waiting for them back in Blighty while they did their duty for the King Emperor in an exclusive outfit like Skinner's Horse. All Reggie did was spend his two years of National Service driving an army jeep.

When Penny returned with the drinks, the same as on his first visit, she sat down beside him on the sofa, saying: 'Do you realise we held hands all the way back down that hill to the car? I hope you didn't…'

'Mind? No, of course not. It was steep and getting dark and you wouldn't have wanted to pitch down to the bottom.'

'As long as you weren't bothered by it, that's all. I didn't want you to feel I was presuming.'

'I didn't think that, so you've no need to worry.' He made himself say: 'And I'm looking forward to that dinner party of yours.'

'Me too, of course. You'll like the others as well, I'm sure. They're quite undemanding.'

He'd be the judge of that. 'What sort of time do your dinners normally end?'

It was bad enough to have to be there at all without being bored witless into the small hours as well. And having to drive home afterwards wouldn't let him do justice to the available drinks.

'It depends. People usually start making their excuses well before midnight. There was a time when guests had a job not to fall over when the night air hit them. But I'm afraid we're all a bit older and more restrained now. Say eleven or eleven-thirty. I'll certainly be in the mood for bed by then.'

As she spoke, he thought she gave him an odd sort of look which didn't last long enough for him to be sure. She'd not dressed it up with raised eyebrows and widened eyes so it probably wasn't meaningful, but it made him wonder if she intended it to be. And if it was and if she did, he'd no way of telling what it meant, if anything, and he couldn't think of a way to find out.

So he didn't respond to it and she didn't repeat it. They carried on chatting as if it hadn't happened until it was late and time for him to leave for home. But he thought about the look, the hand-holding, the reference to bed and their possible meanings all the way back in the dark to Myrtle Cottage.

CHAPTER EIGHT

It was seven o'clock in the evening. Penny arrived at Emma's house thirty minutes earlier after taking a train from Somerset to Clapham Junction, a second train back down the line to Wimbledon, and then a taxi.

She'd decided to phone Emma to tell her she wanted to do some shopping in London and to ask if she might spend the night at her house before returning to Somerset the next day. She fully intended to go into London and look round the West End shops but the main reason for her visit was to see if she could sniff out clues about Emma's possible pregnancy and marriage prospects, in whichever order they presented themselves, if they existed at all. She couldn't make herself put it off any longer.

Emma agreed with the proposal and said she'd make up the bed in the second bedroom for her. It was the room Penny had earmarked as a nursery ever since the morning of the funeral. She'd used it on previous visits, nearly always on her own because of Reggie's wafer-thin tolerance of Giles. She was to leave the next morning after they left for work at six-thirty. If she wanted breakfast she'd have to make it herself, and she was under instructions to make sure her bedroom window was closed and the burglar alarm set before leaving.

She and Emma were in the poky sitting-room, waiting for Giles to arrive. Emma described its furnishing as minimalist but it needed to be sparse in such a small room. And minimalist meant minimal comfort, as Penny was re-discovering as she squirmed about on a cream leather sofa that didn't support her back properly.

The stripped wooden floor bore marks of heavy traffic both old and new. Normal owners, less up-to-date, would have said it cried out for a carpet. Instead, a small rug, patterned in a way certain to be thought meaningful somewhere hot and foreign, lay in front of the redundant fireplace. It was easy to catch your heel in it, she found. A bay window overlooked a thin stretch of shingle and a low brick wall. Beyond that was a pavement with cars parked against it and on it in both directions for as far as the eye could see.

Two steps led down from the far end of the narrow hallway – far in the sense of being more than a few paces distant from the front door. They led to a kitchen that was really no more than a scullery, and to another room with overhead lighting so bright it could have done duty in an operating-theatre. There was a small table with six chairs of advanced design wedged in around it. This arrangement made it look quite a lot like a dining-room, or at least a place where a guest might be asked to sit down to eat.

As happened each time she visited the house, she wondered how a cramped place like this, semi-detached by no more than the width of a shared concrete path, with no garage and in such a crowded street, could be worth as much as her daughter said it was. Her claim about the value-enhancing postcode must be true.

What Emma and Giles called their garden was a back yard with a decked sitting-area that caught the sun for only a couple of hours in the afternoon. A brick-built projection, once an outside lavatory, now served as a shed. Penny had never seen its contents but they definitely wouldn't be gardening implements.

She was drinking a gin and tonic. Emma was drinking orange juice again. It was a good sign, though Penny had read that women were cautioned against drinking alcohol only when they were actually pregnant. Avoiding it as an aid to conception was sensible but only optional. It was too soon for rejoicing.

Unless Emma soon said something to the contrary, it looked as though her womb was still running on empty. Nothing had been said either way during their occasional phone chats or so far today. Penny promised herself that she'd carry on with her policy of asking no questions even though she wanted to. As Emma had told her, it could take time. A second promise, even harder to keep, was to be pleasant to Giles.

Emma hadn't asked about the trip to Winyard's Gap. After giving her plenty of time to say something appropriate, Penny said, 'By the way, I scattered daddy's ashes last week. It was such a shame you weren't able to go up there with me.'

'I explained about that, mummy,' Emma said with one of her sighs. 'It was bedlam in the office at the time and it still is. I really couldn't get away. I only wish I could have.' Looking puzzled, she asked: 'Up where, though?'

'I did tell you. It was at a place called Winyard's Gap. It's just over the Dorset border and there's a steep hill there – hence the up bit – with a war memorial at the top. It's where daddy always wanted his ashes to go.'

'I don't remember him ever mentioning it.'

'No, he probably wanted you to think he was immortal. Parents don't like to go on about that sort of thing to their children.'

'I suppose. All the same, it must have been depressing to have to do it on your own. I hope it wasn't too upsetting for you.'

'I wasn't on my own. I went with a friend.'

'Oh, that was nice for you. Was she anyone I know?'

'It was a he. A man called Alan Baxter who used to play golf at daddy's club. You met him in the Antelope after the funeral service, if you remember. There were two of them there from the club. He was the quieter one, not the fat one with the moustache. He's been very supportive since…you know.'

Emma shook her head. 'No, he doesn't ring a bell, but I met so many people that day it's not really surprising. But I'm glad he's been a help to you. Of course, if you didn't live so far away, perhaps I'd have been able—'

'I know. And you would have, too.' It was the right thing to say and Penny felt she'd made her point. 'Anyway, looking back, I'm glad you didn't find the funeral too much for you. I thought you bore up very well, considering.'

'I tried to. Most of the time I was feeling sorry for you. It was different for me. After all, he wasn't what you'd call young, was he? So it wasn't entirely unexpected. I must have pre-loaded with upset and been living with it in anticipation ever since that first heart attack of his. I didn't want to be any more of a burden to you by making a fool of myself.'

'You wouldn't have been a burden, I promise you.'

Soon after that there was the sound of the front door opening, then closing, and Giles came into the room.

'Hello,' he said to Emma, followed by: 'Hello, Penny. Nice to see you again. How was the journey up? Not too bad, I hope.'

He bent down to kiss her, almost but not quite contacting her cheek and making an affected lost-sheep sound as he did it. He didn't kiss Emma.

He was tall and thin with short bristly hair and rimless glasses. His appearance always reminded Penny of old films about white-coated American scientists busily developing atomic bombs in their laboratories. His pale blue shirt was worn with a single-breasted business suit, but his tie of many colours had a Windsor knot – virtually the Mark of the Beast, according to Reggie.

'I was so sorry to hear about Reggie's passing,' Giles said. 'And it was such a shame that I couldn't get down for the funeral, but I—'

'—was on a trip to Hong Kong. Yes, I remember.'

'Couldn't wriggle out of it, not at such short notice. But Emma here would have explained all that to you. We did write to you, of course.'

It was a With Sympathy card with a picture of an open book and a candle on the front. It needed only the addition of a bell to mark an excommunication.

'So I recall.'

'Good. I'm glad it arrived safely.'

The way he said it make her wonder if he'd expected her to acknowledge it in writing.

He pointed at their drinks. 'I think I might join you two

ladies in one of those. Not the orange juice, of course.'

He sat down on the room's only chair, a sculpted object with chrome supports that doubled back under its seat like the runners on a sledge.

When Emma came back with his drink, he asked her: 'Did you have an okay day? Must be nice to be able to slip away early.' Sarcastic as ever, Penny thought.

After drinking for a moment, he put his glass down and balanced his briefcase on his knees. It was as thin as Reggie's Masonic case which she still had at home, and made her think she must do something about it and its secret contents. It was too special for a charity shop, so perhaps she ought to hand it over to one of the brethren at the Lodge.

'If you'll excuse me, Penny, I must just have a word about some work stuff with Emma.'

'You carry on, don't mind me.'

He snapped open the briefcase's brass locks, took out some papers and showed them to Emma who, Penny noticed, showed less interest than she might have done in what he had to say about them.

'...so I'll talk to Madrid in the morning,' he said, 'and you'd better have a word with the compliance boys. Yes?'

To Penny, he said, 'That's about it for the day. Business done but still in need of tidying-up. And your daughter will see to that for me.'

"For me". That was an odd thing for him to say because it implied his seniority, and Emma always claimed they were at the same level. It sounded as if he was making some kind of point to her.

Dinner was booked at a local restaurant in the village, as Emma and Giles called it. It made their part of Wimbledon sound rural, as though the famous common which began on its edge was rolling countryside.

They walked there together, mother and daughter in front, with Giles lagging behind to make a call on his mobile phone. He'd shed his suit in favour of chinos and a shirt with its sleeves turned back far enough to let passersby see his expensive watch.

Giles or Emma, or both of them, had chosen an Italian restaurant. Rather a good one if he was to be believed. It was small, crowded with slimmer and better-dressed customers than those usually seen in Somerset, but was no more than an old shop with its interior scooped out to make room for tables. Its frontage had been torn down to accommodate big windows with decals of the Italian flag stuck on them.

After they waited inside the door for long enough to make Penny think it was a deliberate way of making them feel insignificant, they were shown to their table by a waitress. She looked Italian enough for anyone with her dark hair, brown eyes and prominent bust but had an East European accent and a relaxed attitude to service.

It took some time for Magda, or whatever her name was, to bring them the drinks they ordered. By then, they'd had plenty of time to decide what they wanted to eat.

Without bothering to consult anyone, Giles ordered a bottle of Chianti. Penny enjoyed hearing his put-on Italian accent baffle the waitress so that she eventually had to ask him to point to his choice on the wine list.

'It's always a good idea to drink the wine of the country,' he told them. Emma asked for sparkling water.

None of them had a first course. Penny and Emma had pasta. Giles's veal arrived quite a bit later. Penny hoped he'd make a show of himself by complaining but he did nothing more than shake his head wordlessly when the plate was put in front of him. There was the usual flourishing of an oversized pepper-mill, and the belated offer of grated parmesan cheese. The up-to-the-minute chic of the restaurant was apparent in the portions; small for the customers and correspondingly profitable for the proprietor. They'd have caused uproar in Somerset restaurants.

While they talked, comparing property prices in Wimbledon with those in Penny's area, Giles suddenly asked: 'Have you had any thoughts of downsizing, Penny?

I was talking to Emma about it the other evening. After all, Farthing's is such a rambling great place that it must be far too much for you now you're on your own. And the profit would be tax-free, of course.'

'No. I couldn't face it. Not to start off again on my own. And what would I do with all my things if I moved somewhere smaller?'

'Auctions, perhaps?'

'Out of the question. As long as I can manage there on my own, I won't even think of moving. I've got a cleaner and a man who comes in to look after the garden. As for money, I'm not exactly tapping at the workhouse door yet, you know.'

She hoped that was true as she was still waiting for Reggie's accountant and solicitors to go through his paperwork. They'd told her it would take a long time, what with his business affairs being complex and hard to unravel. She'd already been waiting for ages. All she knew for certain was that the joint bank account wasn't overcrowded with recent credits.

'I'm sure you're not, Penny,' Giles said smoothly. 'But you are sitting on a large amount of moribund money. The house's value is well above the inheritance-tax threshold and if you stay there you'll never benefit personally from any further increase. It'll only mean more tax for your daughter to pay when you die.'

Emma snapped, 'For God's sake, Giles! Stop it, you can't say things like that.'

'Your mother has to face facts, I'm afraid. It's your inheritance we're talking about, after all. Or it will be one day.' He laughed. 'Unless she's planning to leave it to a cats' charity.'

Looking at Penny again, he said, 'But, joking apart, the point is this; if you did sell and then downsized you'd release a lot of tax-free profit. If you passed that over to Emma at once you'd have to live for only seven more years before it became tax-free in her hands. It's worth thinking about.' He frowned as he said in what Penny guessed was a rarely-used caring voice: 'And yes, I know it's a disagreeable subject but tax-planning is very important.'

The rotten sod knows I've had cancer, she thought bitterly, so he must want those seven years to start ticking away as soon as possible. In which case he could bloody well go on wanting.

'I'm sorry, but the answer's still no. And I'd rather not hear any more about it. Having had one death to deal with, I don't want to have to start thinking about my own. Please don't take offence, but my mind's made up.'

Giles didn't look too put out. 'Well, keep it in mind, that's all I'm saying. If you do have a change of heart, I'll be happy to give you some guidance when the time comes. All right, Penny?'

'If it ever happens, then I might just do that.' But don't hold your breath, she wanted to say.

'I must say it's good to have a sociable evening out with you,' he said after a while, 'and we don't see you that often.' Just in time, he added: 'More's the pity, of course.'

Hearing that, she wanted to break the second of her two promises by stretching across the table and giving him a slap, the sarcastic bugger.

She'd been watching for a sign of a new and closer bond between him and Emma, possibly on account of a shared secret not ready to be divulged to a third party until... what was it women waited for these days, the twelve-weeks scan? They didn't look very relaxed in each other's company and she'd never heard Emma snap at him before, not like that. There was a distinctly chilly atmosphere between them. Nor had he kissed her when he came in. They'd need to do better than that if a baby was on the way. And it certainly didn't look as if marriage was uppermost in their minds.

After Emma and Giles left the house in the morning, she made herself some toast and a cup of tea. There was a low-fat, Greek-style yoghurt in the fridge and she had that with a little sprinkling of Demerara sugar. She packed her overnight bag, washed up her breakfast things, and phoned for a taxi. Then she had a look round the house while waiting for it to arrive. Would they have expected her to do this? She knew she would have.

The last room she looked in was the bathroom. When she used it in the evening and again when she showered before breakfast, she avoided opening the mirrored door of the medicine cabinet. She opened it now, telling herself it was something anyone might do, perhaps looking for sticking-plasters or indigestion tablets. Right at the front of the bottom shelf was an opened box of Tampax.

CHAPTER NINE

'...so if you could get here a bit earlier, that would be perfect.'

Penny's phone call came at five in the afternoon. At the time, Alan was listening to *You Can't Always Get What You Want* on his CD player because he wanted to be reminded of her reason for marrying a man she didn't love and who didn't love her.

It was the same with his ex-wife, apart from marriage not being what he'd wanted or needed. His rushed wedding would never have happened but for Susan's pre-marital pregnancy which never actually came to anything. Marrying your supposedly pregnant girlfriend was what you did in those days and it didn't help to know it wasn't like that now. It hadn't taken him long to doubt the pregnancy ever existed.

Reluctantly, he asked, 'And what sort of thing would you like me to help you with?'

'Not a vast amount. I really only need a hand with the drinks, that's all. And some help with the dishes. It's my first dinner since Reggie, so the sort of thing he used to help with, no more than light duties. Very light duties indeed in his case, and certainly no heavy labouring.'

'I think I could just about do that. Yes, only too happy to help.' To say the opposite would be more truthful but he'd nowhere to turn for relief. 'So what time would you like me to turn up?'

'You remember I told you it's seven-thirty for eight? So perhaps you could get here at about seven. Would that be all right?'

He went upstairs for his second shower of the day, this time wearing a plastic shower-cap. After another shave he arranged his hair in front of the bedroom mirror and lacquered it into place before giving the inside of his wrists a squirt of something fragrant.

As it wasn't to be an evening for suits, he decided on

blazer, grey trousers, and a white shirt worn with an inoffensive tie. All that was left to do now was to make up his mind about which shoes to wear – black or brown. Either colour would go with the grey trousers.

The first and stodgiest headmaster he worked for was on the brink of retirement, so must have been a young man about Twickenham before the war. With his shoulders permanently hunched against a rare outbreak of goodwill, he often shared his views on social niceties with his staff whether they wanted to hear them or not. His rule of thumb for shoes was No Brown in Town. His staff were either old enough to know already or too young to care, so no one ever asked if it applied only to London or to towns in general. Well, bollocks to that. One of the old fool's other strictures was that no gentleman ever wore a blazer after six in the evening. And bollocks to that, too, more as a point of principle than anything else.

Hours too late for him to do anything about it, Alan started to think of a gift for his hostess and what it ought to be. He wished he'd thought of it earlier since flowers were now out of the question as there were no petrol stations on the way to Upper Mendham and the few village shops still in business would already be closed.

His ex-wife invariably took flowers when they were invited out to dinner, and the two bottles of wine he used to take with him were always welcomed. But Penny's guests were likely to be smarter and better-off than his and Susan's were. If he took wine with him they might think it implied Penny would be stingy with her own supply. In that case they could get stuffed. It was going to be wine whatever they cared to think.

He found two matching bottles in a kitchen cupboard. The wine was French, red and three years old. The labels had reassuring pictures of grapes on them and said *mis en bouteille au chateau*. Lacking anything smarter, he put the bottles into one of the supermarket's plastic bags.

'I really do appreciate this,' Penny said as she let him into the hall.

She was wearing a knee-length dress and had the legs and figure to make the most of it, he thought. Before he could say anything admiring about her choice, she was already leaning against him, lightly gripping his shoulders and kissing him on both cheeks like a French general at a medal ceremony.

They were the first kisses of any sort he'd had from her. Were they merely a social gesture or more than that? He couldn't help wondering if they were another step on the way, at least in her mind, to something more, something like romance. No, he told himself, not romance – its old meaning had changed. A romantic tryst now meant having sex without witnesses. Romancing a woman meant having sex with her. It used to mean what troubadours did in days gone by; mooning about while strumming ribbon-bedecked lutes under balconies in Provence. Youthful suitors, it went without saying, not men of his age and certainly not serenading women of sixty. Not that he'd mind initiating a romantic tryst with her but only if he could be sure of not being rebuffed.

'These are for your cellar,' he said, reluctantly returning to the real world and handing her his supermarket bag.

'Would that I had one. Sadly, this place is built on solid rock, so I haven't. And thank you, but you really shouldn't have, Alan, there's no need. Let's go into the dining-room and you can tell me how you think it looks.'

The table there was laid for six, as promised. A carver chair stood at each end with three armless ones on each side. Six candles in matching silver candlesticks stood in a row down the table which had a bowl of stumpy flowers in its centre.

'What do you think of it? Does it look all right to you?'

'It does, yes. I'm no judge but I think it looks rather grand. Now, what would you like me to do first?'

'In a moment. Look, I'll want you to sit at the end of the table here,' she said, patting the arm of the carver chair further from the door. 'I'll sit at the other end, facing you.'

He thought about the seating and the seniority it implied. 'Are you sure you want me to sit at the head of the table? Shouldn't it be for one of the other two men?'

'No, not at all. You're effectively my co-host this evening. And don't get the wrong idea about the others – they're just neighbours. Perfectly pleasant but you might say they're for socialising with, not for swapping intimacies. The nearest anyone gets to that is boasting about how brilliantly one's children and grandchildren are getting on. Either exaggerating their successes or making them up completely, it doesn't really matter. Everyone does it and no one cares or takes any of it seriously.'

They went into the hot kitchen. Something important was happening in the oven and there were saucepans with vegetables in them on the stove.

After putting the bottles away, she started to tell him the duties appropriate to a co-host and – what she'd not said – an unpaid helper. His first task was to sort out the drinks the guests would want when they arrived, though she was sure the two women would have soft drinks from the fridge. The men, these two, anyway, invariably drank whisky before the meal and perhaps he could see to that too.

'I don't know if everyone does it,' she said, 'but I keep a little notebook with all my guests' likes and dislikes, all their allergies and intolerances and those bloody annoying fads and fancies of theirs. That's how I know what they'll want.'

She went on to tell him the whisky and port were in decanters on the dining-room sideboard. He knew that already, having seen them there among the ranks of other bottles and remembered her telling him she kept her alcohol supplies in there as a drink-control measure. She said the men would expect to drink port with the cheese that he'd need to bring to the table when the time came. The women wouldn't drink port but might fancy some of the sloe gin that was also on the sideboard.

It was going to be Hobson's choice of white wine to

drink with the meal as the first two courses were fish; smoked salmon to start and fish pie after that. So much for his red offering, he thought.

'Any special needs for afters?' he asked.

'No, it's only a summer pudding, nothing complicated. Now when we're all together in the drawing-room, you can ask them what they'll have to drink. As I say, it'll be whisky and soft drinks but they need to be asked all the same. And don't forget me whatever you do. I'll have whisky as well just to keep things simple. When you get a moment after that, perhaps you'd take the wine out of the fridge, open it up, and put four – no, five bottles in those cooler things in the dining-room. It's best to be on the safe side.'

'I think I can remember all that.' She'd enough to do without him cocking things up as the evening progressed. 'You mentioned dishes on the phone...'

'Just help me cart them in and out. And put the vegetable tureens on the table just before you need to bring in the pie.' She showed him where in the kitchen's acreage he'd find everything when the time came. 'I'll tip you off when you need to get started.'

All that seemed clear enough and could have been worse. 'Before you sound Action Stations, may I just say how nice you look this evening?'

'You may, indeed, and thank you. And I might say you're looking none too dusty yourself. I hope they'll think we make a handsome couple.'

"A couple". There she went again, another possible clue to think about. 'I'd better get ready,' he said. 'It's quarter past so they'll be here at any minute.'

'They'd better not be. Seven-thirty means exactly that and you'll be able to set your clock by their arrival. It's not like London. My daughter tells me that up there, when people are invited for dinner at eight, they think nothing of turning up at half past as cool as you like. Actually, eight would be thought a bit old-hat. Eight-thirty's more usual, I believe, and then they turn up at nine. It wouldn't do down here, I can tell you, not in this village. We stick to the rules here.'

The other guests arrived exactly on time. There were no cars in the drive so they must have walked from their houses. Penny welcomed them and exchanged kisses with them all. They were only cheek-to-cheek affairs with no lip contact.

Both women brought flowers, but the men, who were wearing brown shoes, had brought no wine with them. Penny introduced him, reminding them who he was and of his connection with Reggie which only Alan knew was untrue. At the mention of Reggie's name, they made consoling noises and looked uncomfortable.

The two men, Brian and Peter, spoke pleasantly to Alan, telling him how pleased they were to meet him and how good it was that he was able to be on hand to help their hostess. Given their Upper Mendham provenance, their politeness surprised him, even if it stemmed from relief that they weren't being pressed into domestic service themselves.

Their heavyweight wives weren't too bad, either. One of them looked as though she ought to have an old-fashioned name like Dorcas, but was called Mary. The other, with features too small for her face, was Helen. All four, men and women, looked to be closer to Reggie's age than to his widow's.

Penny ushered them into the drawing-room where, as instructed, Alan asked them for their drink orders. When he'd sorted out the women's soft drinks in the kitchen he handed them over before hurrying into the dining-room to pour modest whiskies for the men and a large glass for Penny. As he'd be driving later, he limited himself to a pauper's measure. He lit the candles and switched on a pair of lamps before assembling the whiskies on a tray and taking them back into the drawing-room.

After a few minutes spent chatting, Penny went back to the kitchen still clutching her glass. As she left, she winked at him, whispering, 'Leave them to it in about ten minutes.'

Peter and the two wives fell silent when Brian asked Alan if he was retired. He said he was, but used to be a schoolmaster. Instead of the responses he was expecting and usually got; the ones about "all those holidays" and "getting off home at three-thirty", both couples murmured approvingly. Mary told him education was more important than ever these days, whatever that meant. The other three agreed with her. It was an opportunity for the men to tell him what they'd done for a living but neither of them bothered to.

He had a moment of indecision about the way to serve the food before deciding to do it in accordance with what an ex-colleague claimed to be the Tory Party's motto: Give to the Right, Take away from the Left. No one commented, so it must have been correct or else they were too polite to say otherwise.

All said they enjoyed the starter and the fish pie. Penny drank more wine with both courses than anyone else but that was only to be expected after her labours in the kitchen.

After he'd cleared away the dishes for her, he brought dry biscuits and several examples of European cheese-makers' craft to the table. As Peter was sitting on Penny's right, Alan guessed he was the senior male guest so he set down the port decanter by him from where it was soon sent shuttling back and forth across the table between him and Brian. All three women and Alan declined it.

It had gone off pretty well, he decided when the guests had left. The conversation was cheerful throughout the meal and never truly controversial. It was good to have found Penny and her guests taking care to involve him without asking him too many personal questions. When asked, he gave them his views on the state of the local roads, and an anodyne version of his real thoughts about the County Council. No one spoke with much heat except Peter who had such strongly-held opinions on the current Middle East situation that his goblin's face contorted with passion while he told everyone about them.

When he wasn't speaking or being a waiter, Alan had caught himself idly wondering about the sex lives of the two couples who seemed quite fond of each other. They were long past it now, he imagined, but presumably went at it hammer and tongs in days gone by. Supposing they kept it going for an average of once a week for – how long? Say forty years to be on the safe side. More frequent sex to start with, less so later on. That made about two thousand P.Bs of S.I, or Prolonged Bouts of Sexual Intercourse as a P.E. master – a P.T. master in those days, of course – once described such activities to him. Prolonged or otherwise, it was still a fair tally. Well, good for them if he was right.

But beyond looking encouraging and interested he had nothing to contribute to the mild bragging session about their children and grandchildren that Penny forecast. It was noticeable to him, and he wondered if the others also noticed it, that she had nothing particularly admirable to say about her daughter. It made him think Emma's absence from Winyard's Gap was still unforgiven.

As the other guests clustered by the front door saying their goodbyes, Peter shook Alan's hand and said quietly: 'You did really well this evening, Alan, old chap. It can't have been easy for you.'

Had he been a butler rather than a helper, Alan thought, this would have been the right moment for Peter to ease some folding money into his hand.

It was only just after midnight when he and Penny had finished clearing away and were sitting side by side, drinking coffee at the kitchen table.

'Alan, I can't thank you enough,' she said. 'It was a lovely evening for me, and I think they all enjoyed themselves, don't you? You saved me so much work. I only hope it wasn't too boring for you.'

'No, I enjoyed it,' he said fairly truthfully. It was more a question of not having not enjoyed it. 'I'll admit to being surprised as I'd no idea what to expect from four total strangers but they were all very pleasant.'

It was better not to mention he'd feared Helen and Mary would be like the Antelope's harpies, and their husbands like the Antelope's retired warriors, or even carbon copies of Maxwell bloody Tyler. He mentally bestowed on them one of the highest honours in his gift; that he didn't quail at the thought of meeting them again.

Without warning, Penny put her hand on his. 'I'm so glad,' she said, running her fingers over his knuckles in what felt to him like an abstracted way rather than any sort of caress. All the same, it came as a surprise.

'And having you here was so nice for me,' she told him.

As she spoke, she gave him another of those looks of hers which he again hesitantly categorised as possibly meaningful. But like the one she gave him after visiting Winyard's Gap, he didn't know what it meant or what she expected him to do about it.

When he was much younger he might have taken a chance on kissing a woman after being on the receiving end of two looks like those, and he toyed briefly with the idea of it now. But to carry it off successfully meant pushing back his chair and then turning awkwardly, and for her to make both moves at roughly the same time. Even if he'd not misread her signal – if it was one – and she didn't shove him off, the move would end up being ungainly, uncomfortable and potentially embarrassing for both of them. Rather than make a fool of himself, he took the easy way out by doing nothing. Besides, he told himself, he was by no means match-fit and would have liked to be given more notice. It was a shame and perhaps a missed opportunity, but there it was.

The romantic tryst would have to wait.

In the meantime, and in the absence of any reaction from him, she'd withdrawn her hand unobtrusively without saying anything about it. He'd no way of telling if she was disappointed because she went on talking about the evening without giving him a single clue to work on.

CHAPTER TEN

"...such a pleasant evening and we both really enjoyed that fish pie of yours. Thank you so much for inviting us. On the way home we all agreed how nice your new friend, Alan, was, and how helpful he was to you. If only Peter would take a leaf out of his book! Love, Mary."

The two thank-you cards were on the doormat when Penny came downstairs the next morning. As long as guests and hostesses lived not too far apart, cards were slipped through letterboxes without any preliminary ringing or knocking at the door.

Mary's favourable reference to Alan made her card stand out from the usual bread-and-butter acknowledgements. After praise for the food, merited or not, any mention of fellow-guests was rarely more than: "and in such agreeable company" or "and how good it was to be joined by..." Helen's card was similar. After the standard words of appreciation, it read: "...and what a treat to meet someone new. Such a find for you, dear."

It was reassuring to get comments like that and for them to mention Alan. She'd taken care to choose the only quartet of neighbours she could rely on not to question his presence, and the cards showed they approved of him. And thanks to her earlier explanation of his relationship with Reggie, no one looked askance or showed disapproval when Alan sat down at the head of the table and took over her husband's role by pouring the drinks and dealing with the port. It was really an extension of Reggie's role as he never turned his hand to carrying crockery about. He was too busy flirting and concentrating on being the perfect host for that.

She went into the kitchen to make her breakfast. Her sleep had been interrupted by a storm and she was still tired. She'd felt nervous to be alone in the house during the night especially while the bedroom was being lit with flashes of lightning.

Farthing's was reputed to have a ghost, a grey lady, but no one had ever seen her, heard her, or sensed her presence. Penny thought she probably didn't exist. She told herself grey ladies were commonplace in ghostly annals but rarely met with. It was also strange they were so often grey. No one ever claimed to have seen anything like a cinnamon-coloured spectre. All the same, ever since Reggie died she'd been leaving the landing light switched on and the bedroom door ajar.

In the same way that she sometimes thought about the Norman stonemason who shaped the font in St Michael's, she'd lain awake thinking about the people who lived in the house over the years, starting with the Farthings. Generations of men and women in antique clothes and then just dated ones, talking and worrying about news reaching the house of Boney, the Crimea, the Boers, the Somme and D-Day. And all those fears of crop failure and bankruptcy, old age, disease and the routine infant deaths. How many gentlemen farmers, how many of their wives and children, had died in these bedrooms, in her bedroom? Were their coffins carried down her staircase, their passage marked by the striking of a clock like the one in the hall?

She did some different thinking while she was making her breakfast. The evening went well enough while all five guests were still there, eating, drinking and chatting away. It went wrong only when she and Alan were alone together in the kitchen afterwards which was exactly the time when things ought to have got even better. It was embarrassing now to remember it but she eventually convinced herself she'd not put him off beyond recall. His failure to respond to that ill-managed little advance of hers had made her think it might have.

But on his way out he surprised her by kissing her cheek and giving her a semi-hug that was over and done with before she could hug him back as she wanted to. It must mean something. Even that modest display of affection helped compensate in small measure for the way he ducked out of giving her the other sort of kiss she'd been hoping for in the kitchen.

Helen's "such a find" comment was encouraging. She must have been thinking of more than his skills as a waiter. It could imply she suspected Penny of hoping her friendship with this new man might develop into something more substantial. It was easy to believe that Helen, given a free hand, would have liked to add: "particularly after the way Reggie carried on." People never said anything about that in her hearing, possibly for fear of freeing skeletons from their own cupboards. Rumours thrived in a small community and it was galling to think her neighbours might have spent years speculating among themselves about Reggie's adventures and feeling sorry for her because of them.

She looked around the kitchen while she drank her black coffee and ate a thin slice of toast, trying to imagine how the room would look to a visitor seeing it late at night for the first time.

Its sheer echoing size was daunting, and the wooden chairs and unforgiving lighting made it a hopeless place to expect much of a response, if any response at all, to her mildest of overtures. The drawing-room would have been better and she realised now, too late, she ought to have suggested going in there for coffee. The lighting was softer and more flattering, and the seating more comfortable. Much more suitable for lulling him into making the next move.

From what she knew of him, he'd have been too nervous of getting it wrong to try anything on without her first giving him an even brighter green light than she had.

Until she put him right, he doubted that a man with a bus pass in his pocket could even go on a date. With a thought like that in his mind she clearly still had some way to go before he could be brought under starter's orders.

It was half past ten. She normally held herself back from going into the dining-room to make her first drink of the day until about eleven, but the siren song from the half-full wine bottle in the fridge only a few feet away wasn't to be resisted. She took the bottle out and poured herself a glass.

Her feelings for him needed sorting out. With a drink inside her, it didn't take long. She liked him, enjoyed his company and looked forward to more of it. She also fancied him physically – quite a lot, in fact – but with mental reservations about his possible reaction to her operation's legacy. If the two of them ever got that far.

Love could be ruled out, even the wistful sort she used to experience while day-dreaming about Mick Jagger and how wonderful it would be to go out with him with all that would entail. The lack of a love aspect made it easier to accommodate the non-love feelings she suspected Alan had for her. She'd made all the running, and things could have turned out a lot worse. With less luck, such as not meeting him in the supermarket and less subsequent care on her part, her involvement with him could have begun and ended when he dropped off Reggie's golf kit.

With her own mind clearer, she hoped his wasn't confused about the extent of her intentions. He wasn't to know it, but of the handful of single men she knew in the right age range, he was the only one worth a second thought. The bachelors and widowers were grimly locked into old age. The married men were yoked to their wives and spent their retirements taking them shopping or to the doctor's surgery and pottering about doing pointless things at home. Their only redeeming feature was their obvious gratitude for having so far avoided the regular culls of men of their age. Alan, then, was a rarity and worth cultivating. A desirable companion in every sense who, with luck, had several years still to go before his warranty expired.

'You are a shameless bitch,' she said aloud, shaking her head but not in disbelief. It might as well have been: 'Goodbye, Reggie and our forty-odd years together. And step forward, Alan, your day has come.'

It was time to go into the garden to see if her gardener needed to put in an extra afternoon each week from now on to keep it under control. On the way out she paused to wind the hall clock. Above its arched dial there was a small painting of a Nelsonian ship flying an unfeasibly large flag. She'd asked Reggie why that sort of decoration was perfectly acceptable two centuries ago but if a modern clock pictured an aircraft-carrier it would be thought impossibly vulgar. He was on his way out at the time, probably to play golf or visit a client or some woman he pretended to be in need of his professional advice. He hesitated before telling her: 'Styles change, Pen, that's all,' and off he went. It was a significant moment; the first time she found him at a loss, and happened a good twenty years ago.

It took her a long time to walk the full extent of the garden's walls where the ivy was already inching between the honey-coloured stones in defiance of the gardener's spring-time chemical assault. While poking about in the flowerbeds she found enough weeds flourishing in them to make his extra hours worthwhile. She went back indoors to phone him.

After making her call she thought it would be useful to find out from Alan if he had any more thoughts about the evening and to hear if he'd anything to say about the after-dinner events in the kitchen. It was eleven-thirty now so he was likely to be playing golf till lunchtime. Her cleaner was due to arrive soon so the best time to call him was when Mrs Watkins left after doing her usual three hours. That would avoid any worry about being overheard.

When she rang him in the afternoon it took him so long to answer that she thought he might still be out.

'Sorry,' he said when he finally picked up his phone. 'I was ironing and had just got to that tricky bit by the shirt collar. I daresay you'd know all about that. I ought to have got the hang of it after all these years, but I haven't. I'm so slow at it, too. It's all those fiddly little pleat things above the cuffs that cause the trouble.'

What a dog's dinner he must be making of it. She already knew he was no good at ironing, and that beige shirt of his proved it.

'So, how are you, Penny? Recovered from last night's exertions yet?'

'I'm fine. Look, the reason I'm ringing is to thank you again for your sterling efforts.'

'No need, Penny, and thanks again for your hospitality. As I told you, I enjoyed the evening. Rather more than I feared, to tell you the truth. Spending several hours with four strangers can be something of a strain. There's no possibility of an early escape from a dinner – not a socially acceptable one at any rate.'

That sounded okay, no problems so far.

'I'm glad you didn't escape and I'm relieved to hear it wasn't too much of a trial.'

'No, I found them all perfectly easy to get on with.'

She wished she knew more about his house and which room he did his ironing in so she could imagine him in there. He said he lived in a cottage but that meant very little in Somerset. Some of the tiniest cottages in Upper Mendham had names like The Grange and Field House. There were also big old houses like hers with misleading names like Clematis Cottage. Reggie told anyone who'd listen that the owners of the tiny cottages were like the bookies who called themselves turf accountants.

'And that Peter chap said a few kind words to me as they were leaving.'

'Really? What did he say?'

'Oh, nothing much,' Alan said, suddenly sounding defensive. 'But I'm glad you're feeling all right. By my standards, it was a late night.'

'I feel a lot better than I'd have done if it hadn't been for your help.'

'You already thanked me for that. I must say I'd not expected to hear from you again so soon. I hope you didn't call earlier as I was playing golf this morning, an early start at eight-thirty, first match out on the course.'

'How did it go?'

She knew a little about the game from having to show an interest when Reggie talked about pars and birdies and occasionally moaned that slack course maintenance had denied him a victory.

There was a resigned sigh. 'The usual, I'm afraid. What we call army golf – left, right, left, right.'

She'd not heard that expression before. 'At least you had a good day for it after that storm during the night. The garden's soaked this morning.'

'Yes, there was casual water all over the place, and bits of tree scattered about the fairways. Mind you, the greens were holding,' he said without explaining what it meant. 'Such a change after all the dry weather.' He added mysteriously: 'We even managed to get a bit of backspin now and then, so it wasn't all bad.'

She'd no idea what he was talking about. Without meaning to, she asked: 'So you were quite relaxed about the evening, were you? Nothing you weren't happy about?' It sounded so pointed. Trying to sound more casual and less direct, she said quickly, but neither casually nor indirectly enough for her liking: 'Or anything at all, really?'

He was so slow to answer she thought he might have stolen away to do some more work on his pleats. It was so much easier to talk to him face-to-face.

'I don't think so, no,' he said at last.

'That's good.' She waited for him to say something more.

Eventually he did. 'Look, Penny, I'm glad you rang. I've been thinking about how we talked a while back about hospitality and repaying it. You remember? Well, I wouldn't want you to think I'd forgotten so I—'

'You don't have to do that.'

She heard him laugh as he said, 'I hope that's only because you know I can't cook. No, what I was about to say was I'd like to take you out for a meal some time. Not immediately, but not in the too distant future. What do you think? And only if you fancy it, of course.'

'I'd love to,' she said without hesitation. What a surprise, she'd not expected that so soon. 'Do you have anywhere particular in mind?'

'I've not given it much thought because I didn't know how you'd react. What about the Coq au Vin? Would that do?'

'The cocoa van? Lord, I must stop saying that or people will take me for a yokel. But isn't it a shame we can't show off by arriving there in style in your friend's van? Thank you, though. Do you have any idea at all when we might go?'

'I'll have to consult my bulging engagement diary before I can say for certain. No, only joking. You could write all my engagements on the back of a fag packet. How about in a couple of weeks or so? Or would that be too soon for you?'

'Of course not.'

"A couple of weeks or so." It was a long time to wait to see him again, and he'd thought even that might be too soon. After his suggestion she'd hoped for better.

Later that day, she added "New cards" to her shopping list. Those she found on her doormat that morning, one with a picture of a thrush, the other of a robin, were from the same RSPB selection she recently bought but hadn't yet had an opportunity to use. If she had different ones to respond with after future invitations from Mary and Helen they wouldn't be able to flatter themselves that she was copying them. It was an important consideration in Upper Mendham.

CHAPTER ELEVEN

'Is that wreck of a car of yours still behaving itself?' Jimmy Hargreaves asked. 'Silly question, really. It must be or you wouldn't be here. Can't see you splashing out on a taxi.'

'Pretty well, on balance,' Alan said. 'It ought to be, considering all the things I had to pay for to have put right.'

It was worth dwelling on its unreliability as justification for borrowing Jimmy's van earlier in the summer and as a non-monetary reservation fee if he needed to again.

'And I don't remember if I mentioned this before, but I had to put up with a couple of people calling me the cocoa-van man,' he said, recalling Tyler's unfettered laughter. By contrast, he remembered Penny's similar comment with no resentment at all.

The two men were sitting in bright sunshine at a small metal table in the back yard of the Coq au Vin. An opened bottle of wine and two glasses stood between them. It was Tuesday, always a non-golfing day because of the Wendmore ladies, and there was still an hour to go before the bistro opened.

Jimmy, the proprietor and chief cook, was in his early sixties, had a florid complexion and spoke with an unashamed London accent. He was wearing the white smock and chequered trousers often seen in cookery programmes on TV but rarely in real life. Each time they met, Alan resolved not to look too intently at the display of broken veins on Jimmy's nose and so far today he'd succeeded.

'The old cocoa-van-man business still happens to me, too,' Jimmy said, 'but it's never been all that funny. Not exactly a side-splitter, wouldn't you agree? Having said that, it's probably not a bad bit of P.R. for me to be seen out and about in it. But I often wonder what possessed me to give the place a French name. I must have had the idea of offering the locals a bit of much-needed class.' He rolled his eyes. 'Class? Down here in the sticks? Don't make me laugh. And Coq au Vin of all things. Do you know, Al, I've not had that on the menu since the first few months? No one ever asked for it, not once. And it was intended to be my signature dish.'

He took a gulp of the house red and swilled it noisily round his mouth before swallowing. 'Not bad, that,' he said thoughtfully, frowning and smacking his lips. 'I must get some more in.' He went on: 'I ought to have called the place Ham, Eggs and Chips – that's my most popular offering. Or *Jambon, Oeufs et Frites*, if I wanted to baffle the locals even more than they are already.'

'Still as popular as ever, is it?'

Jimmy nodded. 'Always has been from the day I opened. Can't imagine why when you can get H.E.and C. or J. O. *et* F. from any of the local pubs, and cheaper too. Or Sausages and Mash, S and M, except I can't use that for fear of people mistaking it for something more interesting. But on the plus side and unlike most pub menus, mine says everything's locally sourced. Which is fair enough. Waitrose is local.'

Alan shifted his chair to bring his face out of the sun. 'You used to have all kinds of fancy stuff on offer when you started here.'

'That was my wife's idea. To start with, if you remember, the food was all enrobed with this, drizzled with that, a *mélange* of something else. But it didn't take us long to catch on. Of course, as even you may have noticed, we still put on something of a French show; checked tablecloths, an apron and striped T-shirt for Kylie.'

'What, the waitress? I thought her name was Claudine. I've called her that for years and she never said anything.'

'Get a grip, Al. Kylie's her given name. I don't suppose you can call it her Christian name. You don't remember there being a Saint Kylie, do you? No, Claudine's her name when she's being a French waitress. We tried getting her to do a French accent at one time. Didn't work, so I had to settle for dressing her up to look like a Breton fisherwoman. If we had a male waiter instead of Kylie, I'd put him in a bloody beret. But I'm happy to have her as she's easy on the eye and that pays dividends with my ageing male customers. Not that our French ambiance stops there. Don't forget the Charles Trenet CD I have droning away in the background. And I've just got my hands on some accordion music. Can't get more Frenchy than that.'

'I suppose it went with the *canard* à *l'orange* and *bouillabaisse* I used to see on the menu. I can even remember having – no, not having, being offered *surprise de crabe.*'

Jimmy laughed aloud. 'You're right, I remember that too. But the end result of the old surprised crab often left the customers as surprised as me. For instance, putting loads of anchovy essence in it while I was under the influence. That was a bloody surprise to one and all, I can tell you.'

Alan joined in Jimmy's continuing laughter. 'Even so, you must admit it's still a popular place for people to come to. You've often had a good few customers in when I've been here. At least on a Saturday.'

'Can't argue with that, Al. Another of those?' Jimmy said, offering to refill Alan's empty glass.

'Just one more, thanks, and that'll do for me. That's the trouble with you being stuck out here in the middle of nowhere. Having to drive here means I can't take as much advantage of your hospitality as I'd like.'

'There are such things as taxis, mate. If you weren't so tight, that is. It's easy for you, I'd have thought. Inflation-proof pension from the Ministry of Education flooding in each month. Your chief worry must be working out what to spend it on. Me, I still have to work for a living.'

'You can't be doing too badly.'

'No, mustn't grumble. The wolf's still some distance

from the door but I think I can hear him howling now and then.'

Alan decided to come to the point, aware that the second part of what he had to say was going to cause equal measures of disbelief and mirth.

'Apart from the pleasure of your company and a couple of free drinks, the reason I'm here is to put a double portion of cash into your coffers.'

'Blimey, a double portion, eh? Don't tell me you've found someone prepared to put up with you for the duration of a meal. A table for two? One of your golfing chums, I suppose. Did you have a bet and the loser had to pay?'

'No, I'm entertaining a lady.'

There was renewed laughter from Jimmy and he slapped the table hard enough to make the glassware shudder.

'Blimey again. Well, good for you. About time you had a bit of the other, if you don't mind me saying so. You've kept that quiet, I must say. Anyone I know?'

'You cheeky bugger. Yes, she is. At least, she claims to have been here before. With her late husband, a chap called Hallows. Reggie and Penny Hallows. He died a while back and I went to the funeral service as one of my golf club's official mourners.'

'And you've gallantly stepped in to help her through her grief ever since, have you? Very altruistic.'

Alan was ready for the sarcasm but didn't want Jimmy to pursue the matter too far.

'It's not exactly like that, but you may recall them coming here. It must have been some time back. From what she told me it would have been in your *canard à l'orange* days.'

Jimmy screwed up his face and leaned back on his chair. 'I'm trying to think,' he said. 'Hallows, you say? Name definitely rings a bell. Posh bugger, yes, that's why I think I remember him because I don't get many of them in here. Tall, well set-up, seventies perhaps? That sound like him? Yes? Attractive wife, too, now I come to think of it. As you'll have noticed we don't get many of them in here, either.'

'Sounds about right, Jim,' Alan said, thinking of the photo in Penny's drawing-room and finding he wished she'd not kept it on display. For all she said about not loving the old brute she wasn't exactly hurrying to clear the decks of his memory.

'Yes, he once made a fuss about the wines. As you know, it's always me who shows customers the old *Carte des Vins*. I wouldn't trust Kylie with it, you see. She's gormless enough to recommend white wine with everything just because she likes it herself. Not that he was complaining about them, you understand. No, if he's the bloke I'm thinking of he only wanted chapter and verse about them. An all-too-rare event out here in the boondocks, as you can imagine. It's not as though we pretend to be the Somerset branch of the Ritz. But whether it happens or not I always put on a bit of a show.'

Alan groaned. 'I've seen you and had to listen to you in full flow. Nasty.'

'Maybe so, but it has to be done. You know: excellent example of whatever the wine happens to be, well-rounded yet supple and long on the palate. A perfect choice to accompany…and then I reverently mention the dish the customer has his eye on. Usually works, and of course I invariably give all my wines a remorseless testing before putting them on the list. I often get them on special offer at one of the low-end supermarkets. Surprisingly good, some of them. But I always insist on buying ones in bottles that have proper corks and not screw-caps. Looks classier. But when a customer's fresh from giving his tastebuds a good work-out with gin or whisky *apéritifs* – I always make a point of calling them that – he wouldn't know a French *rouge* from a Uruguayan *tinto*. If there is such a thing.'

'Yes, but I still need to take this Penny out for dinner. She invited me to a meal at her house and I have to repay the compliment. There were other guests there as well, not just the two of us,' he added quickly. 'I can't do it at my place because—'

'—you can't cook. Yes, hence your regular attendance *chez moi*. Just as a matter of interest, what did she feed you with?'

'The main course was a sort of fish pie. Quite tasty.'

'Nursery food, really. It's pretty popular for all that especially among the senior citizenry. Reminds them of the good old days. I occasionally do something called a Stargazy pie which is the same sort of thing. A Cornish dish, I believe, as if I care. But as it sounds like she knows what's what, it's probably best for you to steer her away from that if it's on the menu when you come.'

He was silent for a moment as if uncertain what to say next or how to say it, before asking: 'Er,..Al, do you have intentions about this lady, as they used to say? Only if I'm not intruding, naturally.'

The answer needed thinking about because it was important to damp down Jimmy's expectations. Given the slightest hint of anything more than blameless friendship he'd assume Penny was under siege and that he, Alan, hoped to get his hands on more than her housekeeping money if he'd not already broken his non-scoring spell of many years' standing. If Jimmy had an inkling of that he'd spend the evening leering at Penny behind her back and smirking while offering him unwelcome gestures of encouragement.

He'd wanted to be more responsive to her after the dinner party. Rusty from lack of practice, taken off guard and fearful of getting it wrong, he'd passed up a real opportunity to make progress. If she felt slighted, and he couldn't blame her if she did, there might not be another one. Despite letting her down and embarrassing himself, he still hoped there would be. At least he'd given her a peck on the cheek and a mini-hug before he left.

There was a time in his courtship days when a protocol existed for what he had in mind. A little bit of this, a little bit of that, followed by what Jimmy called a little bit of the other. But did it apply to mature adults? To men and women not in their first flush who knew exactly what they were after and didn't want to waste precious time getting it? He'd no idea and no one to ask. Certainly not Jimmy.

'Hard to tell, Jim. I'm not saying I wouldn't but at the moment we're no more than two friends cast adrift on the sea of...you know.'

'*Sea of Heartbreak*, by Johnny Cash? Or would *Only The* bleedin' *Lonely* by Roy Orbison be more apt?'

'I wouldn't put it like that. And she's always mentioning her husband. Rather too often for my liking. She certainly misses him.'

'But she would, wouldn't she? If I were you I'd take things at an easy pace. There's no point in spooking the mare before you've mounted it, as they say in horseracing circles.'

'Stop it. Look, I need to make a reservation.'

'I'll go and get my book. Any thoughts about when?'

'Say about a couple of weeks from now. The trouble is I'm not keen for it to be a weekday evening. Often when I've come during the week it's been like the *Mary Celeste* in here. There again, it can be crowded and full of drunken geriatrics on a Saturday. And I may have to give you a ring to cancel and arrange another evening if she can't make it then.'

'All right, Mr Fussy. I'll make what we *restaurateurs* call a provisional booking. I don't normally accept them unless they're from a friend. Don't like being messed about, you see. You'd be amazed how many no-shows I get even after supposedly firm bookings. That's why I ask for a contact number. Then if they just can't be arsed to turn up I get on the phone to them and give them a bollocking. I mean, wouldn't you?' He waggled the bottle. 'Sure you won't have another?'

'No, I don't want to drink away your hard-earned profits.'

'I'll get it back in spades, mate, don't you worry.'

He wandered off, unhurriedly crossing the yard and

passing the Coq au Vin's wheelie-bins with their attendant flies before disappearing through the open back door of the kitchen. From inside the low-slung building came the sounds of a helper, probably his wife, chopping some foodstuff on a board.

There was no side to Jimmy, Alan thought, which made him a good chap to be with, one who needed no topic-filtration before being spoken to. He was easy to relax with, always cheery, liked a spot of banter and never took offence. His cooking, his or his wife's, was always reliable and occasionally excellent.

Jimmy returned with a book in his hand. Sitting down again, he opened it, riffled through the pages, and said, 'Here we are. This might do you, Al; Wednesday, tomorrow fortnight. I've already got some bookings. Let me see, yes, four tables, fourteen covers. Should suit you, I'd have thought. There could turn out to be more by then but all the ones who've booked so far have been here before and aren't the type to go chucking food around the place or breaking into community singing, let alone expressing themselves in experimental dance. Will that suit milady, do you think? If so, shall I put you down?'

'If you would, thanks. Say for about eight. Yes?'

Jimmy scribbled in his book. 'All done.'

'And could you do me a favour, Jim?'

'Now you're asking for the moon. What favour; international cabaret, karaoke?'

'I'll ignore that. No, I don't normally have a starter as you know but she might. So if you could have avocado and prawns on the menu I'd be much obliged.'

It was one of his favourites as long as the avocado wasn't so hard that it needed a crowbar taken to it. 'I can't speak for the lady, but I'll certainly order it if it's available.'

'How exceedingly retro of you, so very nineteen-seventies. Are you planning to turn up on your Lambretta in an Afghan sheepskin coat and velvet loons?'

'Stupid bugger.' Giving Jimmy a no-nonsense look, he

said, 'One more thing. I don't want any trouble from you. No foolish grinning, nothing like that, know what I mean? Oh, and don't bother going into your wine connoisseur's stand-up routine, either. She probably knows more about wine than you do.'

'Bit of a drinker is she?'

'Piss off.'

When he phoned her later, Penny accepted the date, time and place of the dinner without going off to check her diary or keeping silent while pretending to. It looked as if her post-Reggie social life was turning out to be no more vibrant than his post-Susan one.

'I'll pick you up around seven-thirty and drive you back afterwards,' he told her firmly enough to show he meant what he said. 'That way you'll be able to have a drink without worrying about it.' The perfect host, he said to himself. With any luck it'd pay dividends.

'Are you sure, Alan?' She sounded so doubtful he almost wished he'd not offered. 'I really don't mind driving if you'd prefer me to. You live between here and Netterton, so it's on my way. But it'd have to be in the Range Rover because I've managed to sell the little BMW. The garage man's coming round to pick it up at the weekend.'

'That must have been a wrench for you, getting rid of it. It suited you.' It was a useful basis for buttering her up, so he added: 'An attractive woman in a sporty little number never fails to turn heads and attract attention, I'd have thought.' He stopped himself from explaining that some of the head turning would be because women of her age weren't often seen driving sports cars.

'And there's the envy and admiration to take into account. But I suppose the Range Rover's more practical.'

'I think so. It's because it's a four-wheel drive and better for driving in the winter. You know what the roads are like then. They're either icy or under several inches of water. And there's really no point in me having two cars. Not now.'

'I see what you mean. But I will do the driving, it's the least I can do. Oh, I nearly forgot. You said you'd been to the Coq au Vin before so you'll know it's not exactly a twin-set-and-pearls sort of establishment.'

'Oh dear, and there I was, hoping to wear my diamonds and furs. Don't worry, I won't show you up. And thanks again, I'm really looking forward to it. And to seeing you again.'

CHAPTER TWELVE

It was time to spruce himself up. Looking comfortably down-at-heel saved him money and from having to think about what to wear but Penny showed him up by wearing smart, modern-looking clothes. If he was to make the most of his Coq au Vin dinner date he needed to match her, much as it went against the grain.

He trawled through the contents of his wardrobe and shirt drawer but, as expected, quickly found he owned nothing that would do the trick. Clothes like his never featured in any Young at Heart range. All they proclaimed were ease of maintenance and resistance to wear.

After experimenting in front of the wardrobe mirror with bland combinations of shirts, jackets and trousers, he resigned himself to investing in up-to-date replacements.

The youthful assistant in the gents' outfitters did no more than raise an eyebrow when Alan came in. With his help, Alan chose a blue gingham shirt, a pair of damson-coloured chinos and, after some urging, a linen jacket in oatmeal. In another shop he made himself buy a pair of tobacco-coloured suede chukka boots. At least they were comfortable and wouldn't need breaking in.

He put everything on when he got home. Standing in front of the mirror, he struck a pose he'd seen Keith Richards adopt on stage. The crouch and the heft of the invisible guitar were accurate enough but nothing else was. It was a shame but he took heart when he remembered how Penny had taken a good look at the pink socks he wore on his first visit to her. He thought it was an approving look at the time so decided to wear one of his pairs of them again.

'Goodness, you *do* look smart,' she said when he picked her up. 'Quite the young blade.' There was no hint of sarcasm in her voice, which was a relief.

She looked pretty good herself in black trousers and a loose white blouse with a lightweight green shawl around her shoulders. He knew shawls like that had a special name but couldn't remember it.

'You're looking very nice yourself.'

Jimmy must have been watching out for them because he emerged from the kitchen to greet them as soon as they arrived.

'It's Mrs Hallows, isn't it? How delightful to see you again after such a long time.' Dropping his voice, he went on in a confidential tone: 'I was so sorry to hear of your loss. It must be desperately upsetting for you. Please accept my condolences.'

He turned his attention to Alan and said more cheerily: 'And Alan, my old friend, it's always good to have you here, especially in such lovely company as you are this evening.'

Switching back to Penny, he said, 'Would you like me to take your pashmina for you, dear lady, otherwise you won't feel the benefit when you go out later on? May I? Good, I'll have Claudine show you to your table. And now I must love you and leave you and get back to my culinary duties.'

The waitress, Claudine/Kylie, in her French sea-goer's T-shirt, black jeans and a gore-free butcher's apron, led them to their table and handed them menus.

'Today's specials are on the blackboard, Mr Baxter. Can I get you something to drink in the meantime?' Her accent was the same as it always was, more Bridgwater than Bordeaux.

'Penny?'

'As we're in French mode I think I might have a Kir Royale.'

That sounded expensive but as Claudine was already looking expectantly at him, he said, 'Make that two, please.'

Jimmy was right about the number of diners. Four of the eight tables were occupied by middle-aged people already well into their meals. Not far enough in the background for Alan's liking, Charles Trenet was coming to the end of *La Mer*. Owing to his previous exposure to it, Alan knew the words by heart. It was also the CD's final track, so Jimmy's newly-acquired accordion music was bound to follow.

'This is nice,' Penny said, looking around her. 'It's very much as I remember it. But that waitress – surely she's not French, even with a name like Claudine.'

'No, she's a Kylie,' Alan said, and gave her an abbreviated version of Jimmy's explanation.

'And wasn't it kind of your friend to pretend he recognised me? Go on, admit it; you briefed him about me, didn't you?'

'Yes, well...'

'I'm glad you did.'

Not long after that, he asked for and soon received half a perfectly ripe avocado and a fair quantity of prawns in a pink sauce, enough to overflow onto his plate. He didn't catch the name of Penny's choice. It resembled the base of a jam tart with no jam in it, and was heaped with strands of cooked greenery with fragments of hard-boiled egg trapped in them. It must have been one of Jimmy's experiments but she seemed happy enough with it.

They then had steaks with green salads, but no puddings or cheese. They each drank a glass of the house white with their first course, and he had no more than a couple of glasses from the bottle of claret they shared with their steaks. As it was a special occasion, he selected the wine from further down the list than he'd ever ventured before. Jimmy hovered by the table but obeyed Alan's prohibition of advice and comment.

During the meal they talked about books they'd read but Alan said nothing about his latest library borrowings in case she thought them boring. They also argued amicably about the six non-Stones records they'd choose to have with them on their separate desert islands. She never mentioned her late husband, and he had nothing to say about his ex-wife. At times they laughed loudly enough for other diners to glance over at them before looking away quickly and getting on with eating and drinking.

'That was lovely, Alan,' she said when they'd finished and had drunk the rather bitter coffee Claudine brought them. 'Thank you, I *have* enjoyed myself.'

'Me too. As you know, I come here quite often but being with you has made this evening very special.'

He smiled at her across the table and reached over to put his hand on hers, thinking it was about time he got round to doing that. After all, it was no bolder a move than the one she made in her kitchen.

'It wouldn't have been the same without you.' He meant what he said. It sounded sincere to him and he hoped it did to her.

'No, it would have cost a lot less.'

So much for sincerity. He'd expected a more affectionate response and must have looked disappointed because she said, 'Oh, darling, I'm sorry,' and moved her hand around to squeeze his. 'That was such a pert thing to say. It's been a super evening.'

"Darling", eh? It was another first, another signal. He said, 'I'm glad you enjoyed it. Would you like a brandy or anything?'

'I don't think so. I'm not sure you ought to either, not with having to drive me home.'

'You're right, better not to. I'll just ask for the bill and we'll be off.'

'As it's supposed to be a French place, you'd do better to ask for the *Guillaume*, wouldn't you?'

'What? Oh, I see what you mean. No, Claudine wouldn't understand that. Or *l'addition*, come to think of it.'

'I hope you had a pleasant evening,' Jimmy said as they were leaving, 'and that you enjoyed the food. The lovely Claudine told me nothing was left over, not even for Mr Manners' sake, as my old mother used to say. It's always a good sign for a *restaurateur* like myself. And thank you so much for coming.'

He shook hands with both of them, helped Penny on

with what Alan now knew to be her pashmina, and held the door open for them. She went out first. As Alan followed her he looked back over his shoulder at Jimmy and winked at him. Jimmy winked back and gave him the sort of exaggerated thumbs-up sign seen in newsreels of wounded soldiers returning from Dunkirk. It must have been hard to hold himself in check for so long, and Alan was pleased he'd managed it.

The car was parked some way down the empty, unlit street. When they reached it, Penny turned to him, saying: 'I'm sorry about this, Alan, but I've wanted to do it for such a long time now,' and put her arms around his waist and kissed him on the mouth.

He'd no time to moisten his lips before it happened, and, after surprise, his first brief thought was that they might feel unpleasantly dry to her if the wine had dehydrated them. Then other thoughts rushed into his head; more surprise, then pleasure, then the realisation that he was already responding without thinking about it.

She reacted by parting her lips and keeping the kiss going, but more vigorously than before. While this was happening he registered that her tongue hadn't yet been involved. It soon was, and set off yet another thought, more reflective than the others. It was his first proper kiss, given or received, since long before his wife left him.

There was no time for any more thinking because she let go of him and said, 'I hope I didn't startle you. It wasn't very ladylike of me, I'm afraid. But it just had to be done.'

They got into the car. 'Bloody hell, Penny, that was unexpected. Unexpected, but very enjoyable, too.'

'I surprised myself but I agree about the very enjoyable.'

When they arrived at her house he left his car in the lane and walked up the path with her towards her front door.

'You'll come in for another coffee, won't you?'

'That'd be nice.'

They went straight into the drawing-room where she switched on one of the lamps and left him while she went off to make coffee in the kitchen.

While she was away, he noticed the photo of the husband-and-wife Hallows was no longer in its place. And when he looked round the room it was nowhere else to be seen. In the subdued light and the silence he asked himself what its absence might mean and whether it had any connection with what happened earlier. He tried to recall her exact words and savoured them when they came back to him. He repeated them silently to himself. "Wanted to do it for such a long time" and "I agree about the very enjoyable" – they were the important ones. How did he feel about hearing them in the first place and now hearing them again in his mind? Very good indeed, he decided.

And she said "darling" as well. It sounded actressy but there was nothing remotely actressy about her. Sadly, what she'd said and done made his reticence after the dinner party look particularly shaming.

'Why don't I put some music on?' she said when she came back with the coffee. 'Just don't ask me to listen to any more of that French warbling or those squeeze-boxes. I think we've had enough of that for one evening. I know, I've got a Thelonius Monk CD here somewhere. It was one of...it's jazz, of course, and half the time it's impossible to guess what tune he thinks he's playing, but it's fairly gentle. Fancy it?'

So it was one of Reggie's, was it? Alan would have thought her husband's tastes would have run to some rubbish by Gilbert and Sullivan rather than to modern jazz, even if Monk's modernity was at least half-a-century old.

'Fine by me.'

Though unappealing, it still sounded a better bet than traditional jazz. Oddly enough, his parents, two of the most sober-minded and anti-fun people in God's creation, had been fond of that. When they heard it on what they called the wireless, they tapped their feet and moved their heads about in time, sort of, with the music.

The piano started tinkling, mercifully at low volume, and Penny came over to sit next to him on the sofa. They drank their coffee in silence while he wondered what to say or do next.

'You know,' he said at last, 'you know when we were talking about dates? I think you were right. We've just been on one, haven't we?'

'I told you so. You see, it is possible at our...even if we're not as young as we once were, and a very nice one it was, too. When I was a teenager, a girl was lucky if a date involved anything better than going on the back of a boy's motor-bike to a Saturday-night dance in a village hall. When you got there your hair was all over the place and took ages in the loo to put right, lots of girls all fighting for a place in front of the mirror. And it was all records, not live music. You drank Coke – or cider if you could get away with it. When it was over, the boy drove you back home if he could get his bike started. Then he'd expect a long thank-you snog on the doorstep while you worried in case your dad had waited up and could see you through the bedroom window. It's no wonder I couldn't wait to get shot of it all.'

She'd come close then to saying a word or two about Reggie. She nearly said the Monk record was his but avoided it when she didn't really need to. The non-mention of his name, now and during dinner, must be deliberate.

'I don't know about you but I'm going to have that brandy now,' she said. 'It's a shame you've got to drive home, so I suppose I'm fated to drink alone.'

He stood up, struggling to accommodate a fully-fledged plan that suddenly arrived in his mind. Its temerity surprised him but he decided to give it a go.

'I'll get it for you. But I'll have a Coca-Cola if you've got one in the fridge.'

'Coke? Yes, I'm sure there's one there. You go ahead.'

He found one, opened it, and emptied it straight down the sink, leaving the tin on the draining-board. Then he went into the dining-room and poured the equivalent of a couple of teaspoons of brandy into a glass. Keeping his eye on the door, he quickly swilled the brandy around his mouth before swallowing it. He added some more to the glass, checked the rim for lip prints, and returned to the drawing-room.

'Couldn't you find one?'

He nodded, handing her the glass and sitting down again. 'I was so thirsty that I drank it in there.'

Monk was still playing. Odd parts of the melody, what little there was of it, reminded him of something he'd heard before – heard but not willingly listened to.

'Here's to a smashing evening,' she said, lifting the glass to her lips.

He edged nearer to her on the sofa.

'It was good to spend time with you,' he said. 'I enjoy doing that, you know. You took me rather by surprise back there but I'm really glad you did. I must confess I'd been entertaining hopes in that direction, if you know what I mean. But not yet, and certainly not there and then. So thank you again.'

She looked directly at him, her face so close to his that he could feel her breath on it. 'My pleasure, darling,' she said softly. 'Literally.'

There it was again. "Darling."

She moved her face even closer, saying: 'You did seem a bit taken aback. I was quite worried for a second but then I needn't have been, I'm pleased to say.'

'I just—'

'Alan,' she said suddenly, 'if I didn't know better I'd say you'd been dipping into my brandy on the sly. I can smell it on you.' She tutted. 'You are wicked.'

'I did just have a drop, I admit.'

There was no answer, so he activated the rest of his plan by saying: 'But I'm sure I'll still be all right to drive home.' He made a show of pulling back the cuff of his new shirt and looking at his watch. 'Yes, there won't be much traffic about by now so I think perhaps I ought to be going.'

She put her glass down and kissed him on the lips. 'It's not such a good idea for you to leave now, Alan, darling,' she said firmly. 'In fact, I don't think I want you to do that at all.'

CHAPTER THIRTEEN

'Uncle George and Auntie Mabel fainted at the breakfast table. Children, let that be a warning: never do it in the morning.'

Alan laughed ruefully when Penny recited this to him in bed the next morning while gently pushing him away from her.

'I don't want you overdoing it,' she told him, 'not at your age.' He was like a child rushing to gobble up all the available sweets before they ran out.

All went well in bed once he got going. She wasn't surprised when he was tentative at first because she expected him to be like that after so long without female company. That was what he'd told her and she'd no reason to disbelieve him.

There was no mutual shedding of clothes in the drawing-room or on the way up the stairs, so it was all very decorous and went on being so. As soon as they reached her bedroom they undressed without speaking and with their backs turned to each other, not that it was easy to see much by the shaded light of a single lamp on the dressing-table. When she sensed he was ready, she switched it off and they fumbled their separate ways into bed.

It occurred to her that Alan might have wanted the light left on. Reggie was keen on seeing what he was doing and kept his interest in the proceedings going for years till she had her operation. The light didn't matter after that because he then lost interest in the whole business, at least with her. He never told her why, and she never needed to ask.

The reconstruction of her left breast after the partial mastectomy was nothing like as successful as she hoped it would be. It didn't quite match the shape of the other one and wasn't properly yielding to the touch. To make matters worse, the areola was distended. She tried not to look at it too often but when she did it always reminded her of a map of the Isle of Wight. So whether by sight or feel it was a cosmetic failure. A remedial operation was an option but she couldn't bear the thought of going through it all again when no one could guarantee a noticeable improvement.

She kept her bra on while they were in bed. He must have felt she had a good reason for doing so as he made no attempt to remove it or explore its contents. Neither of them mentioned it.

They showered in separate bathrooms in the morning. She was touched by his sensitivity when he made sure his back was turned while she got out of bed and wrapped herself in her dressing-gown before going into the en-suite bathroom. It was too soon for mutual nudity by daylight. He was also enough of a gentleman to linger in his own bathroom down the landing till he guessed – correctly, as it turned out – she'd finished drying her hair, putting on her make-up and getting dressed.

'Breakfast in twenty minutes, Alan,' she called to him as she went downstairs. 'Tea or coffee?'

'Coffee, please.'

He came down and sat at the kitchen table, unshaven and with tousled hair, not at all like she was used to seeing him. Still in his new Coq au Vin clothes, he drank the coffee and ate the toast she made for them both. He didn't ask, but it would have been bad manners to offer him one of Reggie's shirts to go home in, so she was glad she'd already distributed them and all his other clothes around the charity shops in Weymouth and Poole. It was a relief to get rid of them and do someone a good turn at the same time. They'd have transformed a man of the right size who was down on his luck.

The Masonic case had also gone, handed over at the Lodge to the man who eventually opened the door to her. He probably had a title like Exalted Guardian Of The Oaken Portal and looked and sounded suspicious when he saw it was a woman who was ringing the bell so insistently. But his attitude changed and he sounded grateful when he saw what she was giving him. That left only the watches, the signet ring and the cuff-links to be disposed of. Selling them, or giving them to Giles, was out of the question, and they were too personal for Alan to have them. They were now in a drawer and it looked like they'd be staying there.

'It's going to be another lovely day, Penny, the fifth one running,' was the only observation Alan had made so far at breakfast.

She waited to hear if he had anything to say about what happened overnight. If he had, she wanted to take the opportunity to compliment him on the shape he was in, to reassure him if necessary. She saw only the vague shape of his body when they were in bed during the night, and only his head, bare shoulders and arms earlier in the morning. He felt lithe and fat-free, no doubt because of his regular tramping around the Wendmore course. But if she said anything complimentary he might take it as encouragement to say something nice in turn about her body and even to ask questions, however well-meant and discreetly framed, so she said nothing.

It was tempting to tell him she wasn't taken in by his ruse with the brandy but it was better to let him have his little victory.

'Penny,' he said after a while, 'would it be rude of me to say you were great last night?'

He kept his eyes on what he was doing which was buttering the last remaining piece of toast without asking her if she'd like it. She wanted to say something about that but this wasn't the time for it.

She giggled. 'Rude? After all that? Surely not.'

'I mean the way you put me at my ease. Helped me in fact, you know what I mean. At the beginning I'd started to think I wouldn't—'

'But you did, and you were fine, you silly man.'

'And then I thought you weren't going to—'

'Well, I did. You needn't be in two minds about that.'

'That's such a relief, darling. It'd been such a long time, as I told you.'

She noted his first use of "darling". Now that he had, it proved she was right to have started it and she was gratified he'd caught on so soon.

'It was the same for me. There, that surprised you, didn't it?'

'Really? Well, you're right about that. I am surprised.'

'Don't be. Reggie was getting on a bit, you know.'

It was true but was as far down that particular road as she wanted to go for now.

'I suppose he was,' Alan said, as though he'd not thought of it before. 'All the same, I—'

She interrupted him. 'You mustn't think I'm trying to bundle you out of here but it's nearly ten o'clock and my cleaner's due here soon. I don't want to start her wondering.'

She stood up and started clearing the breakfast things away.

'The house isn't overlooked at the front so you'll be able to make your getaway without alarming any neighbours. Unknown cars are often parked in the lane, so yours won't have attracted attention.'

In fact her cleaner wasn't due till the next morning but she needed time on her own to think things over, to go through every aspect of what had been said and done since their arrival at the Coq au Vin.

'I'll ring you really soon, Alan, I promise.'

Before she opened the front door to let him out, she put her hands on either side of his whiskery face and purposefully kissed him on the lips for several seconds.

'It's so nice to be able to do that at last,' she whispered in his ear. Information of that sort sounded better whispered than spoken aloud.

He smiled, which made her think how nice he looked when he did that. 'I look forward to it,' he said.

She watched from the doorway as he walked down the path to the lane. She hoped he'd turn round, so was pleased when he did and waved to her at the same time.

After he drove away she went upstairs to make the bed. It wasn't that long since Reggie last occupied it, yet it already looked odd to see both sides of it crumpled from use. She went into the bathroom where Alan had showered. He'd left his damp towel draped over the top of the shower's surround and she used it to mop up the splashes on the floor before taking another one from the airing-cupboard and hanging it over the towel rail. Back in the kitchen, she made herself more coffee.

He was only her seventh lover in forty-four years. She thought back to when she was young, disposing of her virginity as soon as she turned sixteen. Most of her contemporaries at school did that. In those days it was considered a sign of good character to keep it till then. Those girls who admitted to casting it away sooner or even bragged about doing so were thought of as rather fast and were likely to be talked about behind their backs.

The contraceptive pill was available but G.P.s were reluctant to prescribe it to unmarried Somerset girls. They might not even have been allowed to. And the local doctor's fondness for drink and his familiarity with her parents wouldn't have helped.

Despite that, she imagined the nineteen-seventies were a carefree time for the local boys. Talk of free love had already spread. Condoms – or blobs, as they were called around the villages – were soon looked on as impossibly dated compared with what was on offer to women and which made them responsible for anything untoward that happened to them. As a result, the chief form of birth-control for young girls, including her, was to say anxiously, "You will be careful, won't you?" before events went too far. There then followed an anxious time for the girls while they waited for their next period. Hers turned up regularly each month, so she was lucky with the five local boys. Then she was unlucky with Reggie but only after a good many enjoyable, comfortable and informative sessions in his flat.

She hadn't told Alan about Reggie's extra-marital activities. It was far too much information. And those activities came at a price for which the instalments fell due whenever he strayed. When she resented what he did it took no more than a few moments' reflection on her comfortable circumstances to persuade her the payments were worthwhile. Yes, she was a kept woman but she was kept in considerable style. It was what she needed.

Reggie's mother reluctantly accepted the need for a wedding but chafed about the match on grounds of class inequality. The chagrin she felt over her son's misbehaviour and Penny's condition resulted in a hurried civil ceremony. Her own parents had mixed feelings. They were put out by the unseemliness of it all but she imagined they were able to console themselves by thinking about the excellent match their daughter was making and by bragging about it to their friends.

After Emma's baptism, Penny's parents and her mother-in-law never met again. The senior Mrs Hallows made sure of that before she went off to live in Normandy, never to return. The shame visited on her by her younger son cast a long shadow. She was buried there and Penny always suspected it was because, in death, the old lady wanted to be close to her husband again.

Reggie was the first man she slept with. Alan was the second. Making love with the village lads never involved sleep. Not in a bed or anywhere else for that matter. No, she thought now, in retrospect it wasn't making love at all. It was having sex; open-air couplings that took place in secluded bits of local woodland accessible on foot or by motor-bike. There were the five boys from her village, then Reggie. And now Alan, though what she did with him had felt like they were making love, not just having sex.

It was soon, very soon, after Reggie, but she was the one who'd doggedly kept her vow to him to forsake all others, so she felt no shame now. From what she'd read in a recent newspaper survey, there was no hanging about nowadays. Needless to say, the survey canvassed only youngsters' views, because, obviously, older people were thought to be long past that sort of thing. Did she feel a need to take matters further with Alan, and did she still fancy him after sampling the goods, as it were? Yes, she did.

At seven in the evening the phone rang in the middle of a TV commercial that featured a woman in fits of laughter. It was aimed at women who wet themselves when they laughed too vigorously, and offered them an uncomfortable-sounding remedy. She hoped it was Alan who was calling her, but it was Emma.

'How lovely to hear from you. How are you?'

'Not too bad, thanks, mummy. What about you?'

'Never better.' It summed up how she'd been feeling till she answered the phone but she was already apprehensive of what was coming. With worries about miscarriages and fertility jostling for precedence in her mind, she asked anxiously: 'No problems, are there?'

There was a slight hesitation before Emma said, 'No, nothing that can't be sorted out. And you mustn't worry.'

It was a sure sign that bad news was on its way when anyone said that. 'Now you've really made me worried. Please tell me it's nothing serious.'

'It is and it isn't,' Emma said annoyingly. 'The thing is, Giles and I have had a massive row but I don't think it's terminal. It's just that I can't face being with him at the moment. It always ends up with recriminations and with me in tears. Mummy, are you going to be around for the next few days? You're not going off anywhere, are you?'

It was the first Penny had heard of them having rows rather than the spats and disagreements she had with Reggie. If Emma and Giles had real ones they must be about important matters and take place when they were alone. Until her visit to Wimbledon, her only evidence of discord between them was when she'd heard him ask Emma to carry out some task he wanted to avoid doing himself, such as putting out the recycling bins or giving the inside of the windows a bit of a clean. To her credit,

Emma never hesitated to argue with him. When she finished doing that she invariably lapsed into a lengthy sulk whether she'd won the argument or not. It was a default response she used when she was young and had gone on using after she left home.

'No, I'll be here. Why do you ask, do you want me to come up to be with you?'

'Thanks for the thought but, no, better not. It'd probably make things worse if anything. I just need to get away from here for a day or two and thought it'd be nice if I could spend them with you. But only if it's convenient.'

'Of course it is. I'd love to see you and it'll give us a chance to talk things over together away from Giles. But won't you tell me about it now?'

'No, I'm still in the office so I can't go into much detail at the moment. Giles or someone else is always going by my desk, you see. I'll tell you all about it when I come down.'

'And you're sure it's nothing really serious? Promise me?'

'It's only that I need a bit of space at the moment.'

'So when do want to come?'

'I've booked tomorrow off as a day's leave, much to his disgust, I might say, so can I come down in the morning? There's a train that gets in just after twelve-thirty. We'll have tomorrow afternoon and most of the weekend together if I don't go back till late on Sunday afternoon. What do you think?'

'Lovely. I'm looking forward to it. And do try not to worry. I'm sure things can't be as bad as they seem.' She said it despite feeling they were.

Emma didn't comment. 'Can you pick me up at the station? I love being in that sports car of yours. If the weather's nice we can have the top down and let the wind blow through our hair, help me clear my head.'

'I'll certainly pick you up but I don't have the BMW any more. I decided to get rid of it because I don't need two cars now and it's not as practical as the Range Rover.

You remember what it can be like down here in the winter, floods and so on.'

'You're driving daddy's car, then.' There was a silence before Emma continued: 'But he bought that sports car for you as a present, didn't he? And now you've got rid of it.' She sounded disapproving.

'One has to be sensible about these things, Emma. Surely you can see that.'

'I suppose so. At least you've still got the other car, daddy's car, to remind me of him.'

Afterwards, Penny turned off the TV and made a stiffish drink for herself. She settled down with it to try to guess what the row was about and why Emma needed to get away to talk about it. She rarely travelled down to Somerset even when her father was alive, and this was the first time she'd asked to come at short notice.

Penny badly wanted to phone Alan and tell him how worried she was but stopped herself. Like mutual nudity by daylight, their relationship wasn't ready for that – not to trade worries. What other parents said was true: you never stopped worrying about your children. He had none so had been spared all that.

At ten-thirty, after watching the news which was all depressing, she went upstairs to make up Emma's bed.

The train arrived twenty minutes late. As soon as she saw Emma approach the barrier she thought how pale she looked; her urban pallor was more pronounced than ever. The entwined initials of the logo on the smart new case she wheeled behind her were easily recognisable, so whatever the problem was it wasn't lack of money.

They hugged and kissed as they always did when they met but there was nothing more intense about Emma's embrace than usual. She smiled a lot and spoke cheerfully enough as they walked to the car, saying little more than thanking Penny for agreeing to put her up and telling her how good it was to see her again.

'It's nothing to do with starting a family, is it?' Penny said when they were in the car.

She had many questions to ask but made herself stick to the one uppermost in her mind. It was sensible to get the pregnancy subject out of the way rather than keep quiet and leave it hanging in the air.

'As you can imagine, I've been really worried about you since you rang.'

'It does come into it, in fact,' Emma said, leaving Penny more worried than before. 'But can we leave talking about things till we get indoors? There was no buffet car on the train and I'm dying for a drink. Would you mind?'

'I think I could do with one myself.'

She was drinking far too much and too often and ought to cut down, but obviously not now, not yet. As for Emma, it sounded like she wanted a real drink. Not just orange juice or sparkling water. It was another bad sign.

They drove on in silence with Emma gazing out of her window at the passing countryside she'd been familiar with since childhood. She seemed distracted, Penny thought, as she looked across at her. Emma wanted to talk, but only in her own good time.

That time came before lunch when Emma asked for a large gin and tonic.

When Penny asked her if that was wise, she said, 'You remember that trip Giles made to Hong Kong? Well, not long before you came up to see me, he finally admitted he'd been offered a job out there. He'd been negotiating the details since he got back and hadn't told me. I was furious. But the offer's just been finalised. It's a two-year contract and involves a promotion for him and he's bent on going. The problem is that they want me to go with him and he wants me to as well. There's no promotion in it for me, so I'd be doing roughly the same work as I'm doing now. I don't want to go, of course, but I felt I ought to put off trying to start a family while we argued endlessly about it. Not that I'd have been likely to conceive. Not with all the stress.'

That accounted for the bad atmosphere during the Wimbledon visit, then. It was all so disappointing – and not just for Emma.'

Penny protested: 'And you never thought to say anything about it when I came up to see you, not even when we were alone together?'

'No. I made him promise not to mention it, and I wasn't going to either. I didn't want you to be worrying before anything was actually decided, not so soon after daddy died. At the time I didn't know if he was going to take the job or not.'

'Lord, what am I supposed to make of that, Emma? If you did go, you'd be so far away and I'd never see you. I'd miss you terribly.' Her main concern made her say, 'But what will you do about a baby once you've decided what's going to happen?'

'A baby? Yes, what indeed? He told me he couldn't countenance the idea of us being out there with a baby, not with all the socialising we'd be expected to do. He said he was glad I'd not already fallen for one because it would have ruined things for us in the circumstances – ruined things for him, I expect he meant. And he pointed out I'd still be young enough to have one after we came back to England.'

'And you said?'

'I said no to that, absolutely not. I definitely wouldn't want to wait till we got back. It's late enough for me already. And it's not as though I even want to go there. I'd be well out of my comfort zone and there's nothing in it for me, only for him. So I reminded him he'd been fine about the baby idea earlier this year, and told him if he didn't change his mind I wouldn't go.'

'And he said?'

'That I was being silly and stubborn and unsupportive.'

'What a cruel thing to say.'

She could image him saying the words, certain in his own mind that Emma had no right to ignore his wishes.

'Yes. So you can imagine how the row developed after that. I hope he'll back down if I go on digging my heels in, but it'll be with very bad grace indeed. Even if I'd got pregnant I'm not sure I could have faced him constantly carping about it and telling me how I'd let him down. But I'm still determined to have one.'

She started to cry. It was what she often did when she was thwarted, Penny remembered, and she hadn't grown out of it. It was either crying or sulking, or both.

Emma said through her tears: 'Tell me, what do you think I ought to do?'

CHAPTER FOURTEEN

'So what did you say to that?' Alan asked, trying to impart some impetus to Penny's tale of woe.

It was her first visit to Myrtle Cottage and they were sitting in its back garden. She arrived after seeing Emma off on the London train and after phoning to ask if she could look in on him. She'd not told him why she wanted to.

The garden looked reasonably neat which was the best he could ever hope for. After his lunch and a snooze he practised chipping golf balls about on the patch of grass that Brenda and her husband called his lawn. He'd have preferred to brush up his putting but Geoff was between visits and the grass was too long for that.

Caught off guard by Penny's call, he did some urgent tidying-up indoors and changed into a better shirt and trousers while waiting for her to arrive.

Any woman would be bound to find fault with his wheelie-bin's unhygienic but convenient spot just outside the kitchen's open window, so he wheeled it further away where it would more hygienic but less convenient. He then hauled both his unwieldy sun-loungers into a spot where they'd catch all the early evening sun. Finally, he took wine glasses and a bottle of Sauvignon Blanc into the garden.

He knew something was wrong as soon as he saw her. He'd been with her when she looked sad or concerned, but never as worried as she did now. Her greeting was underpowered and she'd scarcely sat down before starting to tell him about Emma's visit.

After hearing what he hoped was most of it, and knowing she'd expect a response, he limited himself to asking his single question because he was the last person to comment on foundering relationships. At the same time, he could see why she might need to have him or someone like him to talk to about it.

She clearly had no trouble recalling her reply to Emma, as she answered at once.

'What could I say? I found myself dropping straight into what I imagined to be marriage-guidance mode. Or relationship counselling, given that they're not married. I went on as calmly as I could about the need to avoid rushing into decisions that might turn out to be wrong. I stressed the need for frankness, each of them needing to listen to what the other had to say and why it was said. Textbook stuff, I suppose. What's more, I went out of my way to hide my abiding dislike of Giles. He's so bloody arrogant.'

She stopped talking long enough to drink some wine. It gave Alan the opportunity to say, 'You don't paint a very attractive picture of him, do you?'

'No I don't, and with good reason. He's a complete shit and I've never known what Emma sees in him. I've always known he looked down on me, seeing me as a mere appendage of my husband. My background obviously isn't as up-market as Giles's and I'm convinced he thinks any social standing I have now is down to Reggie.'

She looked angry now, rather than worried. Alan wasn't sure which he liked less.

'He thinks of me like people did of chorus-girls who married dukes,' she said. 'They became duchesses but everyone knew they still weren't proper aristocrats.'

Giles had a point. The duchess reference was Penny's own story in miniature. Alan was wondering why she resented it so much when she asked him – as if he'd know – how Giles could be so keen to go to the Far East.

'It's supposed to be all humidity and typhoons out there, isn't it?'

'Yes, pretty much,' he agreed, reining himself back from explaining why Hong Kong typhoons were really tropical cyclones. It was another example of his geography knowledge being redundant in real life. He let his attention wander when he noticed an uncollected golf ball nestling in the grass. But this wasn't a good time to pick it up.

'...can't just be for the money,' she was telling him, 'because they must have enough of that. I'll tell you what I think; it's because he'd finally establish himself as more important than Emma as far as their careers are concerned. He's always given the impression that he is already, and this would prove it.'

Needing to show he'd not forgotten, Alan said, 'I remember you telling me you were concerned about them starting a family. That could still go ahead, couldn't it?'

'Not according to Giles. Not with all the socialising they'd be expected to do. You'd think Chinese women and ex-pats didn't have babies.'

'No, I meant when they came back. She'd still be young enough.'

'It'd be another two years. She'd be forty-two by then, nearly forty-three.'

If Susan ever had any interest in babies, she lost it a long time before that. She also lost interest in the baby-making process until her library cavalier re-ignited it. Well, bloody good luck to him. Even regular sex, if it still went on, which was doubtful, didn't make up for everything else – moodiness, ingratitude and bloody-mindedness, for instance – as he'd have discovered by now.

'It's not the best age to start producing,' Penny said crossly, as if he'd suggested it was. 'No woman should be going through her menopause while she's still taking a child to school. The other mothers would take her for a kindly granny doing her daughter a favour. And that's always assuming Emma and Giles clicked for a baby right away.'

Alan thought this over for a moment. 'And how did she take it, this advice of yours?'

'Sulkily,' Penny said without hesitation. 'She's always been prone to sulking. She even went distinctly funny when I told her I'd sold my BMW. Reggie gave it to me as a present and she thought I was being disloyal to his memory.' She held out her empty glass. 'Could you give me a refill, do you think?'

While he did that, she said, 'Emma seemed to hope I could make it all right for her. You know, like an alchemist turning base-metal into gold.'

She drank most of her refill before saying: 'I just don't know about her, she can be such a silly girl sometimes. I say girl, but at her age she's hardly a simpering teenager. The trouble is she got used to her father sorting out her problems before she set up home with her succession of Mr Unsuitables. Giles is the third of them. She won't hear a word of criticism of him from me but it's okay for her to moan about him, so I'm still not convinced they'd ever actually split up. Though I can't bear the thought of her being unhappy in the meantime, baby or no baby.'

She finished off her wine, and Alan refilled her glass without being asked to.

'Let's hope it doesn't come to that,' he said.

It was the best he could do in the circumstances and he felt he was acquitting himself fairly well on the whole.

She was busy drinking again now and it was a relief to have a pause in the Emma narrative. He used it to start worrying about the wisteria that ranged across the rear wall of the cottage. Its wispy shoots had begun to invade the thatch and he'd have to get the ladder up there and cut it back. Geoff might be vague about many of his ailments but not his vertigo.

The wine bottle was empty now. What should he do or say next? As an interim measure, he asked: 'Shall I bring out another bottle?' He would have finished his question with a "darling", but neither of them had used the word since she arrived. She apparently knew the secret of when to say it, so he decided to take his cue from her and not to use it today until she did. Then he'd follow suit as naturally as possible.

'I don't think so, I've got to drive. Quite honestly, I'm fed up with talking about Emma. And you must be totally bored with hearing about her. But I do appreciate the way you've let me ramble on. It's not as though she's your problem.'

Without waiting for his agreement about that, which he'd have given readily if asked, she said, 'What I'd really like now is for you to give me a guided tour of this cottage of yours. I'd quite like to have a look round it.'

It was the first time she'd sounded anything less than fraught. She'd been cooler with him than usual so perhaps it was a turn for the better.

'Let me help you with these things,' she said, getting up.

Her help involved no more than picking up the bottle and glasses and then watching him while he manhandled the sun-loungers back into the shed. As they did on their outward journey, they banged against his ankles with every step.

They went indoors the same way they went outside, through the kitchen. To his surprise, she asked him if it was where he did his ironing. When he said it was, she nodded to herself as if she'd known it all along.

He hurried her past the featureless back room and into the front room where he stood back to let her savour its wonders. Several reproductions of still-life paintings were arranged in no discernible pattern on one wall. Each depicted a table top bearing an unlikely combination of fruit and vegetables in an oddly-angled dish that looked ready to slide to the floor. His wife chose them and then abandoned them, him, and the cottage as having no part in her invigorating new life. He would have done away with them but couldn't think of anything suitable as replacements. But if Penny said she liked them he planned to tell her they were his choice.

She didn't, but what she did say was: 'This is…this is a really nice sitting-room, Alan. I bet it's snug in here when the weather's cold. It's very compact.'

Meaning compact as in small, it went without saying. It was estate agents' code. A boldly-positioned house was one exposed to traffic noise and howling winds. Generous was used as a synonym for parsimonious. But it *was* compact, there was no argument about that, especially when compared with the aircraft-hangar dimensions of her own drawing-room.

She'd also chosen to call his front room a sitting-room rather than a drawing-room. What made the difference? Not that it mattered, but he'd have liked to know. In the Wandsworth house he grew up in it would have been called the front room because it was at the front, and not easily mistaken for the rooms behind it. There were two of them; the back room, never known as the dining-room, where the family ate, and the kitchen. From what Penny had told him of her father's circumstances, her early years were probably spent in something similar.

She made up for it by telling him she admired his bureau, which was one in the eye for Tyler. Thinking now of her own antique furniture, he hoped she'd say she liked his Pembroke table and chest-of-drawers as well. If she did, he'd say they were also chosen by him. But she said nothing else, complimentary or otherwise.

When she wanted to look in his dining-room – or back room, evidently not dependent on where you were brought up – she surprised him by saying: 'I *do* like your beams,' even though they were plainer than the heavily chamfered ones in Farthing's.

He enjoyed a close-up view of her legs as he followed her upstairs and into the bathroom where she admired the shower. He had her at a disadvantage there because it was more up-to-date by many years than the one he'd not fancied lingering under at her house. The water there was a gentle drizzle rather than the tropical downpour his shower produced.

The spare bedroom evoked no comment but she liked the view from the main bedroom's window. They went downstairs and into the front room again. She was looking serious once more and he thought she must be ready for another one-sided talk about the Wimbledon problem. He counted down silently; ten, nine, eight, seven...

And then she said, 'I've got something to tell you,

darling.'

There it was, but it sounded to him that she was now using the word to soften him up before giving him another dose of unwelcome news. He'd had his fill of that.

'It's about something I did,' she said hesitantly. 'And looking back now, I'd have been better off not doing it.'

It sounded ominous. 'Go on,' he urged her.

'All right. I told Emma about you.'

Was that good or bad? He didn't know.

'Did you?'

'Yes, and reminded her about how you'd helped me with the ashes. I told her we'd had a couple of meals together including dinner at my house with friends and had become rather close.'

'What did she have to say about that?' It was bound to be nothing supportive.

'Do you know what? She came right out with it – had we slept together? I didn't want to lie to her so I told her that, yes, we had. Not defiantly or brazenly, you understand, just stating a fact.'

'Oh, Lord. How did she react?'

'With shock and disbelief. It was as if I'd told her I had love-children all over the county or she'd been adopted. She wanted – no, demanded – to know what I thought I was doing, and doing it so soon after her father died. She made the mistake of saying something about his body being not yet cold in the ground. It made me so angry I couldn't stop myself reminding her he'd been cremated and how disappointed he'd have been that she wasn't on hand to help scatter his ashes after all he'd done for her. She didn't react to that at all because it didn't suit her purpose. She said our sleeping together proved how little I cared about him, and how selling the car was just one more piece of evidence of it.'

He was already thinking that if he were the rightly-maligned Giles he'd have thrust old women and young children aside to be at the head of the check-in queue for Hong Kong – anything to get away from Emma. She'd graciously agreed to attend her father's cremation and funeral service but not the disposal of his ashes, and now had the cheek to question her mother's loyalty and sense of morality, the spoilt little madam.

'So what did you say to that?' He knew he'd used the same words earlier and come to no harm as a result. 'Did you tell her to mind her own business?'

'Not in so many words. I was in tears by then. They were pretty much tears of anger, but not of regret about us in case you're wondering. She'd been crying earlier, too, and wasn't far off tears again. Do you know what? I actually heard myself say – to my own daughter, mind you – that if I wanted to sleep with somebody, I would, with or without her prior approval. It's true. If I want to sleep with you or any other man for that matter, then I shall.' She said quickly: 'By the way, you're the only one I do want to sleep with. You know that, don't you? And I hope you feel the same way about me.'

It was a bit premature of her to be hoping that, he thought, but he wasn't going to argue. Anyway, she was right – he did.

Penny continued: 'I told her I was unattached now through no fault of my own. I said I was comfortably off, thanks to her father, and didn't want to spend my remaining years like a nun. Was I wrong to say that, do you think?'

'Certainly not,' he told her promptly.

It was interesting that she'd said nothing to Emma about her father's philandering, no matter how tempting it must have been. It was another sign that Penny was unaware of it. Stranger things happened. Some men even succeeded in fathering and supporting secret children without their wives ever finding out. If Penny did know and ever confided in him about it, he again resolved to say nothing about Tyler's revelations, or that he, Alan, knew already. It would do her no good to know her husband's adulteries were common currency at Wendmore and possibly beyond. He wanted to spare her that. And how much of it had already reached the ears of her neighbours like Peter and Brian, Mary and Helen, for instance? Had Reggie ever done the deed with those two women? Surely not, or only when they were all much younger.

Penny was still going on, and he wished she wasn't. She'd told him she was fed up with talking about her daughter but it was clear she'd not yet done enough of it to stop.

'...it was a horrible experience for me. For her as well, no doubt. Just when I ought to have been helping her we were having a row instead. I really dote on her, you know, and can't bear the thought of her disapproval. Afterwards, we hardly spoke at all. She needed someone to be cross with, and because it hadn't worked with Giles it had to be me. The awful cold atmosphere went on till she caught the train. I have to do something to bring her round but can't think what it might be. But it has to be soon, before she decides what she's going to do. I'd much rather have her stuck out there in Hong Kong hating Giles than have her here hating me. I'm sorry that sounds so selfish.'

Masking his doubts and trying to calm her down, Alan said, 'I'm sure she wouldn't hate you.'

If only she'd talk about something else. Even a few details about the W.I.'s goings-on would do.

He tried again: 'Look, she's angry and upset and doesn't know what to do.' Talk about stating the bleeding obvious, he said to himself. 'She's bound to resent you being with me.' As he said it, he wondered if he and Penny were with each other in that sense and whether that was how she now thought of them.

'You being with me and us having slept together can't be easy for her to accept,' he said. 'Why don't you leave it for a day or two to let her calm down and then go up to see her again? Much better than trying to patch things up on the phone, don't you think?'

'Perhaps you're right. I'll see.'

She sat silently for a moment before treating him to her first smile of the day. 'I'm so sorry to have dumped all that on you. You must have worries of your own. Do you forgive me?'

In the ordinary way he'd have listened to someone's problems, possibly a pupil's or a fellow-master's, maybe commented on them and suggested a solution or maybe not, and that would have been the end of it. But it looked as though Penny's problem had the stamina of a thoroughbred and was capable of going the full distance. It looked like the acute phase was over. He was glad about that but knew further phases were still to come. Even the first and worst could be revisited at will.

Feeling sorry for her was no help. Neither of them had an answer to suit both her ungrateful daughter and the ghastly Giles. Emma could either bite her lip and go with him to Hong Kong and be unhappy or he could stay with her in England and be resentful. It was difficult to care one way or the other, apart from the effect it was having on Penny.

Now, conscious of the lack of conversation since her plea for pardon, all he could think of saying was: 'There's nothing to forgive.'

Hoping she'd be ready at last for a change of subject, he said, 'Do you fancy a bite to eat? I could run to a sandwich, I should think. Or some soup.'

'Actually, what I'd really like is a spot of afternoon delight. I could do with cheering up.'

It took him a moment to know what she was talking about.

'You took me by surprise there,' he said truthfully, wondering if what people said about sexual healing was correct. Either way, he was ready to try it.

'I'd like that very much, darling.'

He'd got the reciprocal use of the word out of the way at last. Then he tried to remember when he'd last changed the bed linen and whether it mattered. Regardless of its state, it would have to do.

'I'm sorry I won't be able to stay the night,' she said. 'It's not that I wouldn't like to but a girl needs to have fresh clothes for the morning.'

'Whatever you want to do is fine with me.' It was getting closer to being true.

'Good. I'll just pop upstairs for a little wash and brush-up. Give me fifteen minutes and then I'll be ready for you.'

After she'd gone, he did some selective cleaning of his own bodywork at the kitchen sink and used a tea-towel to dry himself.

There was going to be no undressing in the dark this time, not for him. Even with the bedroom curtains pulled closely together there'd still be plenty of light. He expected she'd be in bed waiting for him by the time the fifteen minutes were up, so however much light there was he'd be the one stripping off in it.

When he'd finished undressing, she said, 'Before you get in here with me, there's something else I need to tell you. Something very personal you'll need to be understanding about.'

Not another revelation, surely. Not after all those she'd heaped on him already.

'I'll try very hard.'

'Some years ago I had breast cancer.'

'Oh, I'm so sorry.'

'It was followed by a partial mastectomy. That's having one breast removed, you know.'

'Yes, I did know that. But Penny, I'd no idea. Well, just the hint of one. It was because you kept your bra on in bed and I thought you must have had a special reason for doing that.'

'I did, and I was so grateful you were thoughtful enough not to ask questions or do anything about taking it off.' Her voice quavered as it picked up speed. 'So I had a surgical reconstruction and it didn't work properly and it looks horrible and I couldn't face having them try again.'

She began to cry, real tears forming surprisingly quickly and running down her face onto the pillow.

'Penny, darling, I don't mind for myself, only for you.

Please don't cry.'

She sat up and he saw she was still wearing her bra.

'I want you to see for yourself,' she told him. 'If we're to be together at all, we can't have secrets. But if you can't face it I'll quite understand. If you think you can, then come over here.'

He moved nearer the bed and stood naked in front of her. She sat up, unclipped her bra at the back and slipped the straps from her shoulders, holding the cups in place with her free hand. Then she pulled the whole thing away.

An uncommon wave of pity surged through him. What he saw wasn't as bad as he'd steeled himself to see. It wasn't nice, but it certainly wasn't horrible or frightening.

'You poor thing,' he said, bending over her and kissing her wet cheek. 'I'm really sorry for what you must have gone through but you needn't have worried about me. It affects me, of course it does, but only because you're clearly so upset about it. It certainly doesn't offend me or put me off. Not at all.' He'd know soon enough if his second claim was true.

'You're sure?' She wiped some tears away. 'Really sure? You're not just saying that?' She sounded like a child pleading for reassurance.

'No, I wouldn't lie to you.'

He knew he was bound to one day but he wasn't lying now.

'Alan, darling, thank you.'

So it had turned out to be all right for her, or at least better than he imagined she must have been fearing. What a chance she'd taken when they slept together for the first time. All she'd had to do was tell him.

Not long after that, what she'd finally shown him proved not to be the impediment he'd feared it might be. So that was all right, too.

CHAPTER FIFTEEN

Penny felt calmer the next morning. After doing some essential shopping she sat in her garden with a newspaper and a drink. The air was alive with birdsong and the sound of bees, but not wasps. They had to be dealt with when they built nests under the eaves.

Bales, her gardener, who must have been seventy if he was a day, had found a spray that worked well and he could still just about creak his way up a juddering ladder to use it. It had to be done at dusk after the wasps went back to their nest for the night, and again in the morning before they left it. He was also good with moles, trapping several of them each spring, nearly always before they reached the main lawn.

He was in the garden now, weeding the paved path that led needlessly to the empty barns. She could hear the clink of his trowel against the stone slabs.

Her worries about Emma receded a little after she talked them over with Alan. Bless him, he'd listened to her while she went into much more detail than he deserved to hear, and did so while making a good fist of showing interest and not letting his attention wander too far or for too long. All the time she was talking she was inwardly reproaching herself for involving him.

She decided against making another visit to Wimbledon. Giles was bound to be there or about to arrive which would make it impossible to have a serious talk. And Emma wouldn't listen, not while she was resenting what she saw as Alan's unseemly intrusion into her mother's life.

Penny was grateful for Alan's consideration in the bedroom, letting her get successfully through the breast explanation she was dreading. How different his reaction was from Reggie's, which was outright but never explained. There was only the slightest hint of awkwardness when Alan fondled her good breast after hesitating to do so, she supposed, for fear of inadvertently reminding her of the state of the other one. He left that one alone and she didn't blame him for that. She could hardly face having to touch it herself. To her relief he'd not tried to make some sort of point by touching it anyway, to prove its condition didn't matter to him.

Four years without sex with a partner and now two sessions. And how very nice and reassuring they were. Not marathon sessions, but not too abrupt, and with no attempt by him to try anything too dramatic or experimental. That might come later but it was hard to imagine him ever going in for much of it.

It had been at least six years of involuntary abstinence for him and he couldn't have expected them to end in the way they did – no more than she could for herself. She was the instigator on both occasions but didn't want him to look on those invitations as rewards for duties done, the first for waiting at table, and the second for listening without complaint to her droning on about Emma.

Regardless of what her daughter might think, bedding him twice wasn't overdoing it. She wondered if Emma had any inkling of her father's straying, not that it would make any difference to what she thought of her mother's new lease of life.

Finishing her drink and the newspaper at the same time, she looked up to see how far Bales had reached along the path. Not much further at all, it turned out when she saw him straighten up with a grimace from behind one of the choysia bushes that overlapped its edges.

He came slowly up to her and touched the cap he always wore.

Reggie would have preferred Bales to be bare-headed so he could tug his forelock in deference to his betters, a reminder of what her mother-in-law called the good old days when labouring men were properly grateful to have a shiny shilling from a gentleman.

'I be off now, Mrs H, I reckons.'

He was an old man who spoke the way the village boys

still did. Her father never used to. It wasn't what accounts clerks did.

She thanked him and reminded him of his agreed extra hours. She repeated what she said because he didn't always take things in without being told twice.

It was her turn to clean the brasses in St Michael's so she had nothing more to drink with her lunch. In the unlikely event that she met anyone in there who wanted to talk to her it wouldn't be polite to be breathing wine fumes over them.

Her meal was the sort Alan told her he made for himself. She opened a tin of sardines, drained away the oil, and mashed them down onto two slices of toast, topping them with chopped tomato.

She never served Reggie with a meal like that, but if she had, and once he'd stopped moaning about it, he'd have doused the sardine mash with the Tabasco sauce he was addicted to. The bottle still stood in the cupboard where it had been since he last used it. She might as well keep it in case a visitor asked for a Bloody Mary, though she couldn't think who such a visitor might be.

When she finished eating she washed up by hand, making more noise with the plate and cutlery than necessary. It helped make the house sound more lived in and let her feel less lonely.

While she gathered her brass-cleaning kit together she tried to visualise what Alan was doing. He'd have finished playing golf by now and would be back at his cottage, dozing in the garden, watching TV or reading. According to him, those were the only things he did. It was a shame, a waste of a good mind and a sound education. He could still have years of life to spend doing not very much before he took himself off into a care home. Or was bundled off to one for his own good by some branch of Social Services.

Her present situation was like his in many ways. Her adult life was spent dancing attendance on Reggie and looking after their daughter, cooking, entertaining and going on exotic and expensive holidays, usually to places where he could play golf while she stayed at the hotel with Emma.

Now, with years still to go unless the cancer put in a return appearance – a constant fear of hers – the cooking and entertaining were at an all-time low and she had no one to care for or go on holiday with. All too easily she could see herself, older and increasingly haggard, sitting alone at a table routinely laid for four in a foreign hotel while younger holiday-makers and their children bustled about the dining-room, enjoying themselves and ignoring her. Or worse, silently pitying her, the poor old widow all alone on holiday, the one who held everyone up by making such hard work of climbing the aircraft's steps. The alternative was to make a nuisance of herself by initiating a frenzy of inviting neighbours to lunches and dinners just for the sake of having company, and then having to be invited back by them whether they wanted to or not.

She tried to dispel these depressing thoughts by striding purposefully to the church as if she were on an important mission. Once in a while when she was attending to the brasses; an altar cross, lectern, candlesticks and several memorial wall-plaques, someone crept furtively in to sit or kneel in a pew at the back of the church for a few minutes' silent prayer. They rarely spoke to her, preferring to do no more than nod.

On her way to the altar she paused to read the cards that parishioners had pinned to a baize-covered board. It had a notice on it that promised the vicar would pray for their hand-written wishes to be granted. Most had been in place for months but there were two new ones, each as gloom-inducing as the rest. One bleakly asked for prayers that some anonymous person wouldn't die. The other was more conversational: "dear god please let our daughter get better thank you god xxx." Few of the little cards mentioned a name. It saved the writers from being identified and talked about.

She thought of a wording she could use to cover all her concerns: "Please let me have a lasting relationship with this man I know. Please stop my daughter's boyfriend being so unreasonable. Please let her get pregnant soon." That said it all. It was only a step away from entries in lonely-hearts columns. Before Alan came along, hers would have been: "Lonely widow, 60, OHAC, considered attractive. Slim, financially secure, likes the good things in life, WLTM a caring gent 60-70 with similar interests for happy times together, maybe LTR."

She knew some of the jargon: OHAC – Own House And Car. WLTM – Would Like To Meet. LTR, which she used to think stood for Leading To Romance until she heard it really meant Long Term Relationship. She guessed "cuddly" meant grievously overweight, and "fun-loving" was code for a sex-crazed alcoholic. "Likes country pursuits" could mean anything from long walks in the rain to organized dog-fights.

One of the brass plaques commemorated the dozen local members of the armed forces killed in the Great War, or 1914-1919 as the plaque had it, and which seemed wrong by a year but must somehow be right. She gave it an extra-powerful going-over, buffing it back to brightness. As always, her heart went out to one pair of long-departed parents who, like Alan's great-grandparents, had lost two sons.

She resented the way an officer headed the list, regardless of the first letter of his surname. After him came a sergeant, a corporal, and then the rest in alphabetical order.

'But all equal in the eyes of God,' she muttered to herself.

On her way out she stopped by the south door to trail her fingers around the font's cable-moulding.

Back indoors again, she used up some time by walking around the rooms and making a mental note of the furniture she could manage without if the time ever came for her to act on Giles's unsought suggestion about downsizing. She soon concluded she didn't want or need to keep very much of it at all. But the thought of having to live in a practical, easily-managed place like a bungalow on an estate was too awful to contemplate seriously.

If running a house the size of Farthing's ever became too much for her, she'd rather close down its rooms one by one till she was living and sleeping in the kitchen, not far from the downstairs cloakroom. The garden could be left to its own devices. Wild gardens were rather fashionable.

She was dreading the time when she'd have to go upstairs to bed. Foxes gathered near the barns at night and she avoided going there even in daylight for fear of meeting them. The nocturnal barking and screaming reached her through the bedroom window and frightened her much more now she was alone. The house's ancient timbers creaked at night, even now when the central heating was turned off for the summer. The creaking sometimes made her think an intruder was creeping up the stairs.

With nothing more to fill her time before her next meal, she decided to drive over and pay Alan a surprise visit. She hesitated before doing anything about it. Twice in two days, the first soon after a preliminary phone call and now an unannounced visit. She didn't want to frighten him off. If she phoned beforehand it would give him the opportunity to make an excuse if he wanted to. She thought about it some more before deciding what to do.

With her mind made up, and in case events turned out as she hoped, she packed an overnight bag with a change of clothes, her toiletries and make-up. As an afterthought she added her hair-dryer. Alan took trouble with his hair to keep it looking so neat, so she guessed he had a dryer of his own but it was best to be on the safe side.

She put the bag in the Range Rover's rear foot-well where it couldn't be seen through the smoked-glass windows. It was important not to look over-confident or to make him think she took him for granted. Then she had a shower and changed into a new top and a short skirt that showed off her bare legs. She locked up, set the burglar alarm and drove off.

His car was parked in the lane outside the cottage and she left hers near it.

There was no answer when she used the door knocker so she walked down the side of the building to the back garden where she saw him clinging to a ladder and doing something to the wisteria growing high up the wall. He was wearing shorts.

When he saw her he climbed down carefully with his secateurs in his hand.

'Good Lord, Penny,' he said, 'what on earth are you doing here? There's nothing wrong is there?'

'No, nothing like that. I was at a bit of a loose end so I thought I'd look you up. It's not inconvenient, is it?'

He kissed her on the lips, which was a good sign. 'Certainly not. I'm glad you did. I only had the wisteria to deal with and then the rest of the afternoon's my own. How nice to see you again. Though I'm not exactly dressed for visitors, as you can see.' He ran his hand carefully over his hair to remove bits of wisteria clippings from it. 'I'm always nervous of going up there for fear of disturbing wasps. And as I'm here alone, it's unlikely anyone would hear if I fell. I could lie here in a crumpled heap till my gardening chap turned up and found me dead.'

'Then it's lucky for you that I came when I did.'

'It certainly is. Do you fancy a cup of tea? He pointed to a pair of rusty metal chairs outside the kitchen door. 'You sit there and I'll bring it out.'

He was soon back with a tray holding two saucerless cups, two plates, a bread knife, and a tin with a picture of a castle on the lid. He cut two crumbly wedges from a fruit cake and handed her one. The cake was on the dry side but quite palatable.

'I do like to see a woman wearing heels,' he said suddenly.

'Do you, indeed? Any woman in particular?' Oh dear, she thought, stop looking for compliments.

'Yes, since you mention it. You're lucky to be able to.'

Thank goodness he left out *at your age*. He went on to

tell her what she already knew, that many women had crippled their feet through wearing the wrong sort of shoes. Again there was no mention of their age.

'And you've got the legs for them, Penny. But then you know how much I admire yours. Bare legs today, too. I like that.'

When they finished their tea he began to tell her how he did at golf that morning but hadn't got as far as the nine inward holes when she stopped pretending to be interested, and interrupted him.

'Alan, darling, have you ever thought how nice it would be for us to have a little holiday together? I was thinking about it this morning.' She'd only just had the idea. 'Somewhere not too hot and not too far away. The Canaries, perhaps.'

She waited expectantly for him to say something but he was looking at his feet, seemingly fascinated by his deck shoes and their twisted leather laces. Maybe he wore deck shoes for safety because of the grip they gave on the ladder's aluminium rungs. He didn't look like a man who'd be at ease on a storm-tossed yacht.

'It's never terribly hot there in the summer,' she said, 'not compared with the Spanish mainland for instance. We went to Seville once, mainly because Reggie wanted to see a bullfight.' She'd mentioned his name again without meaning to. 'Not my thing at all, frankly. No sea, no beach, no pool, just sweltering heat all the time. It's no wonder they call it the Cauldron of Spain.'

Alan hesitated long enough to make her think he was going to turn the idea down. But he eventually said, 'It sounds like a great idea. I've not had a proper holiday since...since I've been on my own. When were you thinking of going?'

So there was no need to get the rack and thumb-screws out to persuade him.

'Quite soon if that's okay with you. But it rather depends on what's available at short notice. I think a week away would be long enough.'

'Why don't I use my laptop to see what's on offer?'

'Brilliant. It'd be good to get away and leave my family problems to sort themselves out.'

'No news from Emma, then?'

'Nothing. To tell you the truth and I know I shouldn't say it, but I've waited so long to find out what's going on that I'm beginning to lose interest. I want the best for her, of course, and I hope they stay together but I've virtually given up hope of ever becoming a grandmother.'

'That's a shame.'

'Yes, it is.'

The Coq au Vin was closed on Mondays. She couldn't persuade Alan to go to The Firkin which looked all right to her regardless of what he told her about it. By the time they set out in his car to the pub in the next village they'd visited a late-availability website and booked a half-board holiday in a room with a sea view in a Tenerife hotel.

The flight from Bristol airport was on the next Friday morning, and Alan used his credit-card to pay for everything. She said nothing about that but was determined to pay her way and more besides if necessary. After all, she reminded herself, she liked the good things in life.

The baggage limit was twenty kilos each which would be about enough for her and much more than he needed. Would those capacious shorts of his reappear in Tenerife? She hoped not. And she'd definitely have something to say if he wanted to wear sandals with ankle-socks.

Even in the pub's drab interior, she found it easy to envisage lovely food and wine, and lazy days by the pool followed by nights of love to the background hiss of the air-conditioning. It would be a good test for them. Spending unbroken time together and coping with the intimacies of shared bathroom facilities would see to that.

When they came back they spent a couple of hours drinking and watching TV, exactly like an old married couple, she thought. And later, when she went out in the dark on the pretext of getting a breath of fresh air and returned with her overnight bag, he appeared not to be surprised at all – just very pleased.

CHAPTER SIXTEEN

Alan knew the departure lounge would be crowded with travellers. Many of them looked old enough to know better than to wear the ill-assorted clothes they must have chanced on earlier that morning, probably in haste and in the dark. Some were already backing up their breakfasts with elevenses of lager, sandwiches and rolls. Others kept getting up to peer at the flight-departure screens to make sure they'd not been left behind. Fractious children ran about annoyingly. They belonged to parents who looked harassed but did nothing to restrain them. He hoped none of them, children or parents, would turn up at the hotel.

Penny wore flat shoes for the journey. It was the first time he'd seen her without heels since the visit to Winyard's Gap. His sole concession to the rigours of foreign travel was a beige cotton gilet. Its many pockets, some fastened with Velcro and some with zips, bulged with his mobile phone, a wad of Euro notes, his wallet, reading glasses, sunglasses, reading sunglasses, both their passports and the other travel documents. Every few minutes he patted all the pockets in turn to make sure nothing was missing.

'For heaven's sake, Alan, do stop doing that. If you've forgotten something it's too late to do anything about it now. Just try to sit still.'

'Sorry.'

She'd not been herself all morning. This little display wasn't her first sign of impatience with him today, and there was still a week to go.

She was looking round the lounge and surprised him when she leaned towards him and hissed, 'I ask you, what on earth do these people look like? They're the sort you only ever see milling about at motorway services. You wonder where they've come from and where they think they're going. And wherever it is, you hope you won't meet them there.'

It was on the harsh side but he knew what she meant.

'Don't worry,' he told her, 'the odds are they won't be staying at our hotel.' All she did was shrug.

He wanted to sit by the aircraft window but so did she. He wedged himself in beside her with his knees pressed against the seat in front while a child sitting behind him kicked him in the back. Penny's elbow was on one armrest, and a fat man with a tiger's head tattooed on his neck had claimed the other one. Alan settled down to read the brochures from the slot in front of him and to get on with being uncomfortable for the next four hours or more.

Their room looked exactly like those pictured on the hotel's website. It was her idea to specify a double room instead of a twin, a good omen. There were two chairs, a long dressing-table with drawers under it, and a mini-bar. Presumably for lack of a buyer, a trainee artist must have given the hotel the three strikingly bad paintings that were screwed to the wall above the bed.

Alan had no small change, so the youth who belatedly brought their cases up from reception was grinning when he left the room with a ten-Euro note in his pocket.

As soon as the door closed behind him, Alan said, 'Are you all right, Penny? You've been a bit quiet all day.'

It was an understatement but safer than telling her she'd been a pain ever since they set out.

'I've had a splitting headache, still got it in fact.'

'What, all this time?'

'Since I got up. Sorry.'

'Don't be. It's not your fault.'

'Strange to relate, Alan, I am aware of that.'

That was telling him. It was Miss Sharp, straight out of the knife-box, as his father used to say of Susan.

After they unpacked, Penny opened the sliding door that led onto the balcony.

'At least they've given us the sea view we asked for,' she said to him over her shoulder.

The "at least" meant she was upset by more than a headache. That bloody daughter of hers was first in the line-up of suspects as far as he was concerned. For all that, he needed to make the best of things.

He joined her at the rail and looked out over a segment of beach and the placid-looking sea. What they could see of both was bathed in late afternoon sunlight.

'Yes, it looks nice out there,' he said. 'I'm glad we booked a room with a sea-view, well worth the extra. We were lucky to get one at such short notice.'

He'd not intended to mention the extra cost yet. Doing so by accident reminded him he must find the right moment, clearly not now, not in her present mood, to bring up the cost of the holiday. He said nothing at the time of booking but it was his credit card, not hers, that was going to be savaged by the better part of two thousand pounds. He'd hoped to be given a cheque for half of it as soon as the website confirmed the booking but nothing like that happened then or since.

Like so much else, the holiday was her idea so surely she'd not misled herself into thinking he was making her a gift of it, but he had his doubts. If so, well, she could think again. Nearly two thousand pounds might not mean much to her but it was a large and unbudgeted amount for him, enough to pay for three years of his Wendmore subscriptions.

It was already five o'clock. 'Shall I ring down to get room-service to bring us up some drinks?' he asked.

'Let's see what's in the mini-bar first, shall we?'

She went back into the room, bent down to take out a bottle of Cava, and picked up two glasses almost hidden by the bottles and jars of woman's stuff she'd strewn across most of the dressing-table.

No wonder her case was so much heavier than his. She'd brought many more clothes than he had, and what looked like shoes for every conceivable occasion. They included one pair that wouldn't look out of place if a local *hidalgo* invited them to a glittering ball at his Canarian villa. They were ranged along the bottom of the wardrobe, and her dresses and separates took up most of the hanging space above them. His shirts, trousers, gilet and emergency linen jacket, already badly creased, were bunched up in what was left. The dressing-table had four drawers. She'd taken three for herself and left the bottom one for him.

'This doesn't look too bad,' she said, showing him the bottle which wasn't as cold as it ought to have been. 'I suggest we make a start on it. It'd take them ages to bring drinks up to us and then they'd be bound to have got the order wrong.'

They sat at a little table on the balcony where he wrestled out the Cava's cork and filled the glasses. In the distance a few holiday-makers were still sprawled on the beach or walking about aimlessly. It was good to see how few children were down there with them.

'How's the head now?'

'It's still not right but it may be starting to clear. I had some Panadol in my wash-bag. Silly of me, I should have had them in my hand-luggage. Still, better late than never.'

'Good.'

He needed to ask if she'd heard from her daughter, if only to get it out of the way. It was another of those tricky decisions. If he did, it might set her off again. If he failed to, she might think him uncaring. He decided to take a chance.

'Not a word,' she said. 'And I don't want to put pressure on her as she must still be going through hell with Giles. I sent her an e-mail instead to say we were going on holiday, where we were staying and when we'd be returning. She never replied. But I can't bear not knowing what's happening so perhaps I'll call her this evening after dinner when we've settled in properly.'

'Do you think it'd do any good?' He didn't have to try to sound doubtful.

'Probably not, and I don't want her to think I'm desperate. I'll have to see, but at least she'd know we'd arrived safely. I know I told you I was losing interest in it all. But that was then. In fact I've been worrying about it ever since and it's been on my mind all the time. I suppose she might just have something to tell me.'

'See how you feel later when you've had a chance to unwind.'

'Possibly.'

She looked him up and down, but not in a way to make him expect an outburst of approval.

'I hope you don't mind me mentioning it,' she said, 'but I wasn't sure about that gilet thing you had on earlier. Though I suppose it's practical if nothing else. And I can't imagine why you brought that linen jacket with you. I don't think you'll need it here.'

He inched up a leg of his chinos. 'You may be right.' Better to agree with her than not. 'But I am wearing these pink socks again that you like.'

'So I noticed. I'm getting a bit…never mind. So what are you planning to change into this evening?'

He'd no plans to change at all. 'According to the website, men have to wear shirts in the dining-room. And long trousers as long as they're not jeans.'

'That's to stop them from going in there in swimming-trunks or those awful sleeveless vests. I just hope you're not planning to wear sandals.'

'Certainly not. I'll be wearing these.' He pointed down to his deck shoes.

'Really? I'm going to wear a dress.'

'A new one?'

'New to you, certainly. I hope you'll like it.'

'I'm sure I will. You always look good.'

And on their way to the dining-room, she did. Better, he thought, than a lot of the women they passed. Not better-preserved but better generally.

They waited in the doorway till a waiter found the time and energy to come over and check their room number against a list.

As they were led away to a distant table, Alan noticed men, and not only men of his own age, openly eyeing her in a speculative way. It cheered him up to see them doing that and he hoped she was enjoying the attention as well.

Most of the tables were already occupied. He didn't hear much English being spoken as he threaded his way between them. Instead, a lot of diners were talking in what he thought were Slavonic languages. Many of them looked ill-at-ease with the cutlery, wielding their table-knives in an assassin's grip or holding them like a scribe's pen. He didn't need to be abroad to see that. The pen-holder's grip was widely used in Somerset, and he once saw a man in the Coq au Vin looking at a steak knife as if it were an intriguing novelty.

The few East European women who weren't young, beautiful and well turned-out, were raddled, with hefty shoulders and arms. They looked powerful enough to have been field-athletes when they were young.

He asked Penny if she thought the younger and more beautiful women were the mistresses of their older male companions who mostly looked like all-in wrestlers run to seed, but rich enough to have lots of gold jewellery on show. She told him they probably were.

There were plenty of children in the room. They all looked too busy eating to be out of control, except for one at a nearby table who was too big for his high-chair and cried loudly between the mouthfuls of food his mother was spooning into him. Passing waiters smiled and clucked at him but he went on crying just the same.

Alan's brief feeling of buoyancy ended when an oldish couple sat down at an adjacent table.

Evidently hearing English being spoken, the man turned to him and said, 'I couldn't help overhearing you, old chap. Been here long?'

The woman smiled expectantly. She looked pleased to have her companion's attention diverted.

'We're English, too,' she said unnecessarily. 'We've already been here a week.'

'Have you indeed?'

Penny looked up from the wine list. 'We only got here this afternoon.'

'It's nice to meet another English couple,' the man said,

looking as pleased as a tea planter might do on hearing his mother-tongue spoken after many years' absence in some tropical hell-hole. 'You'll like it here.'

To Alan's annoyance, he got up and walked the two steps to their table and stretched out his hand.

'I'm Roger, Roger Wellbeck, and that's my better half, Jane.'

Alan made himself stand up to shake the proffered hand. 'I'm Alan Baxter and this is…this is Penny.' He sat down again.

'How d'you do? How d'you do? Very glad to meet you.' His wife stayed where she was and simpered across at the three of them.

Alan hoped that would be the end of it but before he could stop her, Penny asked, 'Have you been enjoying yourselves?'

'Very much, thanks, and we've had some lovely weather.' He showed no sign of wanting to get back to his wife.

'I'm glad about that, let's hope it lasts.'

'I trust you'll make time for a trip up Mount Tiede,' Wellbeck said. 'It's a volcano, you know. They even did some film scenes there once. Yes, you ought to go. Of course, old Tiede's dormant at the moment but I daresay it could blow at any time. Sometimes they do. Do you know,' he continued, still standing at Alan's elbow, 'I read somewhere that if it does and the whole mountain cascades into the sea, the resulting tsunami would whistle across the Atlantic and take out New York completely? Leave it flat as a pancake. Makes you think, doesn't it?'

'We must hope it doesn't happen while we're here,' Penny said.

'Oh, I wouldn't lose too much sleep over it I were you. Still, you never know. As I often say to Jane, what will be, will be. Mind you, you'll need your thermals up there.' He laughed loudly.

'We'll try to keep that in mind,' Alan said.

Wellbeck looked pleased. 'Good, good. Well, I'd better

get back to the trough. Hope we run into you again.' He walked away at last.

'Not if I see you first, you won't,' Alan mouthed after him. Keeping his voice low, he said to Penny, 'Christ, let's hope not, eh?'

She sighed. 'You must try to be nice to people, you know. He meant no harm, he was only trying to be friendly.'

'Yes, I'm sure he was. But I came here to be with you, not to be talked at by a bloody vulcanologist.'

'I know, and it's sweet of you to say so.'

Her words and their accompanying smile registered with him as the day's first sign of good humour from her. The protracted headache must have gone at last.

It was Jean-Paul Sartre who said hell was other people, Alan remembered, as he looked stealthily across at the Wellbecks. Sartre would have done better to narrow it down to other people met with on holiday. But it was quite apt considering it came from the *plume* of a chap from the wrong side of the Channel. It sounded as if it might have come from Philip Larkin, never a man to show a sunny face unnecessarily or dwell too long on happiness. He'd been a librarian, too. Alan hoped Susan's pet librarian was already brooding on his self-imposed fate while contemplating his imminent retirement from the pressures of his date-stamping duties.

It was a self-service dining-room. After collecting a mixture of salad bits and pieces and returning to their table to eat them, Alan and Penny went back to the queue at the tepid-food counter. The foreign-looking food on offer there looked uninviting but they both settled for what a card said were pork chops and which looked as though they might well be. Naturally, there was no apple sauce to be had. They added potatoes, odd-looking beans, and gravy to their lukewarm plates and went back to their table. The wine Penny ordered was brought to them when they were already halfway through their meal but they drank it all.

When they'd finished and got up to leave after deciding not to bother with pudding, Alan saw the Wellbecks were starting to work their way through scoops of multi-coloured ice cream. He acknowledged their flutter-fingered waves of farewell with a nod and a taut smile.

Back in their room, Penny changed out of her heels and into the shoes she'd worn during the day. Then they strolled around the hotel's grounds and had a look at the floodlit pool where swimming was banned, *verboten, interdit* and *prohibido* after eight in the evening, and where flippers and inflatable beds were outlawed at any time. At Alan's instigation, they were now holding hands.

Other guests were also strolling about. Some were Spanish, the women wizened beyond their years but immaculately turned out, the men wearing jumpers against the evening's treacherous seventy-degree chill.

'Do you know, I think we're going to have a lovely time here?' Penny said, giving his hand a squeeze.

This was the second sign of her improved mood. It was time to refer obliquely to what she owed him.

'We ought to, considering how much it's costing us.'

'It's certainly not cheap,' she agreed. 'I know, why don't you keep a note of how much you're spending and we'll settle up when we get back? For the whole thing, I mean. You said you'd bring plenty of Euros and I quite forgot to get any from the bank. Will that be okay for you?'

It was satisfying to have got the subject sorted out, and so easily.

'Of course it will.'

After a while they made their way back to the hotel and into one of its several bars where he ordered drinks and signed for them. He was tired now and feeling the effects of the Cava and the bottle of Rioja they shared at dinner, so it was good to sit down and watch the barman at work on their behalf. There was no nonsense here about dispensing gin from an optic. Instead, it was poured out freely from what looked exactly like a real bottle of

Gordons. The tonic was hosed into their glasses from a dispenser that hung like a miniature petrol pump behind the bar.

To one side of them, on a rostrum, a pianist in a white dinner-jacket played mystery tunes on a grand piano, also white. Alan had the same difficulty identifying them as he had with Thelonius Monk's offerings in Penny's drawing-room.

At one point a man approached the rostrum and spoke to the pianist. He could have been asking him to stop playing or, less desirably, to play a request. Whatever he wanted, it was turned down with a regretful shake of the head.

Not long after that, Penny said, 'I think I might just try giving Emma a call after all. She's bound to be back from the office by now. Would you mind?'

'No, you go ahead.' He asked if she'd rather he left her alone to make the call, either in the bar or back in their room.

'Thanks, but I wouldn't bother, darling. It's not as though we'll be discussing state secrets.'

He noted her first use of the word that day. It was like a weather-vane, a reliable guide to which way the wind was blowing, but came and went without warning, he thought with a sense of helplessness. Still, life was better when she did use it.

He stood up. 'I'll take another stroll around the pool and try to work out where the sun will be tomorrow so we'll know where to sit.'

'You don't need to do that. Really you don't.'

'I know, but you might feel more comfortable if I do.'

As he spoke, the pianist stopped playing, bowed in several directions to not much applause, and walked over to the bar. 'I'd do it now if I were you,' Alan said, 'before he starts up again.'

He waited for twenty minutes before returning. When he did, her phone was back in her handbag. 'Did you get through?' he asked.

'Yes, I did. But no, she hasn't reached a decision yet. I expect that means Giles hasn't made one for her. He was there with her so she couldn't talk much, and she's probably trying not to cause me any more worry. So I've no idea what the outcome's likely to be. I said I'd call her again when we got back and she said that would be fine. Despite all her problems, she asked if we'd had a good flight, what the weather was like and so on. And here's something; she mentioned you by name for the first time. She must be mellowing in her old age. I have to say I'm a bit relieved.'

'And at least she didn't have any bad news for you. That's something to be grateful for. If she had, you'd have been on edge about it for the rest of our stay here. As it is, darling, you should try to forget about it for a while. Let's just concentrate on enjoying ourselves.'

'I'll try. It'll give us a proper chance to get to know each other better. And thanks for staying so understanding. Yes, I know, I keep having to say that to you but I don't want her and Giles's problems to get in our way. There's no point in letting that happen.'

'That's the spirit. Why don't we have another drink and then get an early night?'

'Sounds good to me.'

On their way out of the bar they saw the Wellbecks sitting a long way from the pianist's rostrum. He was talking animatedly to his wife. Alan guessed he was telling her something fascinating about tsunamis he'd forgotten to tell her before or felt she needed to be reminded about. Neither of them looked up as he hurried Penny out, taking advantage of the cover afforded by the exotic-looking plants in terracotta pots that stood about the room.

'We were lucky there,' he said as they waited for the lift, and she laughed as she agreed with him.

She got ready for bed in the bathroom, emerging from it in a nightdress which was green and silky and reached her knees. Try as he discreetly might, he couldn't discern any part of her body through it.

When he was packing he'd debated with himself about the wisdom of including pyjamas. The sight of them was unlikely to set her senses aflame, quite the opposite in fact, but to spring into bed without them might seem presumptuous.

He'd no serious regrets about the way his body looked but she was in relatively better shape than he was, even allowing for that breast of hers which she looked on as a major defect but caused him no problem at all. He hoped he'd made that clear to her by word and by deed.

Before he went into the bathroom, she said, 'I hope you don't mind, but I'd rather not...you know, not tonight anyway. I'm absolutely shattered after the flight and the amount of drink we've got through, and I don't think I'd be at my best for you. But if you like, I can...'

'There's really no need, thanks all the same. No, let's keep it on hold till we've had a good night's sleep. I feel a bit the worse for wear myself.'

All evening he'd been hoping for considerably more than she'd just offered him, especially as she'd readily agreed to his suggestion of an early night, so he was surprised by the sense of relief he now felt. He took his pyjamas from his drawer and changed into them.

By the time he got into bed on what had already become his usual side she was almost asleep with the thin duvet pulled up tightly around her. All he could see of her was her blonde-streaked hair and he brushed his lips against it before turning off his bedside light. She murmured some words he didn't catch. Then, but for the unremitting sigh of the air-conditioning, there was silence.

CHAPTER SEVENTEEN

They were among the last guests to go down to breakfast. Most of the foreigners had spurned the cooked food on offer. Instead, they were eating cereal with pieces of fruit scattered on it and following that with slices of cold meat and cake, not always on separate plates.

'We might as well be in Warsaw or bloody Kiev,' Alan said as they watched the goings-on at a nearby table.

For themselves, he and Penny constructed as near as they could get to proper English breakfasts by taking curiously-scented sausages, scrambled eggs and very small rashers of wrinkled bacon from the trays at the counter.

While they drank their coffee they watched a trickle of women sidling up to the places where bread rolls and packets of butter were on offer, and then furtively loading selections of them into their beach bags before moving on to squirrel away apples and bananas.

'I've see people do that in better hotels than this,' Penny said. 'If it's there they'll take it, never mind the notices asking them not to.'

She immediately regretted mentioning those better hotels. There she went again, boasting about what Reggie's money was able to buy. It was her money now and she'd welcomed the warning prick of conscience that stopped her from urging Alan to look for a more stellar hotel when he was searching on his laptop. More stars, more expensive, more luxurious, possibly a suite like those she was used to staying in. She must take more care not to embarrass him.

But he said nothing more than: 'And I've seen them do it in worse hotels, too.'

It sounded pointed but she hoped it was no more than a statement of truth with no undertones.

After breakfast, he bought a newspaper from the shop near the reception desk. Among the foreign papers in the racks, German, Scandinavian, Dutch and a couple printed in Cyrillic, only the *Daily Mail* was British and he took the last remaining copy.

Now he was reading it in full sun on the balcony, using his reading sunglasses and wearing a one-size-fits-all golfer's cap against the glare. She'd not seen it before but decided not to comment on it. A tuft of his hair like an embryonic ponytail stuck out through the gap above the fastening at the back. At least she now knew how he kept his hair looking so tidy. She'd heard the hiss of his hair-lacquer spray through the bathroom door and, while exploring later, saw the aerosol can peeping out of his sponge-bag.

He agreed with her suggestion at breakfast that they needed only a light snack on the balcony for lunch. It was better than eating in a local restaurant if they could even find a likely-looking one without having to walk miles to do so, and preferably not one that relied on enticing customers with coloured photos of the meals on offer.

They both remembered seeing these on previous holidays. It was as if no one could imagine what a pizza looked like without a picture of one to look at. Reggie always sought out quality restaurants on foreign holidays but Penny suspected Alan and his wife always ate in the other sort.

'I'll leave you with your paper while I go out to find a shop,' she told him. He was sure to be out there on the balcony with it for some time. 'Can you let me have some Euros?'

He put his paper down and went inside to open the safe on the floor of the wardrobe. He chose a four-digit code the previous evening and now took several attempts to open the door with different combinations of it. Rising from his knees with a grunt, he peeled off some notes from his wad and handed them to her. She reminded him to make a note of the amount.

With the money safely packed away in her shoulder-bag, she strolled the short distance to a row of shops a receptionist told her about. As she kept to the shaded side of the street she noticed parts of the pavement were uneven and many kerbstones were broken or missing. Several walls had man-made holes in them. As well as being repositories for discarded cigarette packets, they had skeins of electric cabling dangling in them at a height convenient for a child's questing hand. When Emma was a toddler she had to be dragged away from holes like that on Spanish holidays and nothing seemed to have changed.

The supermarket was no bigger than many high-street shops at home. Unlike any of them, it had plastic dinghies and inflated green crocodiles dangling from its awning.

A woman came up behind her as she went in, and said, 'It's Penny, isn't it? We met at dinner last night.'

It was Jane Wellbeck, who looked care-worn. Penny smiled at her, glad Alan was elsewhere.

'Yes it is, and yes we did.' She looked around but there was no sign of Jane's husband. 'Roger not with you this morning?'

'No, he's gone off in a taxi to play golf somewhere. God knows where, but Roger seems to think he does. Look, on that subject, I'd like to say sorry about the way he went on at you and...'

Penny saw the woman eyeing her bare wedding finger. It was only two days since she removed her ring and there was a thin white mark where it had been. Either Alan hadn't noticed it or, if he had, he didn't know what to say about it, if anything.

'Alan,' she said, without adding any details.

'Yes, of course – Alan. He has a habit of doing that, you see. Roger, I mean. It's so mortifying that he doesn't seem to realise people want to be left alone, left to their own devices on holiday. They certainly don't want to have to listen to his travelogues. I always warn him not to badger them but he can't help himself.'

'No, really—'

'For instance, he's got no one to play with at this golf place he's gone to. It doesn't matter to him, though. He's taken off with all his paraphernalia in the hope of latching on to some poor souls and making up a threesome or foursome, or whatever it is they do.'

'There's absolutely no need to apologise. No harm done at all, I assure you.'

'I'm so glad, dear. I just hope that rubbish of his about Mount Tiede hasn't encouraged you to plan a trip up it,' Jane said anxiously. 'Mount Tedious would be more apt. When we went there the other day it was certainly one of my more boring days for quite some time, I can tell you. You wouldn't believe how many of those I've had. More than my fair share, certainly. So,' she continued, 'you're doing a bit of shopping now, are you?'

'Just some nibbles, really. Oh, and some indigestion tablets if they've got any. We had the pork chops last night and I've been paying the price ever since.' Their texture had reminded her of the biltong that Reggie insisted she try on one of their South African holidays. 'I expect there's a regular demand for Rennies here.'

'I know what you mean. We always try to stick with pasta of one sort or another. That or steaks, provided they're well done. You're just asking for trouble when you eat any sort of underdone meat when you're abroad. Oh dear, and you say you had pork so it's no wonder you're suffering. And you need to be careful with salads. Who knows where the water comes from to wash them in? And ice cubes as well. Still, I'm sure you don't need me to tell you that. I imagine you're a seasoned traveller and, thanks to Roger, I've had to become one too since he retired. When he was still working we used to take our caravan down to the West Country, places like Newquay or Bude, but he's got the travel bug now. We even went to a Greek island last year.' She rolled her eyes and said in a low voice as if in fear of being overheard by a passing Greek: 'My dear, the less one says about the toilet arrangements there the better. I tell you, left to my own devices I'd still be going to Cornwall and take a chance on the weather. Men can be so contrary, don't you think?'

'Mm. Well, I suppose I'd better be getting on. Alan will

start to think I've got lost or been sold into slavery. He does tend to worry.'

That wasn't strictly true, she thought. She must have said it to give Jane a sense of womanly solidarity about the fallibility of men.

'Of course you must, and I mustn't hold you up. I'm only here to buy a paper if I can find one. They'd sold out at the hotel. It's strange the way there are always stacks of foreign ones left over but it never occurs to them to put in a bigger order for the British ones. After all, we four aren't the only ones here.'

'I wish you luck. Are you here for another week?'

'It's back to Sheffield on Thursday for us. We've had lovely weather here but I can't say I'll be heartbroken to leave.'

'Such a pity. Well, try to make the most of what's left.'

'I'll do my best. You too of course, dear. Bye.'

How depressing it must be to have to explain away a husband's shortcomings. It was bad enough having to apologise for Emma when she was young and badly behaved. That poor woman must have done a lot of apologising for her husband on foreign holidays and on Cornish caravan sites. At least Reggie was no trouble, not in that way. He drank too much and became boisterous but would never humble himself by striking up an unwelcome conversation with a stranger. His bonhomie drew strangers to him, so he had no need to.

Once inside the supermarket's cool interior she started to think again about what Emma said on the phone. Much of the version of it she gave to Alan was true; for instance the parts where Emma asked about the journey and mentioned him by name for the first time. Rather than cause trouble, she'd omitted to tell him how her daughter prefaced his name with "that man you're with now."

By the time she reached the end of the supermarket's first aisle she'd made up her mind not to spoil the holiday by getting depressed again, and not only because it was unfair on Alan.

She found some Rennies at the end of the second aisle in a medical section where packets of disposable nappies were displayed alongside tampons, condoms and babies' dummies. In the third aisle she put a packet of mixed nuts and another of small salted biscuits into her wire basket, together with a piece of wrapped, unfamiliar cheese that looked like Cheddar but had holes in it. She added a bottle of red wine to go with lunch, and a bottle of dry white to be kept cool, not cold, in the mini-bar.

There was no sign of Jane, so Penny was able to walk back to the hotel on her own. The bag was heavy and she had to change it from hand to hand several times before she arrived there.

A yard-high thermometer was fixed to a shaded part of the wall next to the hotel entrance. She converted the twenty-six degrees centigrade it showed into seventy-nine degrees in proper Farenheit terms – perfect. She'd try to talk Alan into having a swim after lunch.

When she reached the room she found him asleep on the balcony with the *Daily Mail* on the floor, its pages fluttering in the warm breeze. His head was thrown back and his mouth was open, not an attractive sight. Those teeth of his, were they his own? He'd never said anything about them, but then why should he? If they were real it was nothing to brag about. If not, he'd want to keep it to himself. She was sure there was no denture-cleaning solution in his bathroom at home or here in the hotel.

It struck her that she was already reverting to her pre-Reggie days by using the word denture like her father always did. It was another of the things Reggie put her right about very early on, insisting it was only the working classes who called them anything other than false teeth. Apparently there was a book about it by some famous writer. Nor was there any of that fixative stuff in the bathroom, the sort they advertised on TV. When it came to artificial aids, Alan knew about her contact lenses but had never asked about her teeth, all of which were home-grown.

He soon woke up. 'Successful trip? Did you manage to get any tablets? I could certainly do with a couple if you did.'

'Yes, and things to eat and drink. Anything much in the paper?'

'Not really. I skip the bad stuff, you know. Doesn't leave much else. But the forecast says next week's going to be hot and sunny, at least as far as Wednesday. They don't commit themselves beyond that. The only mention of our part of the world is Bristol. It was cloudy there yesterday. We could have told them that, couldn't we? And it forecasts rain for Somerset. Which is good, it serves them right.'

She laughed at that, glad to be back with him. 'You are a sod sometimes, you know.'

'Quite likely, but imagine how annoying it would be if it was pouring with rain here and hot and sunny there.'

'I bought two bottles of wine in the supermarket. Shall we make a start on the red now?'

'I think I fancy a real drink before that. Let's go down to the bar for a couple first.'

Back in the room after finishing their scratch lunch on the balcony, she suggested it was time for a swim.

'Actually, I think I'll have a snooze if you don't mind. But you go ahead if you want to and perhaps I'll join you down there later.'

'You were sleeping when I came back from the shop. If you do any more of it you won't get a wink of sleep all night.'

He grinned at her. 'Ah, promises, promises.'

'That's enough of that, my lad,' she said, pretending to be cross but secretly pleased. 'Besides, I don't want to be in the pool on my own, not without someone there to look after my things.'

'What things?'

'For goodness sake, Alan. My robe, my towel and my sunglasses for a start, and my sun lotion. And my room key in case you take it into your head to go off somewhere while I'm away.' Did men never think of practicalities?

'I'm only thinking of you. You're not supposed to swim straight after a meal, let alone after a couple of large gins and half a bottle of the local vino. Cramp and so on.'

'That's after a proper meal, silly. It's not as though we've just dined on roast swan and jam roly-poly, is it?'

'What about the drink?'

'You're a fine one to talk, I must say. So what do you suggest we do instead? That's instead of us going swimming and instead of you sleeping your life away.'

'There used to be a time when I liked to swim.'

'Used to?'

'Until I started to think of it as a sort of allegory for life itself. It put me off.'

It sounded profound, the last thing she expected to hear from him. 'How do you mean?'

'It's like this; when you enter the pool it's like being born. The water rises imperceptibly to accommodate you. You move about in it, influencing some bathers by getting in their way and helping others by making way for them. You don't attract much attention unless you do a lot of splashing about and making waves. And then, sooner or later, when your time's up, you leave the pool. The water rises, again imperceptibly, to mark your leaving which hardly anyone's noticed. See what I mean?'

'I think so,' she said doubtfully. 'But it wouldn't be quite the same if you were in the sea. Wouldn't that be better?'

'No, it's always full of kids paddling, and seaweed and stuff. I'll tell you what; if you're bent on not giving me a moment's peace, let's go for a stroll on the beach. We've not seen it yet, except from up here. I suppose we could have a swim in the pool after that if you really want to.'

'I'm sure you'll like it once you get in. But you're not planning to go out for our stroll in those trousers, are you? You'll be so hot in them.'

He sighed. 'I didn't want to get my legs burnt. But I'll put my shorts on if you like.'

When he'd changed into them she saw they were the pair he wore up the ladder in his garden, the yak-coloured ones with more pockets that even he could find uses for.

She told him to take off his socks. They were the pink ones again – how many pairs of them had he got, for heaven's sake? 'Otherwise you'll look like a day-tripper at Minehead.'

Music was playing when they went outside, but it soon stopped. It came from the hotel's Penguin Club for young children, many of whom were milling about in a cordoned-off square by the paddling-pool. Their parents looked on approvingly. From their voices they sounded exclusively English and German.

'Perhaps it's a truth and reconciliation club,' Alan suggested. She gave him a shove and told him to keep his voice down.

A man stood in the middle of the square. He was rigged out in a blue-and-yellow costume that made him look like an ice-cream seller, and was trying to arrange the children into columns. Penny was impressed by the way he did it, patiently cajoling them without losing his temper. Once in place, they were encouraged to hop about in fits and starts as they imagined penguins might do. When they'd hopped enough, and several had picked themselves up off the ground, the man bellowed in English, and then in German: 'Now, the Penguin Club members will march smartly to the music. Just like little soldiers.' By the time he switched to German, the English contingent had already set off. 'Not yet!' he yelled. 'Wait for the music!' They came to a ragged halt and some started sniffling.

'Those blond-haired German kids look as though they're members of the toddler branch of the Hitler Youth,' Alan told her, still more loudly than she'd have advised.

As he spoke, the music started again and the columns lurched fitfully off to the strains of the *Dambusters' March* blaring from loudspeakers. The admiring parents, English and German, watched their children and used their mobile phones to film them, oblivious to the irony of it all.

Alan and Penny left them to it. 'It's curious to think that some of their great-grandfathers could have been old enough to have fought one another in the war,' he said.

'According to Reggie, he'd never met a German who admitted having been in the forces. He said they all claimed to have been ambulance drivers working miles from the front line.' She'd mentioned him yet again. Taking Alan's hand, she said, 'You don't mind me talking about him, do you? It must get on your nerves, the way I keep dragging his name into our conversations.'

'You carry on. He was part of your life for longer than I'm ever likely to be. At my age, I mean.'

He'd heard more than enough from her about Reggie when they were at Winyard's Gap, but his name had kept cropping up ever since. Alan rarely said anything about his ex-wife, and when he did it was always unfavourable. She was pleased about the one and relieved about the other.

They walked on the beach for half an hour, dodging flying frisbees and beach balls as they went. After a while, she suggested it was long enough after their lunch for them to have their swim.

The Penguin Club members had dispersed by the time they went back to their room to get changed, and the erstwhile barrack square was deserted.

She'd last worn her costume in Barbados the previous year. It was all one colour, mid-blue, and cut high in the leg making her legs look longer which was the whole point. She had a few spidery thread-veins six inches or so above one knee but they were hardly noticeable under the spay-tan she'd been applying twice daily ever since the holiday was booked. She spent no more than a few seconds wondering whether the costume was now too young for her before dismissing the idea.

So he'd brought his swimming shorts with him after all. They had only two pockets and were the sensible type not designed for showing off or posturing in. It was a relief not to see him digging out a pair of knitted trunks and defending them on the grounds that if either of them was going to attract attention it would be her. She wore a pair of flip-flops, he wore his deck shoes. Without his socks, his feet looked bigger than they really were.

When they found somewhere to sit they took off the white towelling robes that were supplied with the room. He then surprised her by striding to the deep end, diving straight in with scarcely a splash, and starting to swim steadily down the pool, raising his face from the water to take a breath only every four over-arm strokes. She was impressed. It made her hesitant entry down the aluminium steps into the shallow end look weak. Now and again she saw his progress hindered by less proficient swimmers but he made little detours to avoid them. He must think it was part of that strange allegory of his.

She'd never mastered the crawl or anything approaching it, being unable to stop her legs from moving like a frog's rather than beating up and down. Instead, she used a breaststroke to propel herself slowly across the shallow end and back. Children constantly got in her way and she put her feet down till they moved off to get in someone else's. The air temperature was hot but the water wasn't very warm and she'd soon had enough. She climbed back up the steps and sat down before checking no one had rifled their beach bag. Several men were watching her and she made sure she held her stomach in even though it wasn't necessary.

Meanwhile, Alan was still ploughing his way up and down the pool and she put on her sunglasses to see him better. His hair was plastered to his head. She'd kept her own head well out of the water, not wanting him to see her looking bedraggled. He'd not seen her like that in their room, thanks to the latitude allowed to Spanish electricians which let them install hair-dryers in bathrooms. To do that at home was considered an invitation to suicide, an absolute kiss of death, never mind its convenience.

He emerged at last and came over to stand by her, tousling his hair so drops of water splashed on her.

'You can stop that as soon as you like,' she said, flicking at herself.

'Not bad, Penny, sixteen lengths,' he said rather breathlessly. 'The important thing is to pace yourself. It's supposed to be enjoyable, not a race.'

'Well done, my hero. I'm amazed at how good at it you are. I thought your only exercise was playing golf.'

'I've not swum for years but I'm glad I let you persuade me. In fact I think I'll do some more of it tomorrow.'

She handed his robe up to him. 'Here, put this on or you'll get a chill. And then you can give me a spray with the sun lotion.'

The holiday was their first proper test, she told herself, and she was getting on well with him. She'd been tetchy at first but he must have realised it was only because of her headache and her worries about Emma, so hadn't reacted to it. So far, he'd been patient and uncomplaining about her Reggie-based reminiscences. His table manners and bathroom etiquette were unexceptionable. He was clean-shaven, smelled nice without overdoing it and took trouble with his hair. She already knew he was solvent but not how careful he was with his money. Not tight exactly, just prudent. One thing he lacked was dress sense, but all that needed was a light feminine touch on the tiller to guide him. Given time, she'd be able to sort him out.

There were five more days to go, five days of discreetly observing him at close quarters. He was probably weighing her up at the same time, more keenly now because of her moodiness the previous day, so she'd have to be careful. But any minor doubts she might have had about his suitability to become a longer-term partner were dissolving fast.

CHAPTER EIGHTEEN

The journey back to Bristol proved to Alan that foreign travel was also hell, never mind Sartre's other people. Abroad was bearable if the weather and the hotel were good. The problem was getting there and back.

The airport in Tenerife was heaving when they finally arrived there. They spent a long time finding the right desk, and when they did they had to inch their way forward in a long queue before they could check in. There was more of the same before they were allowed to pass through airport security. For him this involved removing his belt, shoes and gilet as part of the process of weeding out would-be bombers. All the travellers looked cross enough to have violence in mind, but not glum enough to be contemplating imminent self-destruction.

Take-off was then delayed for an hour because of a work-to-rule by unidentified workers. The seat-kicking child from the outward flight wasn't behind him this time, but Penny bagged the window seat again and then dozed all the way back to England with her head propped uncomfortably on his shoulder. At least they'd not come across the Wellbecks again. They must have spent the second week of their holiday exploring other non-features of the island and dining late as a result.

There was a delay of more than half an hour at Bristol before their cases arrived on the baggage carousel. When they did, his was short of a wheel. Hers arrived intact.

At her urging and yet more expense, he'd booked a taxi to take them to and from the airport. He'd worried during all the delays that their driver would have given them up as a bad job and gone off to do a spot of mini-cabbing. In fact he was waiting for them in the arrivals hall, brandishing a piece of cardboard with BASTER HALLOS scrawled on it in black crayon. When he caught sight of them among the throng he made an extravagant show of looking repeatedly at his watch, shaking his wrist about, and then holding the watch up to his ear as if to check it was still working.

Alan invited Penny to spend the night at his cottage but she told him she'd no clean clothes left for the morning. Nor had she any hormone replacement tablets left, and needed to be regular about taking them. She also wanted to go home to get her hands on an important letter she was expecting. So she declined with thanks and gave him a lingering farewell kiss in the back of the taxi as compensation.

Her use of HRT was news to him. Susan used it and claimed it did her a power of good. It made him wonder what the hell she'd have been like without it.

He forgot to close the bedroom curtains when he went to bed and woke up much earlier than he wanted to. He breakfasted on buttered crispbreads because the loaf in the breadbin now sported a verdigris-coloured rash. The opened carton of milk was where he left it by the kitchen sink and had gone badly off in his absence. He poured its remains down the sink, forcing the bigger lumps through the plughole with the back of a spoon.

Going outside to dispose of the loaf, he found he'd forgotten to take his wheelie-bin down to the front gate to be emptied by the dustmen while he was away. It still stood where he'd wheeled it to avoid Penny's disapproval. He'd remembered to lock the front door and set the burglar alarm, though, which must mean old Doctor Alzheimer hadn't arrived yet.

Later that morning he decided to drive over to the Coq au Vin to cadge a coffee from Jimmy Hargreaves and have a chat with him before going on to do the shopping.

It was raining by the time he left the cottage. As he hurried out under his golf umbrella, he saw a fox had defecated on the path. Quite recently, too, to judge by the swarm of flies rejoicing over its copious leavings. The grass was much longer than it should have been.

Back indoors again, he dialled Geoff's number to complain. There was no answer. Alan took out his notebook and made an entry to remind himself not to pay for the missed mowing visit. His jottings were still in it from the holiday, detailing the Euros he handed over to Penny and the ones he settled his bar bill with. He would have used his credit card but remembered in time that foreign currency transactions involved a surcharge. He told her the total before they left Tenerife.

The Coq au Vin's door was open when he arrived and he found Jimmy sitting at one of the tables, reading his morning paper in the otherwise empty room.

'Blimey, it's old Alan Baxter. You're up and about early, Al. I thought Saturday was one of the many days you spent sprawling in your pit, trying to think of something to do.' He paused for effect. 'Unlike some of us who have to work for a living. But I suppose you'd better take the weight off your feet and sit down.'

'Thanks. But you're not exactly toiling at the coalface yourself, are you? I guessed you'd be idling at this time of day so I hoped you'd find a moment to press a complementary cup of your ersatz coffee on me. Look, I've even brought you a little present to soften you up.' He produced from his pocket a slim bottle of chilli-infused olive oil he bought to help while away time at Tenerife airport. 'You can use it to impart a bit of zest to your dishes. God knows they could do with it.'

'Cheers, Al, nice of you.' Jimmy peered at the label. 'Spanish I see. I take it you've been there because I can't remember seeing it on sale round here, not this particular one. Come to think of it, you look as if you've caught the sun.'

'You're not far wrong. The Canaries, actually.'

'So, how did it go? Did you find anyone sufficiently bored to want to talk to you?'

'I did, actually.' He took a deep breath. 'I went with Penny Hallows. You know, the woman who was with me when I came here for dinner.'

Jimmy's eyes widened. 'Did you really? You took the lady on a holiday in the sun? No one could accuse you of hanging about and letting the grass grow. Come on, then, spill the beans.'

'Not *took*, we shared the cost.'

'I bet you did, you miserable bugger. So how long have you been...er, how long have you known her now, two or three months?' Before Alan could tell him, Jimmy went on, his eyebrows at maximum elevation: 'I take it you took full advantage of her widowhood and so on, got down to some carefree sun-kissed filth.'

'We shared a room if that's what you mean. And not that it's any concern of yours but we got on very well together. But just to remind you, I'm a valued customer, so why don't you act like a proper host and get me a coffee?'

'A complementary one, I think you said. But it would have to be, wouldn't it? Nevertheless it shall be done according to thy word.'

He returned with a cafetiére and two cups. 'My wife sends you her regards from the kitchen. Unfortunately, she's too busy to come out here to welcome you in person.'

'That's kind of her.'

'You're right, it is.' Jimmy hunched forward over the table. 'But all jesting apart, you sounded on the serious side about you and your woman getting on well. Does that mean you're thinking of making her a permanent fixture?'

'If we're still being serious, then yes I can't deny I've thought about it. More permanent than it is now, certainly. It's my guess it's crossed her mind, too.'

'But nothing's been said, no discussions or anything like that?'

'Not as such, not as we speak.'

Jimmy poured the coffee. 'There you are, it's freshly made from beans hand-picked in Jamaica's Blue Mountains, or so the label claims. Free to you at the point of delivery just like the NHS is supposed to be. Now, if I were you I'd do something about it before some other love-sick fortune-hunter gets her in his sights. It could do you a heap of good. I got the impression she was comfortably off, sailing through life on a sea of cash. I'll bet she's got a socking great house as well. You ought to move in with her. It'd suit you, give you a chance to move up in society in your declining years, become a country squire, mingling with the gentry and all at no cost to yourself. Remember, Al, I've never caught you hiding behind the door when a bargain was on offer, never known you to pass one up. Look at you now, drinking my profits away. Of course, you'd have to smarten yourself up a bit to fit in with the county set.'

'I thought we were being serious for once. I was, at least.'

'I am, too. It's just that a bit of piss-taking creeps in sometimes. Time marches on, remember. How long have you been living that unwholesome bachelor life of yours?'

'Six years.'

'Quite so, and your days aren't exactly crammed with diversions, are they? A spot of golf, a spot of telly, an occasional read; that's about it from what you've told me. It's not what you'd call living life on the edge, is it? Not for an educated chap like you. And yes, I am still being serious. I mean, not when comparing your life with mine. I know I can't claim to be busy all the time.' He gestured around the room. 'As you can see, I do manage to get the odd moment to call my own, but at least I've got a business to keep me occupied. It may not be much but it is mine. And I've a wife, of course. Our kids have long flown the nest but we've always got both of them to worry about and to keep us on our toes with our hands in our purses. There'll be even more of that when the grandchildren get older. You and I aren't far off the same age and all I can say is I wouldn't want to be facing the future without my missus being with me.'

He laughed suddenly. 'Lordy, I sound like the Duke of Windsor in his abdication speech.' He put on a reasonable impression of a clipped nineteen-thirties voice, saying: '...impossible without the help and support of the woman I love.' Reverting to his usual sub-Cockney tones, he said, 'I don't say I'd have given up my throne for her, but I know what his nibs was going on about.' He finished his coffee before asking: 'Tell me, does your lady friend have kids at all?'

'A daughter, something of a high-flyer in financial circles apparently, lives in London.'

He didn't want to say anything more about Emma. It was bad enough having to talk about her with Penny. No, it was more like having to listen to Penny talk about her.

'I've only ever met her once, and then very briefly. Not unattractive, though.'

'No children of her own, then, what with her being a career woman?'

Alan shook his head. 'No,' he said. He didn't want to elaborate.

'Well, there you are. Two people living separate lives, one divorced, one widowed, both roughly of the same generation. Same needs in life and both presentable to say the very least. And you needn't look at me like that, you know it's true. Getting properly together would make perfect sense. If she's prepared to go on holiday with you so soon after losing her old man – Reggie, wasn't it? – she must have some feelings for you. Were they very close?'

Alan shrugged, not wanting to say too much about that, either. 'I gather they were together for just short of forty years. It must have meant something.'

'Not necessarily. Quite possibly a marriage of convenience. Couples stick together for all sorts of reasons. Better the devil they know, sort of thing, or for the sake of the kids or just for a comfy life. You'd both have to make some adjustments, no doubt. Worth it, though.'

The part about a comfy life was true, Alan thought. For the first time in his life it looked as if getting what he wanted was coming close to matching what he needed. Penny admitted to settling for no more than that when she married her husband, even if the need to have a rich father on hand for Emma was a factor. Would she settle for a similar arrangement a second time, but minus an input of wealth from him?

Without her, his future looked none too rosy. Years – how many, fifteen or so? – not much more than that, of gentle or not so gentle decline with no one to decline with or to care about him. When he could no longer manage the cottage's steep stairs his next move would have to be into a sheltered-housing complex, ideally with a lift that never broke down. That was his father's fate except for the lift. His stingy accommodation had wainscoting with embedded alarm buttons so when the old chap had one of his falls he could crawl inch by inch to the edge of the room and give one of them a prod with his stick.

Beyond that lay an old people's home or, infinitely more frightening, a nursing-home. It wasn't much to look forward to, not when he knew he'd never have the nerve to do away with himself before it happened. Apart from a merciful and pain-free release preceded by an absence of systematic abuse, all he could look forward to in one of those places was being entertained, if that was the word for it, by evening bingo sessions and faltering community singing around a piano.

'You've made me think,' he said at last.

'Go for it, mate. You know it makes sense.'

'It does seem to, I must admit.'

As he drove home from the supermarket he tried to sort things out in his mind to the muted background of Rolling Stones' music from the C.D. player. There were an unusual number of delays on the road so he had ample time for reflection.

On the debit side, Penny said some uncomplimentary things about his clothes while they were away. That was women for you, and no worse than he had to put up with for years from Susan. When she bothered to notice, that was. Then, while they were waiting for the flight at Bristol, Penny looked askance at him and even gave him a mild bollocking when he was doing no more than checking his pockets to make sure he still had all the things he needed and knew where to put his hands on them in a hurry. If she thought him fussy rather than painstaking, she ought to have been with him earlier to witness his problems with the curtains, the bread, the milk and the wheelie-bin. That would have shown him in a different light. She was also sharp with him once or twice during the holiday, but that might stop when her pain of a daughter sorted herself out.

While waiting for a set of temporary traffic lights to change, he wondered if it was doing him any harm to have a fault or two, so long as he took care not to overdo it. It never worked with Susan, of course. In her view, vulnerability merited derision followed by exploitation. Other, nicer, women were said to like their men to have a hint of vulnerability. It gave them the chance to put chaps right about themselves, all in the guise of taking them under their wings and being helpful. He could make do with that.

There was only one short stretch of dual carriageway between the Coq au Vin and Stratfield, and one lane was coned off to protect an absentee workforce. While he crept along the open lane he thought some more about his feelings for Penny. He'd never mentioned love to her and nor had she to him. Perhaps it didn't matter, not at their age. He hoped it didn't. Love was sure to mean bending to another's wishes, but so had his time with Susan. He hadn't loved her but still spent most of those years canted over at a forty-five-degree angle to accommodate her whims. Leaving that aside, how did he feel about being with Penny on a more permanent basis? Subject to time off for good behaviour and golf, he felt surprisingly carefree at the prospect.

He could write off one potential problem. He'd no doubts about his sexual desire for her or his ability to put it into action, which wasn't bad considering the only desire he'd felt during his barren years was for a putt to drop or for a nice sit down. She made all the running till his brandy ploy set the scene for their first PB of SI, so the match was now all-square.

As for the future, her husband's goat-like libido had kept going for an extra decade, though the constant prospect of fresh conquests must have kept it on the boil. He, Alan, was unlikely be troubled by them, so he'd have to hope for the best. And there were always chemical aids to perk him up if and when the need arose.

She slept with him, went on holiday with him and evidently enjoyed his company. It was all good. What he had to do now was hurry matters along; he'd been drifting for six years.

As he turned his car into Stratfield's main street he turned up the C.D's volume. It was playing the Stones' 1964 record, *Time Is On My Side.* Time might have been on his side back then when he was in his teens, but it wasn't now.

CHAPTER NINETEEN

Alan invited Penny to have Sunday lunch with him at Myrtle Cottage and surprised her by saying he'd do the cooking. She was apprehensive about what the meal would turn out to be but pleased to have been invited so soon. One of the first things she did when she arrived was to hand over her cheque for the money she owed him.

'It's my half of the cost of the holiday and the taxi. The bank wasn't open yesterday, so I converted the Euros you gave me into sterling at the tourist rate from the paper,' she told him. 'I hope you're all right with that.'

'Perfectly so.' He said there'd been absolutely no rush, which wasn't the impression she had. 'And thanks very much.'

While she was in Tenerife, the solicitors had at last finished sorting out Reggie's residual financial affairs with his accountant. She'd been expecting their final letter which was lying on the doormat when she reached home. She already knew the details of his part of their joint will so there were no surprises about the specific bequests the solicitors had made on his behalf. There were three; to the Wendmore club, to a Masonic charity, and a smaller one to his gaga brother, Gerard, who lingered on in a care home in some remote place in the wilds of Yorkshire. She doubted her brother-in-law had any recollection of ever having had a brother at all, let alone a dead one, or that he was capable of grasping the fact that he'd had a windfall. Everything else, Farthing's, investments and money, came to her.

The unexpectedly bad news came in the letter's final paragraph: "In conclusion, and in response to your several telephonic enquiries, we regret to advise we have been unable to trace any record of a Widow's Pension which would accrue to your benefit, or of any Life Assurance Policy in the name of your late husband." That was a real shock. She'd expected one or the other, if not both. What had Reggie been thinking of? A financial consultant who'd made no provision for his widow, especially as he must have thought he'd be the first to die? It was like that old saying: Physician, heal thyself.

She'd known for some time that his business was in decline. His income came from fees and commissions but a shortage of new clients had cut back the fees, and the economic recession had slashed his commissions. The letter failed to spell it out in so many words but she now realised they'd been living beyond his means for years. It was bad enough to find that what he'd left her was so modest, but to discover there was no more to come was dreadful news.

What she now had wasn't small enough to make her experience the chill penury he used to frighten his clients with if they chose to ignore his advice. Not yet, anyway. But she'd have to be careful with what there was, very much more so than at any time during the last forty years. At her current rate of spending it wouldn't last her for more than about five years. Before those years were up, she'd need to think about downsizing. Not to hand over money to Emma as Giles had suggested, but for her own use. She could also inquire about equity release, but not from Giles even if he was still on the scene by then. In the meantime, finding ways to prune her expenses was going to be a priority.

There was some consolation to be had, but not nearly enough of it, from her suspicion that many of her neighbours were in similar straits. Not exactly living in genteel poverty, but having to watch the pennies. Property-rich, cash-poor was what people like them often were these days, and now she was joining their ranks. All dress and no drawers, as her mother used to say before her father told her not to. In his way he was as particular about the social niceties of his clerkly rank as Reggie was about those of his grander one. She supposed she'd have to tell Alan about her new concern and put him right about her financial circumstances. He must think she was loaded, living in a house like Farthing's.

Before he started to prepare their lunch, they took a bottle of Chianti into the garden and sat with it in the shade. He was wearing his golf cap again. Wearing it here in Somerset was no more of a fashion statement than it was in Tenerife, so she said nothing about it.

Trying to make herself sound more cheerful than she felt, she said, 'And what delights are you going to prepare for our lunch?' Two plates were warming in the oven so it wasn't going to be a seasonal salad. 'According to everything you've told me, you're not up to doing a traditional Sunday roast, are you?'

'Not exactly, no. The clue's in the wine.'

It was to be a pasta dish of some unspecified sort. While he was at the stove she had to remind him to put salt into the saucepan of boiling water. She then grated a piece of parmesan cheese for him. Its shrink-wrap was unbroken so it must have been bought fairly recently, possibly with today in mind. The same went for the unopened jar of pesto sauce from which he spooned a good deal into the drained pasta. While she watched, he took two hard-boiled eggs from the fridge, sliced them up, and stirred them into the pasta-pesto mix with a couple of dollops of crème fraiche before turning the steaming mass of carbohydrates onto the plates. With the rest of the wine to help it down, it wasn't too bad at all – just unusual.

While they ate, she told him about her financial problems. There was never going to be a good time so it might as well be now.

He listened in silence before telling her how surprised he was. He must have been, she thought, but he didn't sound put off by her news.

'You'll be able to stay on at Farthing's, though, won't you? I'd hate for you to have to move away from there, it's such a lovely house.'

'I hope it won't come to that but I can't see myself going on many foreign holidays in the immediate future. And I may have to let my cleaner go and do a bit more gardening for myself.'

'I can always give you a hand.'

'What? With the cleaning and gardening?' She managed a laugh. 'I can't imagine you doing much of that.'

'Nor can I. No, I meant with money. I've got a pension, though it's smaller than it might have been because I retired early. And then I had to cash in some of it to buy my ex out of her half of this place. That took all my savings as well, so I've not got much of an income. But there's enough of it for me to be able to give you a hand when you need it.'

'You're so kind to me, darling, but I'm sure I'll get by with a few economies here and there. At least, I hope I'll be able to. Let's wait and see, shall we?'

He said nothing more about it while they finished their meal with strawberries and ice-cream. After clearing away, they went upstairs to bed.

Not that she was keeping a tally, she assured herself afterwards, but she worked out that this was the fourteenth time they'd made love. It was conventional to claim it got better every time, but it hadn't. From the first time at Farthing's it was as good as she ever needed it to be. As an extra refinement, he never failed to find the right words to say before, during and after it. That was a new experience for her and she now saw how important it was and would always have been, if it had ever happened before. The unhurried way he went about it was good, too. In the days before Reggie found the thought and accidental sight of her breast such a turn-off, he was all too often in a rush to get the job over and done with and to move on to other things. Probably onto other women, she thought, but with a lesser degree of resignation now than she used to feel.

After making love, they lay together on the bed but without their bodies touching. Recent experience proved that one or more of their limbs developed pins and needles or cramp if they entwined. While they lay there they laughed and talked about things they'd seen and done before they met, and she made sure she avoided any mention of Reggie's involvement. To talk about him while she was in bed with Alan was like having him gate-crash their togetherness and eavesdrop on them.

Later that afternoon Alan got up and, still naked, went downstairs to make them cups of tea. He wasn't self-conscious about being naked in her presence. Neither was she about being naked herself, not since he showed himself to be so understanding.

When he came back she thought it was as good a time as any to broach another subject.

'By the way, I hope you don't mind but I've brought some clothes and stuff with me in the car. I wonder if you'd let me leave them here permanently so I needn't go home at night after being here during the day. Would that be okay, do you think? Apart from the clothes, it's only a few bits and pieces of other things. A couple of pairs of shoes, and make-up and pills and so on. Hardly anything at all, and they wouldn't take up much space here in your bedroom or on that shelf in the bathroom.'

'That's a great idea,' he said at once, 'but only if I can bring some things over to your place as well. That'd suit us both.'

'And it's not as though we'd be living together, is it? We wouldn't want to cramp each other's styles.'

'Of course we wouldn't, but it would be convenient.'

That was interesting. Her reference to living together had slipped out by accident and hadn't been mentioned before by either of them. It wouldn't be a bad idea at all and would solve a lot of problems. They'd become close, more than close, and he'd be bound to welcome the idea of living with her at Farthing's. She'd have company and a man to look after, and she'd heard of nothing in his life to bind him to his cottage. His reciprocal suggestion to have some of his own clothes at Farthing's must mean he expected to spend more time with her there. So why not permanently? Having his clothes there could be the first step. His money could be a life-saver now, too. It was worth thinking about.

In the meantime she needed to break him in gently to a spot of domesticity.

'Just one other thing. Would you mind awfully if we went shopping together sometime? I'd like to do some cooking for you when I'm here, and—'

'Because I'm not up to scratch in the kitchen?'

'No, of course not.' Of course it was. 'Well, not entirely. But you do seem to be a bit low on one or two things. For instance, that saucepan of yours is on its last legs. I could sort you out, if you like.'

'I'd like you to. You know how much I appreciate your cooking.'

That was reassuring. They'd quickly taken two steps closer to putting their relationship on a less random footing. Good Lord, she thought, rolling towards him and kissing him, that's not taken very long. What on earth would Emma think about it? But never mind her now.

'I really don't know how you've managed so long on your own,' she said. It was another hint so she made sure it sounded as if she was doing no more than thinking aloud.

'Even with you doing more cooking, I'd still want to go over to Jimmy's once in a while. I wouldn't want him to think I was deserting him.'

'We could, yes. If only because you may need to borrow his cocoa van again.'

'There is that.'

They woke up half an hour later when her mobile phone rang, filling the room with the opening bars from *Jumping Jack Flash* which Emma had downloaded for her from her laptop.

She reached out to it on the bedside table. 'Sorry about that.'

'Leave it,' he said in a sleepy voice.

'I can't, it might be important.' She answered the phone, silencing the music. 'It's Emma,' she whispered.

'Fair enough. I'll go and have a shower, leave you to talk in private.' He got off the bed and held up crossed fingers. 'Hope she's all right.' As he padded out of the room he said softly: 'But don't go getting yourself upset.'

He was back after a while, standing in the doorway.

'How did it go?'

'Fucking hell,' Penny said fiercely. It was the first time she'd sworn in front of him, and her accent had reverted to the one she used before Reggie made her change it. 'You'll never guess, but she's pregnant.'

'That's good.' When she didn't reply, he said, 'It is, isn't it?'

'Yes, of course it is. She's not absolutely certain yet but she's used three of those gadgets that women pee on and they all showed positive, so I'm sure she must be. And I bet she made a special effort to make sure she got pregnant while she had the chance; never letting Giles alone for a moment and making the most of every opportunity she had. She's not one to put up with not getting her own way. She must have claimed to be back on the pill as a way of encouraging him to get on with it.'

'That would have been devious of her. Devious but clever.'

'But very like her. When she told him what had happened, his instant reaction was to tell her – that's his way of doing things, as you know, telling people what to do – to get rid of it, to have a termination.'

'How did she respond to that?'

'Refused outright.'

Alan came over, lay on the bed beside her and put his arm around her. His naked body was still damp after his shower. She noticed his hair was dry and more compressed than usual. He must have used the shower cap she'd seen hanging on the back of his bathroom door. She started to cry because he was so nice and because she was so upset.

'What did he say?'

'Typical of him. He said that in that case he wouldn't be able to go to Hong Kong after all. Which was exactly what she wanted the outcome to be, of course. No, it'd be too much family baggage, as he so charmingly put it. She told him there was no chance of her having a termination and how she never wanted to leave England in the first place. But he still wants her to have one. He's adamant that she does and she's adamant that she won't.'

Dabbing her eyes with the edge of her pillowcase, Penny said, 'I do so want her to have a baby after having to wait for such a long time, and I don't want her to go abroad. So I really hope this can finally put a stop to the idea. But then it's possible – even likely, knowing him – he'll go off on his own anyway. I wouldn't put it past him, the sod. And then they'll split up for sure and I can't bear the thought of her being a single parent, not at her age. I remember how scared I was of becoming one myself before Reggie came to my rescue. I wouldn't wish that on her.'

It was Reggie's name again, but she couldn't help that.

She pressed her wet face into Alan's neck. 'What am I supposed to do to sort things out for her? Is there anything, do you think?'

His head rustled on the pillow as he shook his head. 'Can't think of anything for the moment.'

'I'm just so fucking fed up with it all,' she mumbled, but he didn't reply.

Fed up or not, she went on thinking about it all the same. It was what mothers did. Earlier on, she had only her new and unexpected money worries to distract her because their arrival had bundled Emma's problems into the wings. Now they were back in the spotlight.

The worst-case scenario had them splitting up permanently, with Emma staying in England with her baby but without its father who'd be – and she'd checked this – six thousand miles away. What would Emma do then? Go on working after her maternity leave expired, dump the baby on a child-minder and spend all her office hours worrying about it? And when Giles came back after two years there'd be complications, his access for instance. One of them would have to buy out the other one. Either that or they'd have to sell the house and split the equity between them. Could Emma raise the money for a buy-out or to buy a place of her own? And now, Penny thought despondently, there was no chance of financial help coming Emma's way from Somerset.

Alan's voice was little louder than a whisper. 'I expect you've been lying here trying to think of a solution. I know I have. Any joy?'

'No, nothing.'

Her accent was back to normal now and he didn't seem to have noticed its disappearance or its return.

'Me neither, I'm afraid. How would you feel if I suggested doing nothing and letting matters take their course? You say she's determined to keep the child, if there is one. So all you can do is sit tight until Giles finally decides whether he's going or staying. Perhaps he will stay put now that his baby's on the way. As you say, that's what she'd like to happen. But it's not the sort of thing you can sort out with her on the phone, and I don't really come into it. If you went up there to see her...well, I expect it'd all end in tears, and most of them would be yours. She must know you can't help her but you're a handy person for her to unload onto. But not sufficiently handy to go there and interfere. Sorry, but there it is.'

Penny thought about that. 'It pretty well sums up what I've been thinking. There is one thing, though. You just said you don't come into it. You did, you know. But you are involved because I know I'd feel a lot worse if I were on my own. And I'm not, am I?'

'No, you're not. You're not on your own.'

'I've known for a long time that I needed your company. It's really more than that. I need you for yourself, not just for your company. Does that make sense at all?'

Why had she said that without having planned to? It was like one of those unscripted plays where the actors blurted out whatever came into their heads at the time.

'Sorry about that and for keeping on about Emma,' she said. Before he could reply, even supposing he knew what to say, she added: 'I hope I've not frightened you.'

'Don't worry, you haven't.' He kissed her forehead.

His breath smelled of toothpaste, and his body of some recently-applied spray. He really did take care to be as appealing as he was.

'And you must try to stop apologising to me,' he said as softly as before.

CHAPTER TWENTY

After Penny left the cottage early the next morning, Alan offered up a bitter little prayer that Emma and Giles would reach a decision to satisfy her and save him from having to listen to any more about their tedious bickering.

It was the first time he'd bothered with anything of that sort since wishing Reggie posthumous good luck on the morning of the funeral service. Again, he might be addressing nothing or no one but it was worth taking a chance. Billions of people had believed in a deity or a whole clutch of them, even the unlikely ones with elephant's heads or multiple pairs of arms.

His short devotions over, he was reading his paper when Brenda unexpectedly arrived at the front door.

'Hello,' he said. 'You're a couple of days early, aren't you?'

'Yes, I'm ever so sorry, Mr Baxter, but I just looked in to see if I could do your cleaning today instead of my usual day,' she said, speaking quickly and looking flustered. 'Geoff's not been too well but he's feeling a bit better this morning. I had to pop out to get a bit of shopping, so I thought while I was out I'd take a chance and look in on you.'

'You're in luck, Brenda. I usually play golf on Mondays but my friends can't make it today. That's the only reason I'm here.'

'Will it be all right, then? I'd like to get it out of the way this morning in case he feels worse later on and needs me to be with him. As it is, I'll only be able to do your upstairs today because I don't want to leave him on his own for too long. Is that all right?'

'Of course it is. But I thought he was well on the mend. Are you saying he's really not that much better at all? I noticed he didn't do the mowing last week, but…'

'Thanks very much, Mr Baxter, much appreciated. No, I'm afraid he isn't. It comes and goes, you see. The doctor put him on some pain-killers but they've not been much use, not so far. I'm not even sure that doctor of ours has got any real idea of what's causing the problem. You know how it is, they make themselves out to know everything but they don't, not really.'

He couldn't fault her conclusion. They were up-to-speed with flu jabs, no problems with them at all. But much more than that and they either took a flyer by prescribing pills or sent you off to hospital to be dealt with by someone who was paid, rightly or otherwise, to know more than they did.

'That sounds about right.'

'And poor Geoff tells me he's been poked and prodded down there something wicked. He's sorry to have let you down over the mowing while you was away. He didn't feel up to it at all. It's not like him, neither. That lawn of yours must be in a right old state by now.'

'You must tell him it doesn't matter, Brenda, and I do hope he feels better soon. He must have been overdoing things.' For the life of him, Alan couldn't think how that had happened or what those things were. 'And you're not to worry about the grass. Worse things happen at sea, as they say.' It was the sort of thing his old granny would have said even as news of the *Titanic* came in.

Brenda said, 'I know what. Why don't I get our boy Terry to come over and give your lawn a good seeing to? He's self-employed as you know, so his time's his own. As it's you, I'm sure he could come at any time to suit.'

Being self-employed was often used as a local expression for being jobless but that didn't apply to Terry. Alan knew he was a plumber in the sense that he was called on to fix dripping taps and sort out washing machines. He also helped out with his father's gardening duties at busy times.

'If he would, Brenda, I'd be obliged.'

'What about tomorrow if he can fit you in?'

'Perfect. But tell him to go ahead anyway even if I'm not here.'

'Lovely. That is kind of you and much appreciated, I'm sure. Well, I suppose I'd better fetch my apron and cleaning things from the car and make a start.'

As he always did, he carried the vacuum cleaner upstairs for her while she followed with its attachments. When he came down again he slipped her reduced wages into an envelope. In her Chapel-going way she was a prim woman who'd prefer to avoid the taint of commercialism associated with openly handling banknotes in return for services rendered. It wasn't the same thing at all but an errant ex-colleague once told him call-girls had similar scruples.

When she returned, she said, 'All done and dusted, Mr Baxter.' She laughed modestly. 'Hark at me, saying dusted like that. Quite funny, really.' Moving closer to him, she dropped her voice to say, 'By the way, I hope you don't mind me mentioning it, but when I was doing your bedroom I couldn't help but notice there was women's clothing in your wardrobe. And women's shoes. Not that I was prying or nothing. That's not my way as you know but you'd left the wardrobe door open, you see. And then there was women's things in the bathroom and all. Things I'd not seen in there before, not with you living here on your own. I couldn't help wondering if someone stayed here while you was away.' She looked at him expectantly, absently screwing one of her yellow dusters into a ball.

He ought to have hidden Penny's belongings away and made sure the wardrobe door was shut, he realised now the damage was done, if that's what it was. At least Brenda wasn't a gossip, never saying anything about her other clients, but that might be because they lived such blameless lives.

'A lady-friend, was it?' she prompted him.

In her mind a woman who fitted that description could be anyone from a casual female acquaintance to a gangster's moll, so he said, 'Well, a lady who happens to be a friend of mine, certainly. And it was last night, not while I was away. It was time to add a detail or two but he settled for only one. 'Her name's Penelope.'

'I see.' After a long pause, Brenda said, 'Poor soul, how she must have sweltered under that heavy old duvet in the bedroom across from yours.'

'Mm, I suppose so. I didn't think of that,' he said, but thinking of it now. 'She never mentioned it.'

'Penelope, you say, Mr Baxter.' She shook her head. The movement left her permed hair unmoved. When seen from above it reminded him of the top of a cauliflower.

'No,' she went on thoughtfully, 'I don't think I ever heard you mention anyone called Penelope.' She made the name sound as unusual as Persephone or Clytemnestra. 'Not that it's any business of mine, of course, but she must be a young woman. Those shoes of hers...her feet must give her far less trouble than mine do if she can get them on and then actually walk in them. And she left her spare clothes and things here as well? Must be a very forgetful young woman, that's all I can say. Unless she's planning to come back here, that is. Still, it's none of my business.'

He'd been readying himself to mention his relationship with Penny but hadn't worked out how to, or how much of it to divulge. The need might have passed now if Brenda had convinced herself his astonishingly forgetful guest spent the night alone in the spare bedroom. Conversely, she might feel she'd said enough to let him know she guessed what had really gone on, but didn't want to go into the sort of prurient detail that would show her in a bad, non-Chapel light.

He looked at his watch, making sure she saw what he was doing.

'I'm sorry, Brenda, but I'm keeping you from getting off home. And it was good of you to come at all in the circumstances.' He handed over the envelope. 'Do give Geoff my best wishes and don't forget to have a word with your Terry, will you?'

'That I won't, Mr Baxter.'

He led her back through the cottage and out of the front door and then phoned Penny. He needed to brief her about

Brenda.

Knowing she'd expect him to, he started by asking about Emma, but Penny told him she'd had no further bulletins about the fighting on the Wimbledon front. She said it was kind of him to ask, so that made his effort worthwhile.

With some trepidation he sketched out the details of Brenda's discoveries.

'That's not a problem, is it?' she asked when he finished.

'Not for me, certainly. And it's not as though she's a gossip. What's more, she lives locally – far enough away from your village not to have much chance of knowing anyone who knows you.' As he spoke, he remembered Brenda was familiar with St Michael's, but possibly only because it was on her pastor's list of places to shun on doctrinal grounds.

'You mentioned me, then? And you're all right with that?'

'Absolutely.'

That must have been satisfactory, at least for now, because she abruptly changed the subject to ask: 'And why aren't you playing golf today? It's one of your days, isn't it?'

'I usually do, yes. But two of my regular playmates are away on holiday, and the salesman had a conference to go to in London.'

'Seems a bit harsh of his employers to expect him to work when he could be out in the sun enjoying himself, don't you think?'

'He manages his work-life balance fairly well, considering. I'll give you an example. You know how golfers usually wear a single glove? To help their grip on the club?'

'If you say so.'

'Well, we do. They're very thin ones that allow you plenty of feel. That's where most of the grip's concentrated, in the left hand. But only if you're right-handed. Otherwise—'

'Yes, fascinating. Do get on with it.'

She sounded annoyed, annoyed with him. Why was that?

'Sorry. But the point is he doesn't wear one in the summer in case his boss notices he's got one white hand and one sunburnt one, might start asking awkward questions. Subtle, eh?'

All she said was: 'So, when am I going to see you again? Always assuming you can bear the thought of it.'

What was that all about? He didn't ask her to explain, but said, 'We could go on that shopping-trip. I know you're itching to get to work on my kitchen.' It was a good idea to let her think he was grateful for her suggestion and keen to get on with it. Keen to get it over with, too.

'Whenever you like.'

'Okay, we could go this afternoon if you've nothing else on. What about driving over to Bath? There'll be plenty of time and I don't know about you, but I've not been there for ages. I could pick you up at your place at what – about two-ish?'

'If you like.'

They left his car in a Park and Ride place on the outskirts of the city. He used his bus pass for the trip to the centre and paid for her ticket. It made him think. Weren't women eligible for bus passes at sixty? But having one and being seen using it must be too much of a giveaway for a woman who dressed as youthfully as she did.

They spent what was left of the afternoon looking at shops and going into several of them. The only break she allowed him was to lean over the balustrade of the Poulteney bridge with her to look at the river for a couple of minutes.

He found he lacked more than he thought. The bag he was carrying bulged with the new saucepan, an omelette pan and some new tea-towels to replace his old ones. They were in no worse condition than frayed and thin but she told him they were fit only for dusters.

The last shop they visited was a men's shop which catered for the more adventurous man if the window displays were any guide. Urged inside by her, he soon became the owner of a pair of navy-blue shorts, narrower and longer in the leg and with fewer useful pockets than the perfectly acceptable pair which had stood him in good stead for years. She also found him a pair of linen shirts, a blue one he might have chosen unaided, and one – God help him – in mauve.

'And make sure they're still damp when you iron them,' she warned him.

Those were enough to be going on with, he thought, but quickly found he was wrong to think that. Instead, she pressed him to buy a pair of liver-coloured moccasins, noticeably less comfortable than his deck-shoes or chukka boots but obviously more to her taste.

'And you want a new dressing-gown,' she said, which was news to him. 'That one of yours could have come straight from the set of that old *Carry On Nurse* film.'

'But you and I are the only ones who'll ever see it,' he protested, 'except for my cleaner.'

'I certainly hope so. I wouldn't want anyone to think I was with a sad old man.'

'I'm not sad.'

'No, but that dressing-gown is. Sad to the point of clinical depression. And while we're at it, you can get some proper new slippers. You needn't think I've not noticed those awful furry objects poking out from under your bed.' She nudged him in the direction of the sales assistant who'd been making a poor job of stopping himself from laughing while he listened to them. 'Go on.'

His earlier solo shopping excursion was to buy going-out clothes. Now she was leading the way in setting him up with staying-in ones. He hoped it meant she was thinking of spending more time indoors with him rather than just tidying him up.

While he waited for the new polka-dotted dressing-gown, the scalp-hunter's moccasins, the slippers, shorts and shirts to be rung up on the till, he asked himself if the time would come when he'd be made to buy duplicates of them to keep at her house. Perhaps she was breaking him in gently.

On the way back from Bath they stopped at a large village, almost a town, close to Penny's much smaller village, and which still had a handful of proper shops. She wanted to buy the makings of a lamb-chop dinner, and he silently admired the way she told the butcher exactly what she wanted and was then served with it. In the greengrocer's shop she rummaged through the vegetables on offer before making her choice. Both shop-keepers addressed her by name which was more than he could say for the check-out girls at the supermarket, even though he was a regular customer. The most he ever had from them was a resigned grunt when he asked for plastic carrier bags. They were useful for holding his old newspapers when he had to put them out for what the council claimed to be recycling. He guessed the council's idea of that involved nothing more than dumping them straight into a big hole somewhere out of the way.

He'd known all along that she let him off lightly during their phone conversation about Brenda's discoveries, and that she was merely postponing giving him the third degree. She'd want to know every detail of how he'd explained them away, together with a full account of what he'd told Brenda about her. With that in mind, he was impressed by the way she kept herself in check until now when they were eating.

'I didn't need to explain them,' he told her. 'She seemed to conclude that whoever the woman was, she spent the night alone in the spare bedroom.'

'And how exactly do you think she managed to conclude that?'

'She said something about how hot it must have been under that winter-weight duvet on the bed in there. That was enough for her, I think.'

'But you never thought to enlighten her?'

The way she asked him that made it sound like a hostile question put by prosecuting counsel to an accused in the dock.

'No, I think she was quite satisfied with what I'd said.'

'So let me get this right,' Penny persisted. 'Your cleaner finds a woman's clothes in your wardrobe, and her make-up in your bathroom, yes? I'm surprised she didn't fumble through my knicker drawer while she was at it.'

'I'm sure she—'

'And she thinks it's perfectly normal for a woman to leave them there in case she fancies staying with you again at some future date? Tell me, how many women do you know who travel the country leaving little caches of their clothes wherever they stay? Just in case they fancy dropping in again for the night? I know it happens at hotels in London where film stars keep permanent suites but this is Myrtle Cottage, not the bloody Savoy. She must be really dense, that cleaner of yours. Wouldn't it have been easier if you'd told her about us? Not that it's any concern of hers but at least it would have clarified the situation.'

It wasn't going well, so he said with more confidence than he felt: 'I'm sure she didn't need me to draw her a picture. She must have guessed what had gone on. She asked just enough questions to work it out for herself without actually putting me on the spot. And as you say, it's none of her business. But I did tell her your name was Penelope, and she assumed you were young because of your taste in shoes. You know, heels and things.'

'That was big of you – mentioning my name. That'll leave her in no doubt as to my exact identity, won't it? Let's see now; name of Penelope, wears shoes with heels, uses make-up. Yes, anyone would know that was me. No chance of her mistaking me for someone else.'

'And I did sort of mention a bit about us to Jimmy at the Coq au Vin as well.'

'Sort of? Us? What, drop the odd hint? Let him guess about how we are? Fabulous. To tell you the truth, Alan, I think you've let me down. I get the feeling you're embarrassed to admit to people that we're together. An item, as people call it.' She looked searchingly at him across the table. 'And we are together, aren't we? Or don't you think so?'

'Of course we are.'

'In that case you've got a funny way of showing it, I must say. I told Mary and Helen – you know, the two women at that dinner of mine – about us before we went away and they were both genuinely pleased for me. Surprised, I grant you, but definitely pleased, and said how they'd taken to you at the time. How polite you were and how helpful to me.'

'Did they? I'm glad they approve. Glad for both of us, of course. You don't think they might have felt it was all a bit soon, a bit premature? You know, after losing your husband?'

'No, as I've told you before, they're no more than neighbours. Friendly ones, yes, but not really friends as such, and certainly not sufficiently fond of my husband to want his memory protected. It's not as though he cared much for them or their husbands. He always made a fuss about having to dine with them when we couldn't get out of it.'

'I suppose that deep down I didn't want to compromise you, that's all,' Alan said, silently congratulating himself for thinking of it under pressure.

'You wouldn't have been. In case you need reminding, I'm a widow of sixty, not some shy virgin who needs protecting from scandal. What you told your cleaning-lady sounds as if you're ashamed of me.'

Since getting stuck into the subject, her tone had switched seamlessly from disapproval to aggression. Now it had moved on to anger.

All he could think to say in response was: 'I'm sorry,' and to look suitably downcast.

'I should bloody well think so.'

She'd finished eating. Now she banged her knife and fork down with a clatter, pushed her plate away from her and sat as far back on her chair as she could with her arms folded defensively.

It was the closest they'd come to having a row, he thought, before it dawned on him that they were already in the thick of one, even if it was as one-sided as those he'd got used to with Susan.

Thinking now of women in general and not only of his ex-wife or Penny, he told himself it didn't take much to start them off. And what did she think he ought to have told Brenda? How about saying that, yes, his overnight guest was Penelope Hallows, not of this parish but from Upper Mendham, a widow whose late husband's ashes were so fresh from the crematorium they might still be lightly wafting about on the summer breeze? And yes, he was sleeping with her here in the cottage and at her house, and had been doing so while they holidayed abroad together? And he hoped to do much more of the same? Bugger that for a game of soldiers, it was bound to be wrong.

His earlier peace-making apology had been rejected. It was time to instigate a cooling-off period of the sort that never worked with Susan, but there was always a first time. Penny wasn't going to make such a move of her own, so he decided to go in for some flattery. Something about her cooking might do.

It had been a long time since she stopped speaking and started to look fixedly at her plate.

'Penny, darling,' he said, ' I have to tell you how much I enjoyed that meal. It—'

'Don't bloody soft soap me, Alan. It won't work.'

That was really bad news since he'd no other strategy readily to hand.

CHAPTER TWENTY-ONE

Penny was feeling contrite the next morning for letting Alan over-compensate for upsetting her.

He was particularly attentive after their meal, waving away her half-hearted attempts to help him clear the table and wash up, and insisting she make herself comfortable in the sitting-room instead. When she was settled there he put on a CD for her to listen to while he busied himself in the kitchen where he took far longer than she would have done. Back with her again, he plied her with a succession of drinks till her head reeled.

As well as feeling ashamed of herself she wished she'd not been so unfair. There was no excuse for the way she pitched into him for his failure to be more forthcoming with his cleaner, not when she was equally guilty of fabricating Helen and Mary's approval of her new relationship. Some of what she told him was true. She did meet them at the W.I. hall and they did ask after him. After that she was as vague as he was, if not more.

'Alan? Yes, I've been seeing quite a lot of him,' she told them. 'He's been so kind to me, you know, helping me through a bad time.'

Neither of them said much in reply beyond telling her that, yes, he was very pleasant and any woman in her position needed a sympathetic ear. When they wandered off to talk to Joan Atkinson about the W.I's next fund-raising event they hadn't all put their heads together to whisper to one another with stealthy glances in her direction as she feared they would.

The drinks took hold at the same rate as the growth of her self-reproach. Her attitude gradually changed during the evening from frosty to properly affectionate. Normal relations were restored by the time they went up to bed, but she'd still not apologized. She wasn't sure how to, so settled for being extra nice to him.

She woke twice during the night. The first time, she lay

awake listening to his steady breathing which he occasionally punctuated with the soft snorts she was getting used to. While lying there in the dark she worried she might be cramping his style by spending so much time with him so soon. They returned from Tenerife on Friday. Now it was already in the early hours of Tuesday and she'd already been with him on the Sunday and again yesterday.

It was hard to know what to do next. If she suggested spending today together he'd feel he ought to have suggested it himself. If she didn't, he'd think she wanted more time to herself. She'd been faced with that dilemma before but not since she was seventeen and going out, or not going out, with Ricky from the garage, her boyfriend, or not her boyfriend, at the time.

When she woke again shortly after five o'clock, Alan was sleeping restlessly and taking up more than his fair share of the bed. She lay on her back in the narrow space left to her with one leg hanging over the edge of the mattress. She felt tense and tried to relax by doing a breathing exercise: five deep breaths in, hold, then seven smaller breaths out, hold and repeat. It was said to help Tibetan monks get in touch with the spirits of their ancestors but she hoped it wouldn't happen to her. It didn't, and failed to relax her, too. If anything, she felt more tense than before.

To the background of the birds' dawn chorus, she spent a restless half hour fretting about Emma, Giles, and their intractable problem. There had been no follow-up phone call from Wimbledon and she was reluctant to make one of her own. She tried to convince herself it was because Giles might be with Emma when she called, or even answer the phone himself, but she knew the real reason was her fear of hearing yet worse news.

Thinking about it brought back a vivid memory of how frightened she was to phone the hospital to hear the results of her breast-tissue biopsy, and how much more frightening it was when they refused to tell her over the phone, insisting instead that she visit the hospital again for an urgent appointment. That initial call had set in motion a storm of bad news and she now wanted to postpone hearing any more for as long as possible.

Reggie would have gone up to Wimbledon to read the Riot Act to Giles and knock some sense into both of them. Now she'd no one to turn to for comfort apart from Alan, and she was wary of involving him any further. It was nothing to do with him, never mind what he said to the contrary.

It might have been different if she had women friends to confide in. She'd not kept up with the girl friends she had before she married. They and their eventual husbands lacked Reggie's earnings and could never afford to live in a village as smart as Upper Mendham. They gradually drifted away from her in her new privileged life and she did nothing to stay in touch with them. Nor did Reggie encourage her to.

The replacement friends she made in the village were nearly all gone now. All of them were older than she was, nearer Reggie's age than hers, and many were now dead. Or "gone on", as her parents used to say. The survivors went into sheltered housing or care homes, down-sized elsewhere to be nearer doctors, hospitals and shops, or moved away to live close to their grown-up children. When they left the village, their big old expensive houses were taken over by younger, affluent buyers who showed no interest in village life or in making friends with their new OAP neighbours.

As far as she knew, all the grown-up children were happy and successful. If they weren't, their parents were unlikely to advertise it. Parents often blamed themselves in secret for their children's shortcomings, but she didn't. Her unwanted involvement in Emma's continuing problems didn't represent much of a return on the money Reggie had invested in his daughter and was scant compensation for her mother's unvarying love.

She started to cry then, but softly so not to disturb Alan.

He'd already seen and heard enough of her doing that. It really was all terribly unfair on both of them.

That morning she again made use of the clothes and make-up that were the cause of all yesterday's trouble. Breakfast was nearly ready when she eventually came downstairs in one of her spare pairs of jeans and a top she wasn't really happy with.

The meal didn't amount to much: coffee, and boiled eggs with toasted soldiers. He'd put little heaps of salt and pepper by the side of her eggcup, which was thoughtful of him. They had more toast with marmalade, and raspberry yoghurt to finish. She said nothing, and would have preferred to eat the yoghurt first but he was too slow to get it out of the fridge for that.

'Everything okay for you, darling?' he asked.

She smiled at him. 'Lovely, thanks.'

It was vital that she have another word with Helen and Mary, ideally one at a time, about the true state of affairs between her and Alan. Not because it was any of their business but because either of them might bump into him somewhere and he might mention the holiday.

To tell him the truth now was out of the question and too late anyway. A straightforward apology to him for her behaviour with no mention of her subterfuge was the best course. She ought to have done it much sooner.

'Alan, darling, I've been thinking. I'm sorry I was such a bitch to you last night. I can't think what possessed me.'

He looked surprised. 'You weren't,' he said. Then, almost immediately: 'Yes, you were, actually. It wasn't like you at all.'

'I know, and you didn't deserve it. I was very unfair to you.'

'You don't need to—'

'I do', she insisted. 'If I were in your shoes, caught unawares like that, I'd have told that cleaner of yours more or less what you did.' That was as far as felt able to go. 'About the same, in fact. I know you were only doing your best to be discreet, not disloyal at all.'

'I'm glad we've got that sorted out,' he said with a long sigh. 'I don't like us to be at cross purposes. Look, let me make it up to you, get us back on an even keel. You did all the cooking last evening and paid for the food as well, so why don't we go over to the Coq au Vin for lunch later on? My treat.'

'I'd love that. Thank you.'

She knew what Emma would make of this scene of domesticity. A middle-aged couple facing each other across a kitchen table so small that their plates almost touched, the room smelling of coffee and of toast left too long in the toaster, and all at nine-thirty in the morning with everything pointing inescapably to their having spent the night together. Instead of being pleased for her mother, Emma would be angry and have something bitter to say about her father's memory being debased.

Alan was still doing his best to please, Penny thought gratefully. It must be the reason for his wearing the new mauve shirt that still showed a faint noughts-and-crosses grid pattern from being folded away in a drawer. He'd tucked it into a pair of blue jeans she'd not seen before. They were faded beyond the needs of fashion and some of the seam stitching was hanging loose. It was worth a mention if only to save him from himself.

'I hope you don't mind me saying so, Alan, but I'm not at all sure about those jeans you've got on this morning.'

He looked down at them. 'It's only a spot of egg-yolk. It'll soon sponge off.'

'No, not that.'

'What then? I'm rather attached to them, had them for years.'

'It looks like it, darling. They're almost flared, a real link with the past. So much so I'm surprised they haven't got flower-power patches on them.' Before he could say anything, she added: 'And they're really baggy at the back.' She almost told him how Reggie used to describe the effect. He never wore jeans, never owned a pair, but always had an expression ready for use when he saw men trailing folds of loose denim behind them: the elephant-arse look.

'The thing is, as men get older their bottoms tend to shrink. That's what happens, and it's certainly happened to yours.'

'Do you think so? I've always thought I looked okay in them. Besides, you often wear jeans, like today for instance.'

'Not like yours, I don't. And my bottom's not like yours, either.'

'I know. I like your bottom.'

'I did get that impression. So we're both very lucky, then, aren't we?'

He made a play of shaking his head resignedly. 'I tell you, being with you is costing me a fortune. First of all it was the holiday, then the shirts, shorts and all the rest of the stuff, and now you want me to ditch these.'

'You can't put a price on looking good. In my understated little way I think I'm transforming you.'

'I know. And, yes, I suppose I do appreciate it. All right, I'll wear those new shorts when we go to lunch.'

'I don't think you should. Why not wear those chinos you wore the first time we went there?'

'And what about this shirt you made me buy? Could you face being seen with me in it at the Coq au Vin?'

She'd already decided the colour was wrong.

'No, wear the new blue one, it's less sudden and more suitable for a restaurant. After all, where we're going isn't exactly like a beachside café in Bognor, is it?'

'Jimmy wouldn't think so. What about these pink socks? Are they still okay for you?'

She got up, came round the table and kissed him under his ear, taking care not to disarrange his hair.

'Certainly they are. I can hardly imagine you in any others.'

The Coq au Vin was having a quiet day. Only two tables were occupied, one by an old couple who seemed to have lost the gift of speech but not of eating with their mouths open, the other by a man with a full beard but no moustache. It made his face look as if it had been pushed through a dense ginger-coloured hedge.

Jimmy greeted them and showed them to a table.

'Claudine's got the day off today,' he told them, 'so you'll have to put up with my brand of table service, I'm afraid. But perhaps you'll do me the honour of taking a drink with me before you order.' He sat down heavily at Penny's side. 'What would you care for, my dear, *apéritif-*wise?'

After he returned with their gins and tonic, large for Penny, small for Alan, and his own large Scotch, and they'd taken meaningful drinks from them, he recommended they had the steaks he had in stock.

'Ten ounces at least, all of them.'

Alan laughed. 'I know all about your recommendations, Jim. You need to get rid of stuff that's been hanging about in your kitchen, absolutely on its last legs.'

How rude he was being, especially as Jimmy was so polite to them when they were there before. It must be a man thing.

'*Au contraire*,' Jimmy said to her. 'Don't you listen to his foolishness, my dear. He's to fine dining as I am to mountaineering. If I were ever tempted to go in for that sort of thing, my wife would plunge one of her boning knives into my manly chest. The last thing we need during a recession is to kill off our few remaining customers with a dose of salmonella.' He pointed at the window. 'You'll have noticed that little sign there; five stars, the maximum the authorities award for food hygiene. But seriously, I do really recommend those steaks, they're the best I've had in for some time.'

Alan asked her what she thought. 'Do you fancy one after all that nonsense?'

'I think I might.'

Jimmy said, 'And may I tempt you to one of my delicious starters?'

Alan answered for them both, rather quickly, she

thought, but then remembered who was paying.

'No, just a salad and a few of your oven-ready chips.' A little too late for her liking, he raised his eyebrows and asked her: 'Okay for you, too?' She nodded, and he said to Jimmy: 'As I'm driving I'll have one of your bottled beers. In a clean glass if you've got one.'

Penny asked for a demi-carafe of the house red. Jimmy said, 'Thy will be done,' and went off to the kitchen.

Alan looked out of the window at the pewter-coloured sky.

'I think it's going to rain,' he said. 'I'll just nip out to the car and get my umbrella in case we need it when we leave. And I'll have a pee as well while I'm at it. For some reason that G and T's gone straight through me.'

'Thanks for sharing that with me, darling.'

When Jimmy reappeared with the wine and beer he sat down with her again.

'I hope you don't mind me saying this while he's away,' he said, 'but Master Baxter happened to mention *en passant* that you've been seeing something of each other. But I do hope I'm not stepping in where angels fear to tread.'

'He told me he'd mentioned it to you, yes.'

'Good. Gave me no details of frequency or intensity or anything else of that nature, of course.'

'Of course.'

'Now I don't want to talk out of turn, but if you ask my opinion, which you won't, I have to tell you he's a very lucky man to have met you.'

'He'd be pleased to know you think so. I am, too. Thank you.'

'But I do hope he won't get to hear of it. Those few words are meant only for your ears, dear lady. And I wouldn't dream of suggesting to you that you're also fortunate to know him because it'd be like congratulating a girl when she gets engaged – it's just not done. But I've met all sorts in my calling and I have to say he's one of the most decent chaps I've ever had the pleasure of taking money from. Chaps like him are worth a guinea a box.'

'I must say you're very rude to each other.'

'Yes, I know we both take the…the mickey, but that's no more than badinage, you know. A little banter to help us through the day.'

'Don't tell him I told you, but I happen to know he's very fond of you and loves coming here. I remember you were kind enough to lend him your van when his car was off the road.'

'Ah yes, the old liveried horseless carriage.' Jimmy broke off to finish his whisky. 'Lovely,' he said admiringly as he put his glass down. 'All praise to our Caledonian cousins.' Laughing now, he went on: 'Tell me, do you know what people would have called him when he was driving around in it?'

'The cocoa-van man. Yes, I knew that.'

'Quite so. Though I'd hoped to be the one to enlighten you. Still, do please remember what I said. He really is a top chap.'

'To tell you the truth, Jimmy – I can call you that, yes? – I'm glad you've confirmed what I already know. But two heads are better than one, aren't they?'

'I'm not sure my wife would agree with you, my dear, but let's hope so in this case. And if I'm not being premature, may I wish both of you the very best of luck for the future?'

CHAPTER TWENTY-TWO

'...so it's extremely ill-advised of the present government to make these tests mandatory,' the Shadow Education Minister said testily, as if no one who understood politics would ever think otherwise.

It was a good point, well made, but self-appointed football referee Baxter still had to show the offender a red card. According to the rules of a game he'd invented, any player who wrested four syllables from "mandatory" had to be penalised.

Alan often played his game on mornings when he got up in time and wasn't playing golf. This rainy morning there were only ten minutes to go before the final whistle at nine o'clock and the team of radio presenters and their guests was already reduced to seven players. The rules were getting too tough for current usage. Any day now he'd have to decide on "surreal"; whether or not to let it describe any faintly unusual or mildly surprising event.

During the weeks since Tenerife he'd built up a store of his clothes at Farthing's, and Penny had added to hers at Myrtle Cottage. He once saw Brenda looking at items of his and Penny's underwear hanging companionably together on his rotary clothes-line. But as she said nothing about it he decided he and she must have reached a mutual but unspoken acceptance of the situation.

Terry was now coming weekly to do the mowing and light weeding. He did both better than his father ever did.

Geoff, meanwhile, was reported to be bearing up well after an unspecified abdominal operation. "Down there", was all Brenda said about it.

He'd be replacing his son any week now which was a problem in itself. Terry's plumbing skills weren't often being called upon and he sounded grateful for the chance to make money from gardening while he could. Alan would have liked to make him a fixture at his father's expense but it would be bound to cause a family rift.

Brenda might take her revenge for his abandonment of her husband by flouncing off and leaving him to do his own cleaning.

As far as he and Penny were concerned, he thought the next stage of their friendship could be the exchange of tokens of permanence. Not the giving and receiving of rings, heaven forbid, but of house keys and burglar-alarm codes. It meant bidding farewell to his privacy, what little there was of it, but that was okay. There was nothing incriminating for her to find if she went scouting around the cottage in his absence – no stash of porn on top of his wardrobe or under his bed, for instance. If she agreed it would prove she trusted him to keep the relationship going or even to crank it up. The development wouldn't compromise their agreement that they weren't actually living together. Not yet, anyway. If it worked, it might lead inexorably to a welcome invitation to move in with her.

It was important not to frighten her off by being precipitate. One step at a time was the way to do it. Once the first one was taken he'd be able to return from golf to whichever house he was staying at and find lunch waiting for him. If it was true that women liked to feel indispensable or to be encouraged to feel that way, she might want to take charge of his ironing and make sure he never ran out of essential supplies when she was staying with him. The shopping trip to Bath showed she wasn't averse to at least some of that. They'd be spending much more time together, so they'd both be winners.

The rest of the day stretched before him in ordered tranquillity. He was due to have dinner with her at Farthing's and to stay the night. After lunch he'd have a doze and follow it with a long rest while watching cricket on TV.

With nearly three hours to go before he needed to open a tin and to make toast, the phone rang. It was Penny. Without asking him how he was or what he was doing, she told him she was sorry but he couldn't now come that evening. With her voice awash with world-weariness, she said, 'It's Emma, you see.'

It always was. 'What's the problem?'

It was a reasonable question as everything he heard about Emma involved a problem. If not about her fertility or Giles, it was Hong bloody Kong. At least he'd not asked what the problem was *now*.

He felt apprehensive but went ahead anyway. 'It's not bad news, I hope.'

It was a forlorn hope because only ill-tidings ever came from that quarter, but he had to ask.

'Yes, it is. I've only just got off the phone to her.'

There was a pause he wished had lasted longer if only to give him more time to prepare himself for whatever tragedy or pseudo-tragedy was coming.

'They've split up, her and Giles. She's had her pregnancy confirmed and she's keeping the baby. So that's the good news, if you like. He's buggering off to Hong Kong which is good news for me in a way but definitely bad news for her. He's overcome his normal lethargy and has already moved out. To his mother's, wouldn't you just know it? He's staying there in Epsom till he leaves permanently.'

Alan groaned inwardly. 'That's such a—'

Rather than let him tell her what it was, she said, 'In a way I'm relieved they've made a decision. God knows, they've taken long enough over it. It's not the one I'd have chosen for them but at least it's an end to all that shilly-shallying.'

'I really am sorry to hear about that, Penny,' he told her as soon as he was given the chance. He knew there was more to come from her. More bad news, that was. Its advance party was already well dug in because it looked like he'd now be tapping at the door of the Coq au Vin for his evening meal.

'Yes, I'm sorry too. But it's time to be practical now there's something definite to work on. I've got to try to sort things out properly. To help her sort them out, I mean.'

'I can see that, darling.' He used the word even though she appeared to have forgotten its existence. 'But why—?'

'Why can't you come over this evening, you mean? Because I'm taking the train up to Wimbledon to see her, that's why. She's taking the afternoon off work and wants to talk to me about money. But unlike you, she doesn't know about my new financial situation. I think it'll come as a nasty shock to her. I'm taking the train that leaves just before twelve and ought to be at her house by three. I'll get a late one back this evening. It'll give me a few hours with her.'

Thinking she'd expect him to offer, he said, 'Right. And I'll be going with you.'

The time of the train to London would be too early for him to have lunch beforehand and the train back would make it too late for dinner, he thought morosely.

'You can't do that,' she said at once. 'She'll think you're sticking your nose in. She may or may not be reconciled to our being together but...'

'But she's not exactly crazy about the idea and wouldn't welcome any involvement by me, I know. But I still want to come with you.'

He went on to explain he didn't need to come into Emma's house with her and could easily find things to do, and parts of Wimbledon to visit, while she was talking to her daughter. As he told her this, a ripple of nostalgia trickled over him. It made him think he wouldn't mind having a wander around Wimbledon as it was years since he was in the area.

He'd done some mild courting there in his youth, mainly in the back rows of the town's three cinemas, often interrupted by the searching beam of an usherette's torch. And then there was the Wimbledon Palais. He was too young to go to the Saturday-evening dances there in the mid-sixties but he and a few classmates sometimes took the bus to see the evening bouts of professional wrestling. It would be good to see the old place again.

'And I don't like the idea of you having to travel back here at night all alone and feeling depressed,' he said. She was always downcast after talking to and about her daughter. A possible obstacle occurred to him. 'Emma didn't suggest you stay the night, I suppose?'

'She did say I'd be welcome to but, frankly, I didn't think I could face having to go through it all this afternoon and evening and then again in the morning. As it is, I haven't a clue about money and haven't actually got much now, but I imagine it'll give her a chance to talk about them splitting up and how it's affecting her and what she plans to do about it. I always like to see her but I can't say I'm looking forward to meeting her today.'

'In that case I'll definitely travel with you. Give you a shoulder to cry on, but let's hope it doesn't come to that. At least let me do that for you. What do you say?'

'As long as you can find something to occupy your time up there and don't mind waiting while I'm with her. Yes, in that case I would like you to come. Thanks for offering.'

'At least it looks like you'll still be getting that grandchild you've set your heart on, and it'll be here in England which it wouldn't have been otherwise.'

And she'd have plenty of opportunities to spend time with it, travelling up and down from Somerset to baby-sit. She might be looking forward to it now but wouldn't be so keen once it started. She'd get calls like "Oh, mummy, would it be okay if I left little Nicholas/Nicola with you for a week while I'm at a seminar in Germany? It'd be such a help and I know how much you love having him/her. You'd be only too pleased? Really? It's so kind of you. So when do you think you could come up here to collect him/her?"

'I know. The baby part's good, even if nothing else is.'

They drove separately to the station and arrived in good time to buy their tickets. He used his credit card but didn't draw her attention to it.

'You never know for sure if they'll be serving food on

these trains, so I made a few sandwiches to sustain us,' she told him when they sat facing each other across a table in a half-empty carriage. 'They're cheese and tomato. I hope that's all right with you, darling.'

So the word had boarded the train with them. He must have done or said something right. Relieved about that and the sandwiches, he said, 'Good thinking, darling.'

Returning to the reason for the journey with less reluctance than he could have foreseen earlier, he said, 'But what's puzzling me is why she wants to talk to you about money. From what you've told me about her job she can't be short of it, and I'd have thought it was a bit early for her to have concerns about child maintenance. Their solicitors will sort all that out for them. And if Giles is on a good salary, I doubt there'll be much of a problem.'

'God, I hope you're right. I know he's a sod but I think even he would step up to the mark, money-wise. I imagine it must be about mortgages or pensions or future school fees. Oh, and before I forget I'd better give you a note of Emma's address.'

She took a notebook from her handbag, wrote in it and tore out the page.

'I've put her phone number down as well but don't ring unless it's an absolute emergency. Now that I think about it, an earlier train back would be better. I reckon three hours or so with her will do. I don't think I could face more than that. I know, why don't you hover unobtrusively some way down her road at about six? I'll have had more than enough by then.'

'No problem at all.'

As they left Wimbledon station, Penny said, 'I hope you can find something to do to pass the time.' She looked up at the grey sky. 'At least the rain's stopped for you. Go into a book shop and have a look in an A to Z to see where her road is, or get a taxi. I'm going to get one now so I'll leave you to it. Don't forget; be in her road around six and try not to look too furtive. We don't want you getting arrested for loitering with intent and I'll try not to keep you waiting. Where are you heading off to now?'

He told her about the Palais.

'I hope you're not disappointed. It's probably unrecognisable after all these years.'

As they kissed goodbye, he said, 'Promise you'll not get too upset.'

She shook her head. 'Believe me, I wish I could but I'm prepared for the worst, so I won't make promises I can't keep.'

'At least try not to.'

He walked away down the Broadway. It looked more prosperous than he remembered it, with better shops and many more restaurants. There were fewer charity shops than in most Somerset towns, and no boarded-up shops at all that he could see. He crossed the road to look at the theatre where his parents had taken him to see pantomimes as a child, and made his way by degrees past the tube station and along to the site of the old Palais.

He was ready to be disappointed, and he was. It was inevitable that he was now looking at housing instead of a Palais de Danse. Did the occupants know their ground floors were once jitterbugged on by G.Is, strutted on by the Beatles, the Rolling Stones and the Kinks, or wrestled over by Milo Popocopolis, the Golden Greek? Of course they didn't.

On a whim, he walked back to the tube station and boarded a Tooting-bound train to have a look at the Art Deco cinema where he first saw the Rolling Stones on stage. It was now a bingo hall.

Disappointments like that made him think there were no longer any traces of his personal yesterdays. He caught himself looking back more and more these days, mainly because his age didn't allow him much future to look forward to. He was running short of links with his past, and his personal new order hadn't replaced them with anything he much cared for. Apart from Penny, that was. He cared for her and today proved it. Otherwise he wouldn't now be standing on a windswept corner of South

London, poorer by the price of two return train tickets, buffeted by the noise of traffic, and with hours to kill before he had to pilot her through whatever new worries her daughter was heaping on her at that very moment.

CHAPTER TWENTY-THREE

Penny asked the taxi driver to drop her off in Wimbledon village, some distance from her daughter's house. A walk would do her good and give her a chance to stretch her legs and get some fresh air after being cooped up in trains for hours. She also wanted time on her own to think about what to say when she got there. Emma was sure to want money from her and expect to get it, though the possibility of that happening was now non-existent. The news would come as a disappointment and needed to be broken gently. It was like those signs that cautioned shoppers against asking for credit; refusal often offended.

She felt guilty for wanting to put the meeting off for as long as possible. The feeling stayed with her, nibbling at her conscience while she walked slowly down both sides of the central street, using up time by lingering in front of shop windows displaying the sort of unusual and desirable things she rarely came across at home.

It was already half past three when she looked at her watch, and she'd told Emma to expect her by three. Alan was due to start his loitering about six. She was glad to have suggested they take an earlier train back. The time she'd left herself would be ample for anything her daughter had in mind.

'I'd started to give you up for lost,' Emma said, showing Penny into the sitting-room. 'I suppose the wretched train was delayed, was it? Still, you're here now.'

Stepping warily over the rug with its significant pattern, Penny sat down on or in the experimental chair with its sledge-like supports. The only difference she noticed in the room since her last visit was a magazine about mothers and babies that lay open on the sofa, drawing attention to Emma's new mother-to-be status.

Emma must have seen her looking at it. 'You see, mummy, I'm already getting prepared and there's so much to learn and remember. It's all new and exciting. I can't bear the thought of having to wait till the baby's born before I find out whether it's a boy or a girl, and I want to know as soon as possible. I bet you'd have liked to know in advance what you were going to have.'

Everything was in such a rush back then that Penny had little time to worry about what sex her baby was going to be. Besides, there was no easy way of finding out in those days. Reggie wanted a boy and spent more time discussing the names of boys than of girls. Emma was an early mutual choice for a daughter as suitably middle-class and neither dated nor aggressively modern, but he couldn't decide between Nigel and Jeremy for a son and heir. Both names complied with the same three criteria that Emma's matched, but he was still flitting between the two right up to the time of her delivery. His mother tentatively proposed Sebastian as a boy's name in memory of a Christian martyr shot through with arrows in Roman times. Reggie said she liked it only because there was a foppish youth of that name in Waugh's *Brideshead Revisited*, and vetoed it. In the end, he and Penny were both relieved to have a healthy child after a difficult and protracted labour.

'It would have been nice, yes, if only to know what colour of clothes to buy. I know it's not like that now. In those days it was pretty much limited to blues and pinks. Or white if you were up-to-date, or yellow if you wanted to make some sort of statement.'

After a spell of asking about Emma's health, if she was taking the right sort of dietary supplements and if she was having any morning sickness, and being more or less reassured on all points, it was time to start on the difficult stuff.

'We've got lots to talk about, I know, and I can't tell you how sorry I was to hear your news. But can I just get one thing out of the way first? Are you and Giles now absolutely determined to go your separate ways with no possibility of either of you changing your mind before it's too late? You gave me the distinct impression on the phone that you were splitting up for ever.'

Emma showed no sign of being angry or close to tears, or anything like that at all really – just excited. How long would that last before it was swamped with concern about the realities of her position?

'I'd always hoped you'd make a go of it with Giles. And yes, I've always hoped you'd marry him. After all, you spent so much time with Brendan and then with that other man that came to nothing.'

'That other man? Roger, you mean. You can mention his name, you know. He was part of my life for almost eight years.'

'I'm sorry. But they both hurt you so much when they wouldn't properly commit. That's all I'm saying.'

'I know, but that was years ago and I was well shot of both of them. But in answer to your question; yes, we are going our separate ways. He's going to Hong Kong and I'm not going with him. He leaves next week.'

'As soon as that?'

'He said there was no point in staying any longer and he needed time to get settled in there before starting his new job. And he's right. We've both dug our heels in and we've nothing left to say to each other. Neither of us ever seems to be able to compromise, let alone give in gracefully to the other, so it's better this way than carrying on fighting and arguing all the time.'

'But you still got pregnant by him,' Penny pointed out. 'How did you manage that? It must have been—'

Emma laughed. 'Not at all. I told him I was taking the pill again so he wanted to make the most of what was still available to him while he had the chance and while it was on offer. And it's not as though I was going to fend him off, was I? He was surprised – if that's the word for it – when I told him I thought I was pregnant. I had to say it was an accident; that I must have made a mistake, forgotten to take some of the pills, or that the batch was faulty. Unlikely, I know, but he seemed to accept it.'

'I guessed you'd have lied to him about being back on

the pill. It's exactly the sort of thing you would do.'

'Don't be po-faced about it, mummy. It was a complete no-brainer from my point of view. And, in a way, it's lucky he's leaving as soon as he is.' She patted her stomach which looked as flat as ever. 'They react to stress, babies do. Even in the womb.'

'But now he knows you're expecting at last, surely he wouldn't want to leave now, not leave you in the lurch.'

'He won't be abandoning me completely because he hopes he'll be able to get back a couple of times a year to see his child. And he'll be here for the birth if he can get away. He says when the two years are up he wants to help me as much as he can, his job permitting, even though we won't be together.' She leaned forward on the sofa. 'I tell you, this type of arrangement isn't at all uncommon these days. It's disappointing, I know, but it would have been much more complicated if we were married. And I'm reconciled to it now. In the meantime we've put this house up for sale and I'm going to have to buy something smaller.'

'Smaller than this? Surely not.'

'Surely yes, a little flat or maisonette. He's not being totally unreasonable for once. As soon as my maternity leave ends he's going to make us an allowance of twenty-five per cent of his net salary.'

It sounded a lot to Penny, more than she'd expect from him.

'I daresay that's better than having to fight him through the courts,' she said, imagining that was the alternative. 'But you told me you wanted to talk about money. If he's giving you a quarter of his salary…'

'Net salary. It makes a difference.'

'Even so. I don't know what he earns but I imagine a quarter of it would be a tremendous help. So what exactly…?'

'I'll tell you. As you know, we've got a joint mortgage on this place. We rented that flat in Hammersmith for far too long while we waited for property prices to fall like everyone said they were bound to. Including daddy, I might say, though I'm not blaming him for a moment. But they kept on rising so we decided to buy after all, only to find we'd bought at exactly the wrong time, right at the top of the market. Prices have levelled out since then with the result that we've not got much equity in it yet, not above our original deposit.'

That was the last thing Penny expected to hear. She'd nothing better to say than: 'I'd no idea.'

'I don't suppose you had. Anyway, some of my half of what equity there is will be swallowed up by the costs of buying a new place – survey fees, solicitors' fees, stamp duty, that sort of thing. What's left after that, plus my savings, will just about cover the new deposit.'

'Well, that's—'

'But I won't be able to afford any new mortgage repayments, not with the cost of child care to consider. And I'd never be able to find anyone, not an au pair or a carer, who'd take on an infant from about seven in the morning till seven or eight at night. That's when I'm usually out of the house at the moment. There are my business trips abroad, too, often at short notice. It means I'll have to leave my job and get a less demanding one.'

'But then you'd have even less money.' Couldn't Emma see that?

'Exactly. Because less demanding inevitably means less well-paid. A low level job with a low level salary. Something local with no commuting so I could fit it in around normal child-care hours. Perhaps even a part-time one.'

'I'd no idea,' Penny said again. 'It never crossed my mind.'

'It's certainly crossed mine, I can tell you. What's more, even if I didn't buy a place I still couldn't afford much rent, not here in Wimbledon. Giles's allowance would cover my utility costs and living expenses and child care, but not my housing as well.'

'I can't see why you don't just stay here.'

'Can't you?' Emma said peevishly. 'Just think about it. Giles couldn't afford the whole of the mortgage on this house by himself, not after handing over a quarter of his net pay for me and the baby, and after buying a place of his own when he came back from abroad.'

'God, what an awful position for you to be in, and now of all times. You must be so worried.'

Feeling she badly needed some comfort, Penny said, 'I know it's far too early but I don't suppose I could have a drink. A proper one, I mean.'

'Of course you can. All this must have come as a shock to you. G and T all right?'

She returned with a full glass. 'But you won't mind if I don't join you.'

After a few sips of what was an uncommonly strong drink with as much gin in it as tonic, Penny asked, despite knowing what the answer would be: 'So where do I come into all this?'

'Mummy, it's really embarrassing for me to ask you, but did daddy leave any money to be put aside for me?'

So she'd been right all along, not that it was any comfort.

'I'm afraid he didn't, no. It all came direct to me. I imagine he must have felt it would all come to you when I died – Farthing's and everything.'

'I'm not being rude, but he must have left quite a substantial amount, mustn't he?'

'Sorry to disappoint you, Emma, but he didn't do that either. And I can tell you it came as a very unwelcome surprise to me when I found out just how little it was.'

She went on to explain reluctantly about the decline in Reggie's business, the raids on capital to fund their high-on-the-hog lifestyle, the lack of life assurance and a pension. And how she said nothing about it because she was ashamed on Reggie's behalf for his letting things slide. She knew it was giving her daughter another stick to beat her with. Emma was always a daddy's girl whose father could do no wrong in her eyes. None of it could possibly have been Reggie's fault.

'...so you see, if you're asking me to give or lend you money for a mortgage or rent, I'm sorry, but no can do, I'm afraid.'

Instead of commiserating as Penny still hoped she would, but knew she wouldn't, Emma said, 'You remember what Giles mentioned when you were up here last? About downsizing? What about that?'

'If there's any downsizing to be done it'd be to provide me with money to keep me going in my old age. It may well come to that. Think about it, Emma. I'm only sixty and could have twenty or thirty years to go. That would take a lot of funding, especially if I end up for a long time in some sort of old folks' home. The fees in those places are enormous.'

'What about equity release?'

'What about it? I'd still need the released money to live on, wouldn't I?'

She let herself think what it would be like if the worst came to the worst and Emma had to come and live with her in Somerset. It wasn't an appealing prospect. Lovely to spend lots of time with a grandchild but not so breathtakingly enjoyable that she'd relish becoming a full-time nanny while Emma was away from the house miserably doing some mundane local job that made no use of her City abilities. Quite apart from the restrictions on her own freedom, there was Alan to think about. She'd never succeed in getting him to move into Farthing's, not with Emma and a baby living there.

A remote possibility remained, so remote as to be almost invisible, but she decided to mention it anyway, if only to show she was trying to help.

'I suppose you might try your uncle Gerard,' she said doubtfully.

She saw Emma's eyes light up at the mention of his name, and needed to damp down any expectations she'd kindled.

She hurried on: 'But I expect any money he inherited

from his mother must have leaked away by now. He sold that house of his in Yorkshire years ago and must have been using the proceeds to fund his care-home fees ever since. And he can't have had much in the way of savings when he went into it because he was a Master of Foxhounds before the accident and that involves lots of expense and high living. But you never know, it might be worth trying him, though I think you'd be doomed to disappointment.' She paused. 'So if neither of us can help you, what do you think you'll do?'

'I had hoped you'd be able to help. Truth to tell, I rather assumed you would. As it is and after what you've told me, I don't have much choice, do I? I hate the thought of it but I'll have to go in for a termination after all.'

'What? You can't possibly mean that.'

'I can, actually.'

'But what about Giles?' Penny protested. 'What would he think if you had an abortion?' It sounded more realistic and stark to call it that. 'Don't you think he ought to have some say in the matter?'

'He wouldn't think anything because he wouldn't know. I'd tell him I'd had a miscarriage.'

'That's awful.'

Emma shrugged. 'I know, but what else can I do? And don't tell me I could then join him in Hong Kong after all. It's too late for that. All this has made me realise we're not right for each other. We probably never have been. No, it's best if we go our separate ways. It's not as though I've not done it before.'

'I wasn't about to suggest you went with him, I assure you.'

'Just as well. So although I'd love to keep the baby – you do know that, don't you? – I still have to go ahead with the termination. I don't really have any choice. If I kept it I'd be an unmarried mother in my forties with hardly any money. How could I hope to attract another man in those circumstances? I'd want another one to be with because I've never been on my own and wouldn't want to have to start now. What sort of men are single in their forties or older? I'll tell you; gay men and mummy's boys, that's who. Or widowers and divorced men, possibly with children of their own to support. They're not the sort who'd want to take on more baggage in the shape of an additional child, are they? So that's where I am unless you can find a way of helping me out.'

'But I can't, can I?'

'Evidently not. But everything would be so different if you could. As it is, I might still be able to find a single man who'd like to have a baby with me. Women do have them when they're older, even into their late forties. It's a chance I'll have to take.'

Penny gulped at her drink. Breathing hard and trying to keep her voice under control, she said, 'You know I try never to criticise you, Emma, but I must say yours is a horribly cynical attitude. It really does you no credit. First of all you deceive Giles about the pill, then you expect me to help you out financially, and now you plan to deceive him again because I can't do that and because you want to find another man. And you'd actually prefer to get rid of his baby to being on your own? I know his behaviour's not been out of the top drawer but he deserves better from you.'

'Beggars can't be choosers, mummy. Life's hard when you want things you can't afford.'

'Not that you've ever had to experience that, of course. You've never had to go without.'

She knew she sounded bitter but it was no more than the truth.

'Why not rent somewhere cheaper than here? Less fashionable, perhaps? You might even be eligible for housing benefit.'

'Daddy would have loved to hear you say that, wouldn't he? You know what he thought of scroungers.'

'He wouldn't have thought it was scrounging. When he was sixty-five he said that as he'd paid in all his life it was time to start taking something back. So he did. He took his

State Pension the same as everyone else.'

'Whatever,' Emma said infuriatingly. She sounded like the petulant teenager she used to be. 'Even if I could afford to, I wouldn't contemplate somewhere cheaper and I'll tell you why. It's because there are good reasons for them being cheaper. Quite apart from anything else, the schools are so awful. I wouldn't want a child of mine to have to go to one of those. And nor would you. Not after the good one you went to and the even better one daddy paid for me to go to. Good enough for you, good enough for me, but too good for a mere grandchild. Is that it?'

'Emma, let's stop this before we go too far,' Penny pleaded. 'We're both upset now, and there's no point in making things worse. It's best if I go back before we start to say more things we'll both regret. We can talk together another time when we've both calmed down and had more time to think. I'll just have a word with Alan and—'

'So that little liaison's still going strong, is it?'

'Yes it is, I'm pleased to say.' Why couldn't Emma accept it? It didn't affect her.

'He's a lovely man and I'm very fond of him indeed. It's such a shame you won't hear of it. I don't want to be lonely any more than you do.'

'No, don't say anything,' she said as Emma tried to interrupt her. She knew it would be something critical and she was cross enough already not to need an extra helping of upset – so cross that she'd be unable to stop herself from saying something irreversibly cutting in reply.

'In fact he was thoughtful enough to insist on coming with me on the train to keep me company. He's been killing time somewhere in Wimbledon while I've been here talking to you. So if you don't mind, I'll go into the other room and phone him to find out where he is.'

'Be my guest. You wouldn't want me to hear your intimacies.'

Penny went into the miniature dining-room, closing its door behind her. She thumbed the number of Alan's mobile phone.

'Alan? It's me,' she said when he answered. 'Where are you?'

'Not far from you, as it happens. I took a bus up the hill and I've just had a walk over part of the common. Surprisingly enough, much of it looks the same as it did years ago. Unlike everything else around here, I might say. But I didn't know you were going to ring me. How's it going with Emma?'

'Truthfully?' she said, keeping her voice low. 'Not very well at all. But I've decided to leave here early as there's no point in staying any longer. No,' she said when he asked her why, 'I'll tell you all about it when we meet. You've got her address so can you grab a taxi from somewhere and get here as soon as possible? I'll be waiting down the road a few yards from her house, so don't let the taxi go. But whatever you do, don't come to the door.'

'Bad as that, is it?'

'I'd say so, yes. See you soon.'

She went back into the sitting-room where Emma was looking close to tears.

'He'll pick me up down the road. I really do think it's best if I go now.'

'All right.'

At the front door, she turned to Emma and said, 'I'm sorry to have upset you and that I couldn't help.' She stroked the side of her daughter's face. 'I do so hope you find a way out of this mess, without…you know. You've still got time.'

'I know I have. There's no rush. And I'm sorry too.'

'Can we kiss goodbye?'

'Course we can.'

They embraced. 'I'll be in touch soon,' Penny told her. 'I need to get my thinking-cap on and see if I can come up with something.'

'Thanks, mummy, and thanks for coming to see me. Try not to worry about me, I'll be all right.'

'If you're not, I know it won't be for want of me trying.

Just promise me you won't do anything about a termination till you hear from me.'

'Okay, but please don't take too long.'

Penny walked down the road on the look-out for Alan's taxi. On the way, she eased her wedding ring off and slipped it into her purse. It was lucky she'd remembered to put it back on her finger before arriving at Emma's. If she'd noticed it was missing, a bad time would have been even worse.

CHAPTER TWENTY-FOUR

Starting in the taxi, and taking up the theme again at the station, Penny unloaded her news onto Alan.

It began with a trickle of information and conjecture that soon became a torrent. He listened intently, butting in occasionally to ask questions, not only to show interest but also to clarify a point or two of detail she might expect him to remember later. Her answers confirmed what he already knew; nothing he said was going to solve the problem she'd made him share with her. Nor could he reassure her or cheer her up.

She hadn't asked, but in case she was thinking he might have more finances than he'd disclosed, he said, 'I wish I could do more but I already told you how I'm fixed for money.' It didn't help, but she needed reminding.

None too soon for his liking, she reached the end of her tale when they finally boarded a Somerset train a good deal earlier than planned. Within minutes she was dozing with her head on his shoulder. She did that on both their holiday flights and it was no less uncomfortable now. A human head was said to weigh about ten pounds and he could well believe it because hers felt at least as heavy as five bags of supermarket sugar. He made a few cautious attempts to get the poundage to rest against the window but they made her stir and moan softly in her sleep, so he stopped trying.

When she woke up one stop from their destination, she said, 'Where are we going to spend the night? I could get some sort of meal together at my house, if you like. I don't know about you, but I've had nothing to eat since those sandwiches on the way up. I didn't have time to go shopping this morning but I'm sure I can find something.'

'I think we'll have to eat at yours because I've got nothing substantial at the cottage that doesn't need defrosting. But I'll need to be up early in the morning as I'm due on the first tee at nine. I can still cancel, though.

Would you like me to?'

'No, there's no need. But thanks for offering.'

While she made a start in the kitchen he made them both a drink, left hers with her, and went into the drawing-room. Sitting well back on one of the comfortable sofas, he thought again how undeniably pleasant it would be to share Farthing's with her. There was even room for one or two of his own pieces of furniture. His bureau, for instance, would fit in well with her stuff and had some merit of its own despite Tyler's dismissal of its handles. He'd also have to do something about relocating the drinks to this room. Their inconvenient site, well out of easy access in the dining-room, might act as a damper on her drinking but there was no call for it to affect his.

He expanded his range of thinking to include daydreaming, entering a state where everything was possible. Surely it wouldn't be long now before he was invited to move in with her. When he was, he could visualise the two of them routinely eating in the kitchen rather than in the grandeur of the dining-room. He'd wear his new polka-dotted dressing-gown and smart new slippers while having his leisurely breakfast – the cooked sort he'd easily get used to having. After that he might choose to take a stroll around the well-tended garden if the weather was fine.

It would be a relief to get away from Myrtle Cottage's cold slate floors which gleamed with moisture in the spring, autumn and winter, and sometimes in the summer as well. Good, too, not to have to worry about the state of his thatch with its display of bright green lichens. There'd be outings together when he wasn't playing golf. And lunches, dinners, TV, books and bed. Apart from the outings, it wouldn't be a complete change from his present way of life except that he'd have company and, despite it sounding ungracious to think of it in such terms, a housekeeper.

She'd never said anything about loving him. Whatever her feelings were, they weren't in the grand-passion league but then they were unlikely to be at their ages.

There must be procedural gaps to be crossed in strict order when it came to love. They'd be narrow to begin with and easy to traverse: being attracted to, fancying, quite liking. After that they probably became progressively wider and correspondingly harder to cross: being fond of, enjoying being with, missing being with, and finally being unable to contemplate not being with. Did you get better at leaping across the ever-widening gaps? Or did it get harder every time so it took a massive, kill-or-cure, heart-bursting bound to reach the dizzying final stage of actually loving someone?

He hoped he wasn't fooling himself when he guessed Penny was currently at the penultimate stage – missing being with. Now that he thought about it, his own feelings were also lodged there. It was unfamiliar territory for him as he'd never got that far with any other woman. Looking back, it never got beyond stage two with Susan; no further than fancying. She never did anything to make or let him get beyond that. Even the fancying hadn't lasted long. About a year, he remembered.

When he moved he'd have to let out his cottage to tenants rather than sell it. That way, if Penny died before he did, he could use it as a place of refuge when her daughter promptly ejected him from Farthing's. Until that happened, the rental income would be a welcome addition to his reduced pension. As he'd told her, he was willing and able to help her out with money. He'd be able to help her a lot more once he'd got his hands on a regular inflow of rent. Emma would kick up a fuss but she'd get over it. As a bonus it also meant that whatever else happened, she'd never move in with her mother. She wouldn't do that, not with him living there as well.

His performance today must have helped Penny along the path. He'd been quick to insist on travelling up to Wimbledon with her. He unhesitatingly paid for the train tickets and the taxi fare, as well as listening with sympathy to all she had to say.

It wasn't his place to tell her, but from what she'd said, and it was hard to believe she'd left anything out, it was clear to him, if not to her, she was never going to solve Emma's problems. Her shortage of money was the key, and he'd been as surprised as she was to find out about it. Not content with cheating his Wendmore friends at golf, the late Reggie had cheated on Penny in life and was still messing her about in death.

He was carrying on with his day-dreaming when a disturbingly radical and alternative idea arrived unheralded in his mind. Unlike the sudden idea that initiated his brandy ploy, he tried to strangle this new one at birth as it involved a huge compromise, one he'd not given a thought to before. But it lived on, squalling for his attention. Its point-of-sale attraction was its comprehensive solution of everyone's problems, but it needed thinking through to tie up its loose ends. He finished his drink and settled down to do that.

Not much later, Penny called him from the kitchen. 'Your dinner's ready.'

It was ham, eggs and chips, Jimmy's staple dish at the Coq au Vin.

She had little to say for herself while they ate. Rather than set her off and spoil their meal, he waited till they finished eating before he asked: 'Any thoughts about what to do?'

'No. I told her not to do anything silly before I got in touch with her again, though I can't imagine what I'll tell her when I do. But we don't want to go on talking about it. I've had too much of it and I'm depressed enough already. Let's just take some drinks into the drawing-room and try to relax. It's been a bloody awful day for both of us.'

They sat together on the sofa he used earlier.

'I'm so glad you came with me today,' she said, 'I only wish we'd had a better outcome.'

'Do you think she'd actually go through with it? You know, the...'

'Oh, Alan, must we?' After a moment, she said, 'Yes, I

think she will. But I must try to be unselfish because I'm in danger of concentrating on what I want and not what's best for her.'

'In the circumstances, you mean?'

'Yes. Bad circumstances, her bad circumstances. I wouldn't want to be in her shoes.'

'But you'd do anything you could to help her?'

'You know I would, I'm her mother. But there isn't anything.'

'There may be a way.'

That time on his own before dinner was enough for him to think through all its ramifications. He now wanted to hurry her along before prudence had a chance to stop him telling her about it.

'I certainly wish there was,' she said. 'But there isn't.'

'No, listen for a moment. It's all about money, isn't it? There is a way she could have enough to buy a new place outright with no mortgage.'

'You don't think I haven't thought—'

'I said to listen, darling. Now I've a fair idea of what this house is worth and it's a lot more than the cost of the sort of place your daughter needs. A flat or a maisonette, didn't you say?'

'I've already been through all that with her. I told her—'

His voice rose above hers. 'No, listen. If you sold it and gave her enough of the proceeds to buy a little place of her own, perhaps in a place like, say, Kingston – good schools there, and cheaper housing, too – she'd be able to get by on what Giles gave her and with what she could earn.'

'You know I can't do that, ' Penny said wearily. 'There wouldn't be enough left over to buy a half-decent place for me and leave enough for me to live on afterwards as well. Not if I live as long as I hope to. I told her all that.'

He made time for one last piece of thought before saying: 'You wouldn't need to buy another place for yourself, not if you moved in with me at the cottage.'

He knew the implications of that were too much for her

to take in all at once. It had been hard enough for him to grasp them all.

To help both of them along, he continued: 'I know two can't really live as cheaply as one, but try to think of the savings you'd make. There's the upkeep of this house and garden to think of; the fuel bills, council tax, insurance, all sorts of expenses you'd no longer have. And you'd still have quite a bit of money left after selling it.'

There was no response. So, as a further inducement, the only one he'd been able to think of, he said, 'And if you're wondering what would happen to you if I died first there's no reason why I shouldn't leave the cottage to you. I've no one else to leave it to, have I? But if you wanted a widow's share of my pension when I'm gone, I'm afraid you'd have to marry me. It's a bugger, but there it is.'

He had to wait before she said in a wondering voice: 'And you'd really do all that for me? Give up your independence so my daughter can have a way out of her problems?'

'Yes, I would. But not just to help her.'

'What you said about the widow's pension, are you proposing to me as well?'

'Only suggesting it, and only if you'd like me to, of course. But it does seem like a good idea. At least, it does to me.'

She kissed his cheek. 'I can't believe what's happening, you amaze me. And I hope it matters to you as much as it does to me, but now I can tell you at last that I love you. I've not said anything before because I didn't want to panic you. If you want to know, I've loved you for quite a while so it's not just because of you being so kind to me now.' She went on almost at once: 'But before I say anything else, Alan, I have to ask you; do you love me, too?'

His mind accelerated. Despite claiming to love him, she'd not agreed to his suggestion as promptly or as eagerly as he hoped, but there was nothing left for him to offer. He'd never thought of her living with him at his cottage because he'd let himself hope to share Farthing's with her, and he presumed she'd want to stay there.

It wasn't a bad deal he'd put on the table. Not that those affected by it would wind up with all they really wanted, but his offer gave the three of them what they needed. It provided free housing for Emma which would make her more appealing to a potential suitor, even with a child about the place. Penny would get a grandchild, security and peace of mind. He'd have companionship and someone to look after him. That Rolling Stones song from a lifetime ago still resonated.

He'd not lied to her when she made him look closely at her damaged breast, though he'd known he would one day. But his response was so important it might clinch the decision for her. Women – not Susan, of course – liked to be sure about that sort of thing. Penny had already been married once to someone who didn't love her. Would she want to do so a second time?

She was looking intently at him now, waiting for his answer. He made himself wait to see if he might possibly be at least halfway through that final massive heart-bursting, kill-or-cure bound. It didn't take long.

'Of course I do,' he said.

THE END

Lightning Source UK Ltd.
Milton Keynes UK
UKOW04f1915091215

264451UK00005B/337/P